THE CH. ..L R

THE ASSASSINS GUILD, BOOK #1

C.J. ARCHER

"It lies not in our power to love or hate,
For will in us is overruled by fate."
— Christopher Marlowe, *Hero and Leander*

.

CHAPTER 1

Hampshire, November 1598

$\mathcal{O}$rlando Holt had never killed a woman before. He'd assassinated a bear tamer, a viscount, three French noblemen and two Spanish ones, a knight, a painter, a physician, an acrobat in Cathay, and five apothecaries. He had nothing against apothecaries, but he'd come across a disproportionate number during his three-year tenure in Lord Oxley's Assassins Guild. All the apothecaries, and every other target, had been men and thoroughly deserving of the Guild's justice.

Lady Lynden would be his first woman.

He watched her from his hiding place behind a yew bush, the only shrubbery in the walled garden with enough leaves to hide him. Aside from the dozen densely foliated trees lined up against the brick wall where Lady Lynden worked, most of the garden was bare. A few rust-red leaves clung stubbornly to the roses and other shrubs here or there, but they were rare. In contrast, the green leaves of the dozen trees seemed lush and vibrant, and quite out of place amid the autumnal landscape. Unfortunately, he was too far away to use them as cover. Thank God for the yew.

That was the problem with autumn. It was better than winter for shadowing a potential target—less chance of freezing his balls off—but the warmer months offered more places to hide. If he were really lucky, village women would shed their clothing in the summer and paddle in a nearby stream when they did the washing.

He didn't think Lady Lynden would go in search of the nearest body of water and take a dip in her underthings. She was a she-man, as his brother used to call women who wore masculine clothes or liked to do a man's work. Orlando couldn't see Lady Lynden's face from where he squatted, but he noticed the loose calf-length farmer's trousers, the woolen jerkin, and the wide-brimmed farmer's hat, all in dark colors for mourning. She'd rolled the sleeves of her shirt up to the elbows, revealing tanned forearms, and by the way she dragged around a large pail filled with what looked to be soil, he knew she was no delicate flower used to a life of embroidery.

Yet Lady Lynden was a noblewoman. According to Hughe, she was the widow of a baron who had returned home to live in the manor owned by her country gentleman father. She wasn't supposed to be this she-man doing heavy garden work. He knew it was Susanna Lynden because Hughe's client had said she'd be working in the walled garden at Stoneleigh without the aid of a gardener or other servants.

She straightened suddenly and looked around as if she could sense him watching. But he was too well hidden, despite crouching no more than a few feet from her. She sighed and removed her gardening gloves and hat.

Orlando almost overbalanced in surprise. He took it all back. Lady Lynden was no she-man. She was a beauty. Hair of the fairest gold, braided and pinned to her head, creamy skin, an oval face with delicate features, and large eyes. He couldn't see their color from where he hid, but he'd wager they were blue to go with her pale hair and skin. Where her forearms were brown, her face was as English as the queen's.

Yet a description of her individual parts didn't do her justice. She was extraordinary. Her face captivated him, rooting his feet to the muddy earth, and he couldn't stop staring. It had been a long time since he'd seen a woman as achingly beautiful as Lady Lynden, yet here she was in a Hampshire backwater dragging pails of earth around, dressed in men's clothes.

And he was supposed to kill her.

He passed a finger over his upper lip just as his target wiped the back of her hand across her forehead. She glanced around then pressed her hands to the small of her back and rubbed. So the hard work was not to her liking after all. What about the clothes? Did she dress like a man because she wanted to or because it was practical?

Orlando watched as she picked up a trowel and began digging through the dirt in the pail, turning it over. A few minutes later, while her back was turned, he crept quietly away through the ivy-clad arch and out of the walled garden.

He had never killed a woman before, and he wasn't about to start. Not without being absolutely certain she was the murderer Hughe's client claimed her to be. Hughe himself had said the job probably wouldn't be the quick in-and-out that Orlando preferred and that a thorough investigation was needed. That meant doing something Orlando had hoped to avoid, staying.

He raced to the nearby woods and retrieved his pack from the inside of a hollow log where he'd left it. He didn't need to change clothes and he wasn't hungry, having dined at the village inn before coming to Stoneleigh, so he slung the pack over his shoulder. A few minutes later, he was once more leaving the woods and heading for Stoneleigh. This time he didn't creep. He whistled. Loudly.

As expected, Lady Lynden came to the arch of the walled garden to investigate. "Lo?" she called out. "Who is it?"

"Madam, my humble apologies." He removed his hat and bowed

low, sweeping the brim across the gravel path. "I didn't mean to startle you."

"You didn't startle me. I simply came to see who whistles out of tune near my garden." Her voice was like honeyed wine, sweet and thick, but with a hard, flat edge.

"Out of tune? Dear lady, you wound me."

She rolled her eyes, and he was pleased to see he'd been right. They were as blue as a bright summer sky.

"Why are you smiling at me like that?" she snapped, stamping one hand on her hip. The other was tucked behind her back.

"I can't help it. You're a vision of beauty, a balm for my travel-weary eyes."

She didn't blush or smile coyly or do any of the things ladies did when paid a compliment. She merely scowled, scrunching her pretty little nose up as if she found his words, or his presence, distasteful. "You do not put balm on eyes, young man, unless you wish to go blind."

"Young man? I suspect I am older than you." Lady Lynden was four and twenty and already a widow twice over. Orlando was four years her senior, yet he knew when he smiled his dimples gave him the appearance of youth. Those bloody dents in his cheeks were the object of much teasing ever since he'd reached manhood. The only consolation was that women of all ages seemed to take joy in them.

Lady Lynden revealed the hand previously hidden behind her back. It clutched a rather vicious-looking short-handled gardening fork. "I asked who you are," she said. "Answer me."

He held up his hands. His pack slipped down his arm and hung in the crook of his elbow. He wasn't in any danger from the shrew. She might be stronger than the average woman thanks to her gardening, but he was larger and had been trained by Hughe. Women were no match for him.

"Orlando Holt at your service." He bowed again. When he straightened, she was still scowling. It didn't make her any less beautiful. "I was hoping you could give me work, madam."

She lowered her weapon and her stance relaxed. "No, I'm sorry, Mr. Holt. There's no work available here. Try up at Sutton Hall over the fields." There was no flutter of her lashes or wistfulness in her voice when she spoke of her previous home. She had given it up and moved back to her father's neighboring house of Stoneleigh when her second husband died and Sutton Hall had passed to his heir, a cousin. That had been a year ago and she was still at Stoneleigh and still unwed. Orlando wondered when her father would find her husband number three.

"I was at Sutton Hall earlier," he said. "There's no work for me there either." He held his breath. Waited. But his lie seemed to slip by unnoticed. She merely shrugged and turned to go. "Wait!" He caught her arm but dropped it when she tried to jerk herself free with such force that he probably bruised her. He cursed under his breath. He hadn't let go when he should have. Instinct had made him hang on. Instinct and training.

Lady Lynden's eyes narrowed, and if it wasn't for the slight tremble of her hands, he would have thought her unafraid. "I told you. There's no work here."

He nodded at her garden fork. "Then why is the lady of the house doing men's work and dressed in men's clothes?"

"Who says I'm the lady of the house?"

He liked the way she tilted her pointy little chin and the way anger made her eyes grow darker, like the Mediterranean Sea in the late afternoon. He smiled again because he couldn't help himself. She was a shrew, and he enjoyed a challenge.

Pity she was a potential murderess and not a candidate for keeping him warm at night. Although there were no Guild rules stipulating the former precluded the latter, Orlando liked to think even he had enough moral conviction to stay out of her bed.

"You speak like a lady," Orlando said, hefting his pack up onto his shoulder, "walk like a lady and have the bearing of a lady. In my book, if a rose looks and smells like a rose, it probably is a rose."

One side of her mouth lifted in a sardonic smile. "In that case..." She pointed the fork at his face and scanned it down his length to his muddy boots. "You look like a vagrant..." She sniffed the air and pulled a face. "...and smell like a vagrant."

He sniffed his armpit. The stink wasn't *that* bad considering he'd been traveling for three days. "I am not a vagrant. I am, however, in need of good, honest work. Garden work," he added. "I'm a gardener."

She raised both brows. "Really?"

He nodded. "I was most recently employed at Collier Dean, a grand house in Sussex. You've probably heard of it."

"I haven't. Do you have a letter of recommendation?"

"No, alas. I didn't think to get one before I left."

"That was foolish."

"What can I say? I'm a fool." He grinned and received a frown in return.

"Why did you leave?"

"I'm traveling to Salisbury to visit my sister."

"You're from Salisbury? That explains the accent."

His accent was a London one, but she seemed to know no better and he saw no reason to enlighten her. "I thought it time I visited her, but I ran out of money. I used my last coins dining at The Plough in the village." Lie upon lie upon lie, all smoothly spoken. He was an expert at them, as were all the members of Hughe's band, past and present. It was vital for survival to be able to act in any role at any moment with no preparation.

"What type of garden work did you do at Collier Dean?"

"Digging, weeding, pruning." What else did gardeners do? There wasn't much call for it working in the Assassins Guild or at his family's London house. They had a small garden to service their kitchen, but it consisted of a few herbs and such. Certainly nothing like the exotic trees he'd seen backed up against her garden wall. He shrugged. "Whatever was required of me."

"You weren't head gardener then?"

"Head, body, hands and feet." She didn't even crack a smile, so he forged on. "I was under the direction of the lady of the house, a keen gardener like you, madam."

"Did she grow oranges?"

"What?"

"Oranges. Did she grow them?"

"Uh, no." Only a madman would try to grow oranges in England. They were a fruit more suited to warmer climes like Spain. Surely they weren't the trees he saw in her garden. Why would she want to grow them when she could have perfectly good English fruit trees like cherry or apple?

"Then you are of no use to me," she said. "Not that I need a gardener."

He thought it best to keep his mouth shut. Lady Lynden didn't look like she would appreciate him pointing out that her hands were covered in hard calluses and she had dirt smudged on her forehead, or that the pails of soil looked much too heavy for her to drag around. This last he could not admit to having witnessed anyway.

"I'm very busy. Good day, Mr. Holt." She marched off, giving him a fine view of her shapely calves. When she reached the far wall and the dark green leafy trees, she turned around. A flicker of either surprise or irritation crossed her face before she waved him off, as imperial as any queen. "Try Cowdrey Farm," she called back. "It's quite a walk to the west, but Farmer Cowdrey will have work for a strong lad like yourself."

"I'm eight and twenty, not a lad. And I'm a gardener, not a farmer, but thanks anyway."

She turned her back to him once more but not before he heard her muttering, "Beggars can't be choosers."

"I'm not a beggar either. Or a vagrant." *I'm an assassin. And a bloody good one.*

He trudged back along the gravel drive to the road leading into the village. Lady Lynden might have been the most beautiful woman Orlando had ever seen, but she was as prickly as a hawthorn. Ordinarily he would avoid shrews like her but not this time. He had to thoroughly investigate the claims against her and if she were guilty, then he would have to assassinate her.

7

Women who went about murdering their husbands could not be allowed to escape justice.

* * *

SUSANNA LYNDEN SAT on the ground under her largest orange tree and watched the retreating back of Orlando Holt through the garden arch. It was a broad back attached to the sort of shoulders that would be useful for hoeing garden beds and for sinking one's teeth into if she felt so inclined. Which she absolutely did not. She was not ready to take a lover, and she suspected Orlando Holt would make a terrible one anyway, or terrible for *her* at least. Too handsome for his own good and certainly too charming. Men like him never stayed true to their women, and she'd had enough of straying men.

Good lord, she must have been lonelier than she thought. She'd met Holt only briefly, yet her mind had stripped him naked. Perhaps it was time she got a lover. How did a gentlewoman go about obtaining one? Nail a handbill to the post outside The Plough announcing the vacancy? She threw her head back and laughed, startling a yellow butterfly perched on a leaf.

No, there would be no lover for her, or a gardener. Not even a laborer. Pity, because Holt would have been perfect with his experience and his size. She'd be lucky if she could afford the wages of the three servants they currently kept as well as food enough to feed them, her father and herself. The little money they had needed to stretch until she'd found a city shopkeeper to stock her marmalades and succades. Finding someone was taking longer than she expected.

She drove her fork into the soft earth and pushed herself to her feet. Her head touched one of the low-hanging green oranges, and she ducked out from under the canopy. She slapped on her hat and stood back to survey her oldest and strongest tree. Its leaves were a healthy green and the fruits almost the same color. They would turn orange soon and need protecting from the winter. Already the air felt chilly even when the sun was out.

How cold would it get this year? She'd only lost one tree last winter, but the others had dropped most of their fruit. She hadn't been able to give them the full attention they needed while living up at the Hall, and her father hadn't the strength to do what was necessary to protect all of them from frost. This year she'd wanted to try a new housing technique for ensuring their safe wintering, but time was growing short along with the days, and there was still so much to be done. The temporary and somewhat flimsy shelter would have to do for now.

She picked up her pruning knife and lopped off the straggling branches to make it easier to cover the trees. It grew more and more difficult to reach the higher ones, and soon her arms and neck ached. She removed her gloves and massaged her shoulder.

"Those trousers really don't suit you, Susanna."

She ground her back teeth together then turned around with what she hoped was a genteel smile on her face for her late husband's cousin. She had to remind herself that he meant well, but it didn't make his stupidity any less, well, stupid. "I find skirts too restricting in the garden."

Jeffrey—Lord Lynden—squinted and stretched his neck. With the high collar and his chin resting on the stiff ruff, his neck appeared unnaturally long. "Is that dirt on your forehead?"

"Probably. I find I can't escape the stuff out here."

"I suppose not." He indicated the pruning knife. "What are you doing with that?"

"Pruning."

"And what's in the pails?"

"Dung from Cowdrey Farm's cows mixed with soil."

He pulled a face. "It looks like hard work."

"I can manage, and I enjoy being out here with my orange trees." It was true, she did like gardening, but she could certainly use some help. Not that she would tell Jeffrey she couldn't afford a laborer. Any mention of money, or her lack of it, would only bring up the topic of her marrying again, something she wished to avoid. With Farmer Cowdrey having asked her countless times already, she was becoming an expert in avoiding the subject altogether. And avoid it she must. Two disastrous marriages had proved to her it wasn't a state she wanted to enter into again, ever.

"I can provide one of my gardeners to help you if you like," Jeffrey said.

He'd never offered her staff before. Considering he loathed spending money on things that didn't directly improve his own estate, it was quite a generous offer. What did he want in return? "Thank you, but I can manage."

He regarded her closely, still frowning. Jeffrey was always frowning it seemed, so unlike her late husband, his older cousin. Phillip had been dark-haired and silver-tongued, a combination that meant everyone liked him, particularly women. Jeffrey was more serious, hardly ever laughing with abandon as Phillip used to do, and flirting wasn't an art he'd mastered. Most of the village women crossed the road to avoid speaking with him.

Susanna knelt down on the ground and dug through the fertile mix of dung and earth in the pail.

"That reeks," Jeffrey said. "Must you do it now?"

"I have to put it around the trees."

"This moment?"

"I can think of no better one." She stood and eyed the nearest tree several feet away. Her lower back ached just thinking about moving the pail and digging through the dung and soil. "Would you mind dragging the pail over there?"

"Me?"

She turned to look at him and almost burst out laughing. He had his wrist pressed to his nose, the white lace cuff trailing over his mouth and chin like a snowy beard. "I see no one else here."

Half his face may have been covered, but it didn't hide the disgust in his eyes. "This is why you need a man to help you."

She refrained, just, from pointing out that he was a man.

"What about your servants?" he went on. "Can't one of them help?"

"They're busy and too aged for this type of work in addition to their usual duties."

"You should replace them with more able-bodied ones." He took a step back and she sighed. It seemed Jeffrey was like his cousin in one respect. Neither liked to get their soft, white hands dirty.

"Jeffrey, why have you come here?"

"To offer you the use of one of my men for your garden."

He'd come just for that? Surely not. "No, thank you."

"You won't need to pay me."

"No."

"But you can't do this on your own! Look at you. Your knees are dirty and your skin is brown!" He sniffed. "And that smell. It's disgusting and unseemly. A woman of your station should be inside sewing, not mucking about in filth. Admit it, Susanna, you're in over your head with those orange trees. I don't know why you care about them so much. They take up all your time since you came back here. You should have left them to die after your mother's passing." He must have known he'd over-stepped because he had the decency to flush and look away. He knew how much Susanna had loved her mother. The trees were her legacy. She would not let them wither.

"Thank you for your concern," she said carefully lest the wave of emotion washing through her burst out. "But I do not want your help."

He pursed his thin lips so that they disappeared entirely. "Susanna," he finally said on a sigh. "Why do you thwart me so when all I want is to care for you? As my cousin, it's the least I can do. Allow my man to help." His gaze darted away and wandered around the garden, avoiding her. "He's new to my employ but trustworthy. And very strong, very capable. He'll do whatever you ask of him. I highly recommend him to you."

Why was he insisting? What could possibly be in it for Jeffrey?

He wasn't a terrible person, but he never did anything out of the goodness of his heart. If it had been anyone else, she would have thought he was trying to woo her, but being her cousin by marriage meant a union between them was unthinkable as well as illegal. Perhaps he needed her to act as lady of Sutton Hall for some important visitors.

Like his cousin before him, Jeffrey planned on putting Sutton Hall on the map, or at least the map used by the nobility with influence at court. Being a baron wasn't enough for Jeffrey. He wanted to be *noticed*, and that meant having the right people visit and ensuring they were entertained during their stay. Phillip had been a natural host, charming and witty, attentive but not syco-phantic. Jeffrey would have a more difficult time of it. He plodded through conversations, failing to grasp subtle changes in moods or clever retorts. He needed a friend to guide him through prickly political and social situations with high ranking guests, which was why Susanna would be a terrible hostess. She'd learned from her two marriages that being the perfect gentleman's wife didn't come easily to her. She preferred her garden to the ballroom and tending the orange trees to indulging the whims of fat noblemen.

"Susanna, please, I insist. I beg of you to accept my offer to help."

Insist? Beg? Rather strong words for a simple offer. She shook her head and grabbed the edges of the pail and dragged it along the path.

"Whoa, mistress, stop," a vaguely familiar voice said from behind her. Before she could turn around, big brown hands grasped the pail and lifted it. Lifted it! She looked up, straight into the blue eyes of Orlando Holt.

"Where do you want it?" He gave her a smile and a dimple appeared in each cheek. Now that he was closer she could see that he was indeed older than she first thought. Those dimples made him look impish, as if he'd been caught stealing from a plate of sweetmeats. She had the ridiculous urge to press her smallest finger into them.

"Lady Lynden?" he prompted. His smile widened. The man knew what she was thinking. She was certain of it. Curse him.

"Over there," she said, pointing to the nearest tree. She watched as he carried the full pail to the tree. He wore only a jerkin over his shirt, like her, but where her clothes were big and loose, his jerkin stretched tautly over his shoulders and across his back.

"Who is that?" Jeffrey said, coming up beside her. "A new servant?"

"A vagrant," she said and bit back a laugh. Holt had emphatically argued with her over the point only a little while ago. She couldn't deny sparring with him had made her feel more alive than she had felt in months. Odd how such a simple exchange with a stranger could do that. She must have been more desperate than she thought for witty company. It certainly wasn't the handsome and charming male company she missed—she'd had enough of that from her two husbands to last a lifetime.

"My name is Orlando Holt," Holt said, rejoining them. A few strands of his blond hair had flopped over his forehead but otherwise he showed no signs of exertion. He nodded at Jeffrey in greeting. "I'm a servant here."

"You most certainly are not!" she snapped.

He grinned again. Good lord, did he ever *not* smile? "I am. Mr. Farley has added me to his staff."

"You spoke to my father after I told you to leave?" The insolent, devious...*vagrant*! "Go back inside and tell him you'll not accept his offer." When he didn't move, she took a step closer, but that was a mistake because it only emphasized how much bigger than her he was. She came up to the middle of his chest.

"I have offered my services and your father has agreed to my terms," he said, his eyes sparkling with humor. "He is the master of Stoneleigh, is he not?" It wasn't a question that required an answer. The slippery eel knew that. "Besides, I need the work." He held up his hand to stop her, as if he were the master and she the servant. She was so shocked she didn't know what to say. "Cowdrey Farm is too far away and I'm a gardener, not a farm hand."

"Ha!" she managed, annoyed that he'd predicted her argument.

He forked an eyebrow at her and looked like he would say something more, but Jeffrey spoke first. "You should have come to Sutton Hall. There is plenty of gardening work."

"There is?" It was her turn to lift a questioning brow. Holt kept on smiling, not in the least disturbed that he'd been caught out in his earlier lie. Had he been to Sutton Hall at all? He said nothing and she turned to Jeffrey. She could only confront one liar at a time. "Then why were you offering me one of your gardeners if there is so much to do up there?"

Jeffrey blushed to the roots of his bright hair. "Uh...I... "

"So you are the master of Sutton Hall?" Holt asked when Jeffrey failed to complete his sentence.

Jeffrey adjusted his black velvet cloak so it draped more elegantly over his left shoulder, and thrust his chin out. "I'll ask the questions, not you. But I'll have you know that I am Lord Lynden. I am also Lady Lynden's cousin."

"By marriage," she added.

"And so it should be I who provides her with a man to help in the garden. Be off." Jeffrey flicked his long fingers toward the arch. "Tell Mr. Farley you've changed your mind and cannot work here. Susanna," he said, turning to her, "do not trust this stranger. His methods are underhanded and his manner impertinent. Take my man instead. Indeed, let me speak to your father this instant."

She caught Jeffrey's arm before he could move off. "Thank you, but there's no need to drag Father into this. Since he has already employed Mr. Holt here, I must accept. Thank you for your offer, it was kindly done." And insistently. Very. She was glad to be able to refuse without qualms. She didn't want to find out what strings Jeffrey had attached to his proposal.

"You're going to accept this vagrant?" he spluttered.

"I have no choice. Father is the master of Stoneleigh."

He stared wide-eyed at her. The yellow flecks in his eyes glinted in the afternoon sun that had finally wrestled the clouds aside. "I never thought to see you give in so easily, Susanna." He made a miffed sound through his nose, bowed perfunctorily, and walked out of the walled garden. She went to the arch and was relieved to see him gather up the reins of his horse and ride down the long drive to the road.

"So," Holt said, standing with his feet apart as if he'd planted himself there, "what do you want me to do next? We have some time before sunset."

"You, Mr. Holt," she said, pointing at him, "should not get too comfortable. I'm going to see my father and insist he withdraw his offer. You lied about asking for work up at Sutton Hall, did you not?"

"No lie, m'lady. The steward shooed me away. If he lied about the lack of work because he didn't want a stranger on the premises, I cannot be held to blame."

"Well, I refuse to have someone so ... so ... presumptuous working alongside me."

"Presumptuous? I simply saw a job that needed doing and offered my services to do it."

"Mr. Holt, perhaps it isn't clear to you, but we cannot pay you." She wasn't embarrassed to admit it. One glance at the partially patched-up house and the sorry state of the outbuildings would tell him money was scarce.

"I only require food and a roof over my head," he said. "Do you have a barn?"

"The roof leaks."

"The stables?"

"There's no room." It was filled with crates of jars and equipment for making their marmalades and succades. Silver needed her space along with the small cart and tack.

"A spare closet in the big house?"

"You get above yourself, Mr. Holt," she shot back over her shoulder as she passed under the arch.

His chuckle followed her all the way to the house.

CHAPTER 2

"*Y*ou have to let him go, Father," Susanna said.

John Farley patted the coverlet beside him and when Susanna sat down, took her hands in his, dirt and all. "My dear, you've worked yourself into a state. You'll unbalance your humors. Take a deep breath and tell me what ails you."

"Nothing ails me."

"You did not take a breath."

"Father!" Why was she surrounded by frustrating men? She breathed deeply, not because it was what her father wanted but because it helped soothe her fractured nerves.

"There," he said, not letting go of her hands. His palms were warm but the fingers cool. The backs were covered with freckles in every shade of brown, as were his nose and cheeks. The skin underneath was pale and stretched so tight over the bones it looked as if it would fray like an old cloth washed too often. "Better?"

"No," she said, rubbing his fingers to warm them. "There is a man in my garden who will not leave. He says you employed him. I want you to dismiss him. This instant."

Farley sagged into his pillows and regarded her with one of *those* looks. The sort he always gave her when he thought her being

16

foolish or difficult. "I cannot dismiss him. Ah, Bessie, there you are," he said when the maid entered carrying a tray with cup and bowl on it. "You understand, don't you, Bessie?"

"Aye, sir." Bessie was as old as her father, perhaps older. It was difficult to tell. She'd always seemed aged to Susanna, with her rounded shoulders and gray hair peeking out of the front of her large brown caul. She'd worked at Stoneleigh for as long as Susanna could remember. Indeed, all three of their remaining servants had. They were as much a part of the manor house as the stone walls. Susanna suspected they would still be there even after she and her father passed on, haunting the place for generations. The idea appealed to her. The ancient Farley line would end with her, but there would be continuity at Stoneleigh as long as the spirits of the servants lingered.

"Father," she said, heavily. "That man Holt...there's something about him. Something I can't put my finger on. I don't trust him."

"But he's not even been here a day." He took the cup Bessie offered and cradled it in his hands. "How can you not trust him when you don't know him?"

"I've seen enough of him to come to that conclusion. He's...arrogant."

"You say arrogant. I say charming."

"He doesn't know anything about growing orange trees."

"Show me an English gardener who does."

"He, he doesn't know his place," she said.

Her father laughed, making his snowy beard shake and his eyes moisten. "Did you hear that, Bessie? A servant at Stoneleigh who doesn't know his place."

Bessie grinned, lighting up her entire face. Susanna had always loved Bessie's smiles. They were big and bold and brought joy into the dreariest of rooms. "I know my place," the maid said, stirring the bowl's contents with a spoon. "It's doing Cook's bidding."

Farley laughed harder. "Shouldn't you be doing *my* bidding?"

Bessie passed Farley the bowl and took the cup. "I'm more afraid of Cook, sir. She's bigger and has more large knives at hand."

Farley sniffed the steaming broth in his bowl. "Ahhh, and she's a marvel in the kitchen. I don't know what we'd do without her."

"Starve," both Bessie and Susanna said, then laughed.

Susanna's laughter quickly vanished. "Be serious for a moment, Father. Why did you employ Holt without knowing anything about him? It's most unlike you to do something like that on a whim."

"I couldn't help it, my dear. He was so insistent. I couldn't say no." He shrugged as if he couldn't have denied Holt any more than he could stop a sneeze.

He had not always been so easy. When he was younger and Stoneleigh's estate larger, he'd been careful and thorough. His wishes had always been followed and he commanded respect from his family, servants, and the villagers. Never a cruel man, he did, however, expect to be obeyed. And everyone had.

Then many things happened. The first husband John Farley had found for his only child proved to be a wolf in sheep's clothing. Once he'd lost his fortune, he took his anger and frustration out on Susanna, beating her for no apparent reason except that he could. Fortunately he died before the beatings became unbearable, and not a single soul mourned him. At the same time, the weather conspired to ruin the crops at Stoneleigh for four years in a row and money became tight. Farley was forced to sell all productive lands to his neighbors to make ends meet. Then, worst of all, his beloved wife, Susanna's mother, died and he went mad with grief. Her death changed him in other ways too. His health failed, his mind went a little wayward, and all vitality seemed to leech out of him. Where once he was strong and capable, he became helpless and easily led. That's how Phillip had talked him into agreeing to a marriage between himself and Susanna when her father had wanted to keep her at home awhile. To be fair, it was a good match for an untitled widow with a small dowry, and Susanna had desired the man and the marriage anyway. She'd been reluctant to leave her father, but Sutton Hall was only across the fields from Stoneleigh.

With only a few servants to aid her father, the remaining land ceased to make a profit and had to be sold. Weeds infiltrated the garden at an alarming rate, choking out most of the herbs and orange trees which her father managed to keep alive as a loving tribute to his wife who'd planted them. The outbuildings fell apart, and even Stoneleigh itself began to look like a tarnished trinket in need of loving care.

Then there was the loss of her two babies in the early stages of the pregnancies. It had devastated her father almost as much as it had devastated her.

"You will have to say no," she said, digging her heels in. "I don't need him."

"My dear, you do." He sipped his broth. "I know how hard those trees can be in these cold months. I fear you'll work your fingers to the bone and lose your pretty looks."

"I don't care about my looks."

"No, but a husband will. You can't expect to catch another if you look like a tired old hag."

She shot him a withering glare, but he was concentrating on his broth and didn't see. She appealed to Bessie, but the maid bustled about, tidying up the bedchamber, and didn't seem to be listening. "You agreed you would not make me wed again."

Farley glanced up sharply. His face softened and she realized she must have looked quite pale. The thought of marrying again always made her feel ill.

"I'm sorry, my dear, you're right, but that's not what I meant. I won't force you again, but that doesn't mean you won't *want* to marry."

"I won't."

"You may," he said and returned to his broth. "If the right man comes along."

She sighed and shook her head. "None of this changes the fact that we cannot pay Holt. We don't have enough money."

"We could pay him in marmalade." He chuckled but caught her narrowed glare and sobered.

"Perhaps I can offer a compromise," Bessie said.

"Please do," Susanna said, suddenly feeling tired. There was so much to do and here she was arguing with her father over money matters. Sometimes she wondered if he really knew how desperate the situation at Stoneleigh was.

"Offer him board and food in exchange for his work in the garden," Bessie said, placing a folded blanket in a trunk.

It was what Holt himself had suggested. "Yes, but..." It didn't solve the issue of having a man like Holt working in her presence. Too close.

"Tell him he is free to come and go as long as he achieves a minimum amount of work each day, an amount which you both can agree to, m'lady."

Interesting. It sounded like a good compromise. Servants and laborers valued their free time since they were given so little of it. It didn't solve the problem of Holt himself. He unsettled her, made her nerves stretch. He was so much like Phillip in that regard. So...smooth. Phillip had a way of slipping under her defenses without her realizing until it was too late, and then he would get what he wanted. What he wanted usually included forcing her to entertain guests she didn't like or stopping Susanna from visiting the villagers he thought beneath them. Then there were his lovers...so many lovers.

Bessie's sympathetic gaze fell on her. "Since he is in *your* house and you are *his* mistress, he will do as you say or be forced to leave."

Then it will not be like it was with Phillip. Is that what she meant or was that merely Susanna's interpretation?

She pushed her palms down her thighs to still her shaking hands. Her father continued to sip his broth and Bessie bent to the fire and stoked the glowing logs until a small flame leapt to life. The room seemed unnaturally quiet, as if they both waited for Susanna's approval and she realized with a start that she was mistress *and* master of Stoneleigh. Her father wasn't capable of running the place anymore. It wasn't just her home. It was her own little kingdom that she ruled over.

"Very well," she said. "Bessie, please prepare the attic room for him." It was the smallest, most dreary closet in the servants' wing. No point in letting Mr. Holt get too comfortable. He would not be staying long.

* * *

ORLANDO FOUND it difficult to listen to Lady Lynden without being distracted by some feature of her face. Her mouth was so expressive, her lips full and luscious, and her eyes changed according to her mood. Sometimes light and clear, other times dark and tumultuous. To his surprise, when she returned from the house, they were bright blue and merry. Whatever her father had said to her, she now seemed to accept Orlando's presence.

Unless she had got her way and he was about to be dismissed.

"Mr. Holt," she said, striding up to where he stood in the center of the walled garden. "Present yourself to my maid in the kitchen at supper, and she'll direct you to your new room."

He nodded, feeling a little light-headed with relief. It would be easier to search the house if he was actually living in it. *Thank you, Mr. Farley. You may have just saved your daughter. Or condemned her.* Orlando would know soon enough if she indeed deserved the Assassins Guild's justice. Someone—their client—obviously believed she did, but Orlando wanted no doubts before he'd act.

"Now, the rules," she began, and he groaned. "You don't like rules?"

"I love rules," he said. "My entire life has been governed by them." This at least was true. His father's strict rules when he'd been a child, his brother's equally strict rules after he inherited, and society's rules of what was acceptable for a man to do when he was frustrated with all the other rules imposed on him. Hughe's rules were lax by comparison, and they didn't come with a beating if he failed to follow them. Or guilt.

So much guilt.

"We have some time left before we should go in for supper," she said, pushing past him. Her hips swayed, and he couldn't stop staring at the way the muscles in her calves moved beneath her netherstocks. He'd seen women's calves before, but not a single one could compare to Lady Lynden's exquisitely curved ones.

"Mr. Holt," she snapped. "You'll be useless to me if you continue to stare like that."

He blushed like a bloody schoolboy. "What can I do first?" he asked.

"These trees need to be covered during the winter months. I have canvas in the barn and stakes to build a structure. Can you hammer straight?"

"Of course," he said, liking the way her eyes narrowed and her lips pursed. She was trying to categorize him, he guessed, to label him and put him in the appropriate box. She'd already called him arrogant and charming with so much disdain that he suspected his allotted box wasn't kept for her favorite people. He would have liked to prove her wrong, but what was the point? Most likely she'd be dead soon. If not, he'd be gone.

"Come with me," she said and led the way out of the walled garden and around the side of the manor house. At first glance it appeared to be a sturdy stone structure with much of the front wall covered in ivy, but when he looked closer, he noticed rotting window and doorframes. Long arms of ivy reached across some of the windows and one slender stem threatened to get a hold in a large crack in the stonework.

She led him to the barn near the stables. No sound came from the stables, no neighing or stomping or chatter of grooms. There were no horses at Stoneleigh it seemed. No horses, no children, no young men capable of helping in the garden. It was a tomb.

"You're employed for as long as you wish to be, Mr. Holt," she said as they entered the barn. She indicated the wooden stakes leaning against the far wall. "You'll be given food and board and can come and go as you please in the afternoons as long as I am happy with the amount of work you do in the mornings. If this arrangement is not acceptable, you can go to Sutton Hall and ask for work there since it seems they have plenty after all."

Orlando sent up a silent curse. He should have learned more about Sutton Hall and its master before he used it in his concocted story.

"I think I'll stay," he said, gathering up the stakes. They were taller than he by half a body length, but not heavy. He smiled at her because he wanted to smooth away the line that had settled between her brows. "I like Stoneleigh."

"Oh?"

"I want to learn about orange trees."

The line cleared and her eyes brightened. "Of course. They're a fascinating plant." She picked up a box, and he followed her out of the barn, back to the walled garden. "My mother planted them almost twenty years ago," she said, her voice wistful. "She'd always been a keen gardener and liked a challenge. When she heard that her mother's kinsman, Sir Francis Carew, had brought several plants over from the Continent, she asked for his supplier and bought some herself. She and Sir Francis exchanged letters on their techniques for growing the trees here in England. They are the first to attempt to do so, you know."

"Really?"

"It took some experimentation, and they both lost plants to frost but they learned. And now look at them!"

He did indeed look, but not at the trees, at her. It was as if a candle had been lit inside her. Her eyes shone and her cheeks flushed pink. Over a few trees! He didn't understand it.

Orlando dumped the stakes to one side of the furthermost tree and Susanna placed the box next to them. It was filled with hammer, nails, a pruning knife, and other tools.

"What does the fruit taste like?" he asked.

"The ones from these trees are quite sweet. The ones growing further down are the bitter Seville variety, which Mama planted earliest of all. The first crop will be ready in about two months. You'll be gone by then."

And so might she.

He crouched near the bundle of stakes, pretending to inspect them, but in truth his gut churned at the thought of ending the life of the extraordinarily beautiful and vibrant Lady Lynden. Surely she wasn't guilty. How could such a creature be vicious enough to end the lives of two husbands? She didn't fit the pattern of his previous targets. He'd felt no qualms ending the lives of those who committed the basest crimes and gotten away with it, but Lady Lynden was different. She couldn't possibly be guilty. Could she? And if she was, could he do what needed to be done?

He drove a stake into the soft earth, far enough that they wouldn't shift in anything less than a gale. After the first one, he turned suddenly to ask if it was to her liking, and caught her staring at him. Or at his arms, to be precise. He'd pushed his sleeves up to above his elbows and her gaze was fixed on his bare skin.

"Are you pleased, my lady?" he asked, his voice sounding thicker and more seductive than he intended. He didn't mean to flirt with her but he found he couldn't help himself.

She blushed fiercely and quickly looked away. "It will do, Mr. Holt."

He worked until all the stakes were firmly in place at regular intervals along the line of trees. There were twelve of them, all carrying green fruit the size of a child's fist. It wasn't until he parted the branches that he became aware of the number of fruit. The crop would be good if they didn't lose them to frost.

She explained all this to him as he worked. She told him the canvas would protect them from the English winter, so much colder than their native climate. She went on to tell him how Sir Francis Carew had built a wooden structure around his trees which could be removed when the weather warmed. The canvas was simply attached to the top and opened on sunny days, even in winter, and replaced at night. He'd found this the best method in England's cold winters.

"He wrote to me and said his trees like the extra protection, and there is not the hazard of the canvas sides being torn off in strong winds."

The trees *liked* it? She spoke of them as if they were people. "You could build something like that," he said.

"I could if I had six of you here on a permanent basis," she said wryly.

He picked up a mallet and hammered the last stake as far into the ground as it would go. He wished there were six of him too. Then he could continue his investigation without wasting time protecting bloody orange trees from freezing their delicate little twigs off. It was ludicrous. They weren't supposed to grow on English soil, and he was no gardener. He was the second son of a London merchant and a trained assassin, skilled at everything from surviving in the forest to dancing in foreign courts. Hughe had better be bloody appreciating the thoroughness with which he undertook this assignment. If he didn't...

Orlando smiled ruefully to himself. If Hughe didn't appreciate it, there was nothing Orlando would do. He liked being part of the Assassins' Guild and he would never jeopardize his position. The satisfaction of getting justice for victims overrode any qualms he had about taking a life, but most of all, he liked the adventure working for the Guild offered. It kept him from being bored, and being bored was something Orlando needed to avoid at all costs.

He drove another stake into the ground with all his strength, but it didn't drive the sudden, hateful memories away, or the guilt. He'd always have those.

The shimmering golden sun was hovering on the horizon by the time they returned the gardening tools to the barn. The stakes were ready for the canvas to be attached to them, but first the trees needed fertilizing and light pruning.

"We'll start tomorrow," Susanna said, walking alongside him to the house.

They skirted the perimeter of the small kitchen garden and he breathed in the scents of sage and thyme. They were the same herbs growing at his London home, and he felt a little nostalgic for the days when he and his brother would play hide and seek among the rosemary.

"Thank you, Mr. Holt," Susanna said at the door. "You're a hard worker. I'm sorry we cannot pay you better for your efforts." She dipped her head, hiding those beautiful eyes. Was she ashamed of her family's lack of fortune? Or ashamed she'd misjudged him?

"You have saved me from starving to death on a freezing night. I should thank you."

"Freezing? It's autumn, Mr. Holt, not the depths of winter. And here I thought those muscles made you tougher." She swept past him into the kitchen, leaving him staring after her.

She was flirting with him. Wasn't she? It was difficult to tell. Most women softened their caustic remarks with a wink, and some even went so far as to lift their skirts when no one was looking. Lady Lynden left him feeling uncertain and on edge. It wasn't a feeling he was used to.

He removed his hat and went into the kitchen, but Susanna had already passed through. A generously sized woman stood at the central table pounding dough with her massive fists. She looked up, not breaking her rhythm.

"You the gardener, eh?" A tangle of thin red veins spread across her cheeks and nose, and her smile revealed a gap in her front teeth. "M'lady said there'd be an extra mouth to feed for a few days. She didn't say you had the face of an angel."

An angel? That was new. "Orlando Holt at your service." He bowed, eliciting a surprisingly girlish giggle from the cook.

"You can call me Cook," she said. "Everyone does. I've been called Cook for so many years now I can't even remember my own name no more." She giggled again, making her large bosom bounce beneath her apron. "Go and wash up outside." She jerked her head at the door he'd just come through. "When Bessie's finished with the mistress, she'll show you to your room. You're to have supper

26

here with Bessie, Mr. Hendricks and me, and breakfast too. We dine with the mistress at midday every day in here."

"The servants dine with Lady Lynden in the kitchen?"

"That's the way we do things here at Stoneleigh. M'lady says it's too lonely now that Mr. Farley must stay abed so she likes to dine with us. She has her supper with her father in his room and breaks her fast in her own parlor, but for dinner we all come in here. She says she's too dirty after working all morning in the garden to sit in the dining room so the kitchen it is." She slammed her fist into the dough then picked it up and placed it on a cloth laid out on the table. "I know it's probably not how things are done where you come from." Her gaze was challenging, defiant, daring him to make fun of the arrangement or her mistress. He wondered what Cook would do if he did. Hammer him with one of those paws?

"I think it's a fine arrangement. I wouldn't want your mistress to be lonely." He ducked out through the door and found a pail of icy water and a scrubbing brush in the corner of the kitchen garden. He washed up and was about to return inside when he heard a man speaking.

"...just turned up, out of the blue," he said.

"Does he know the master can't pay him?" That was Cook.

"Aye. They offered him board and food but no money."

"And he still took the job? He must be desperate."

"That's the thing. I know there's work up at Sutton Hall, but this man Holt said he'd been round there and got turned away. There's probably work at Cowdrey too, but he says he's a gardener, not a farm laborer."

"Aye, there's a difference you know. The old mistress told me that once. She said gardeners got more knowledge so they're smarter."

"You think this Holt fellow has a brain?" The man snorted.

"He might have. Just because he's got a face like an angel and the seams of his jerkin are popping apart trying to cover those shoulders doesn't mean he's got wool between the ears."

"Humph."

"So you think he's lying about asking for work over at Sutton Hall?" Cook asked, her tone challenging.

"Could be."

"Hendricks!"

"Well, none of us know him. And he...never mind."

"He what?"

"He looks at Lady Lynden like..."

Orlando pressed himself against the wall and leaned closer to the open doorway.

"Like what?" Cook prompted. She sounded indignant, defensive. Orlando liked her even more.

"Like he wants to...you know..."

Cook clicked her tongue. "They *all* look at her like that. She's a beauty, and any man with eyes in his head goes a little foolish around her."

"Yes but he's...I don't know. There's something about him I don't like."

"You haven't met him!"

"I've seen him through the window just now. He's got a swagger about him."

"Well, I never thought I'd hear *you* judge someone before meeting them, Mr. Hendricks." The sound of chopping filled the strained silence. Orlando thought the man called Hendricks may have left, but then Cook spoke again. "You can't protect her forever."

A deep sigh then, "I know. I know, Cook. But something tells me this man Holt is going to bring trouble to Stoneleigh."

"If he does..." *Whack* went the knife on the chopping board. "...I'll slice his balls off."

Orlando winced. "Slice whose balls off?" he asked as he entered the kitchen.

Cook looked up at him but continued to chop the turnip with a precision that would make Hughe pleased if she was one of his band. A thin man covered in so many wrinkles he looked like a crumpled piece of parchment sat on a stool near the hearth, stirring the contents of the cauldron hanging from a hook above the fire. The suspicious Hendricks.

Orlando nodded at him. "Well met, sir." He held out his hand. "Orlando Holt. Gardener."

"John Hendricks, manservant." He took Orlando's forearm with a grip so hard it left behind red marks on his skin when he let go. "I hear you're helping the mistress in the garden."

"Aye."

"For how long?"

Orlando shrugged. "Until it's time to move on. I'm just passing through."

"Weather'll get bitter soon," Hendricks said. "Don't leave your departure too late."

"I won't. I hope to arrive at my sister's place in Salisbury by Christmas." He peered into the cauldron and breathed deeply. "Ahhh, I haven't smelled a broth that good in an age."

"It's beef broth left over from dinner. There's bread and cheese to go with it." Cook waved her knife at the bench seat on the other side of the table. "Sit, Mr. Holt. Hendricks, fetch the marmalade."

"Why do I have to fetch the marmalade when he gets to sit?"

She thrust out one plump hip, making her skirts swish across the flagstones at her feet. "Because he doesn't know where the pantry is and you do." She pointed the knife at a door leading off the kitchen. "And when you get back you can take the dough to the bakehouse and put it in the bread oven. It should be ready by now."

Hendricks eyed her knife. "I'm supposed to be a gentleman's groom of the bedchamber," he mumbled but softened it with a smile that made his wrinkles bend.

"And I'm supposed to just cook and Bessie's supposed to just be lady's maid." She waved her knife at the door. "Now go fetch the marmalade before poor Mr. Holt starves to death."

Hendricks's smile was replaced by a scowl. "He doesn't look like he's going to starve anytime soon," he muttered as he stalked into the adjoining pantry. He came out holding an earthen jar as another woman entered the kitchen. "Bessie, meet our newest member of staff before he expires from lack of marmalade."

Despite himself, Orlando laughed, and if he wasn't mistaken, Hendricks almost cracked a smile but held it in check. The thin old man wasn't so bad after all. Orlando rose and bowed to Bessie. "We've already met," he said. "Bessie was kind enough to grant me an audience with Mr. Farley."

"I could hardly say no when you said you wanted to help my lady in the garden." He guessed her to be aged about fifty like the other two. She had a smooth, friendly face with golden flecks in her green eyes that made them merry and spirited. A caul covered all of her hair except for the front and she stooped a little, as if her back pained her.

"Ignore Hendricks," she said with a mischievous twinkle in her eyes. "None will expire from lack of marmalade at Stoneleigh. We have enough to feed the queen's army if they pass through."

"Heaven forbid," Cook wailed. "Don't talk about armies and wars coming to Stoneleigh."

"So where did such a handsome devil as yourself blow in from?" Bessie asked Orlando.

Cook's knife stilled and Hendricks paused at the doorway, the cloth-wrapped dough in his arms. The only sound was the crackle of the fire and Orlando's heartbeat. Every time he spoke a lie he wondered if he'd be caught out, if he'd gone too far and under-estimated his audience. This time was no exception. Country folk weren't always simple. Some traveled. Others might have family in other counties.

"I worked in the garden of Collier Dean in Sussex."

"Who's the master there?" asked Hendricks.

"A gentleman by the name of Tindale." The harder his heart beat, the smoother his lies became.

"And you were gardener?"

"Aye." The shorter his answers, the less likely he was to be caught out. Hughe had taught him that and a near-fatal experience had driven the point home.

"Is Tindale nobility?" Hendricks went on.

"No."

"Does he farm his land?"

"He has sheep."

"Did you—"

"Hendricks!" Cook and Bessie cried together.

"Leave him be," Bessie said.

"Off to the bakehouse with you," Cook scolded, shooing Hendricks out the door with a shake of her knife. "Don't mind him, lad," she said to Orlando. "He's just jealous a younger and more handsome man has come into his domain."

Bessie burst out laughing. "Aye," she said. "He's used to us fussing over him, but now you've come along with your dimples and long eyelashes and he thinks we'll stop."

Hendricks flirted with the other servants? Orlando liked the old boy more and more. "I'm sorry my presence upsets him."

Cook dismissed his concern with a wave of her hand and ladled broth from the cauldron into a bowl. Bessie disappeared into the pantry and returned a moment later with bread and a wedge of cheese which she set on the table. She handed a knife to Orlando and he sliced up the cheese.

"Ignore Hendricks," Cook said, placing a bowl of broth in front of Orlando. "He's just set in his ways."

A ribbon of steam drifted up from the bowl, and Orlando breathed in its spicy aroma. He was starving. "Has he worked here long?" he asked, sitting down.

"Going on thirty years," Bessie said, sliding into the seat beside him with her bowl. "Cook and I arrived about the same time as each other, a few years later."

"That's a long time. Have you always been the only servants at Stoneleigh?"

"Goodness no," Cook said. "There were more than a dozen of us once all crowded around this table. Stable boys and maidservants and two gardeners too."

"Really?"

"Oh yes," Bessie said as Cook pulled over a stool and sat at the table with them. "They did all the hard work the mistress couldn't do on her own. That's Mistress Farley, Lady Lynden's mother."

"When did she die?"

"Three years ago. Her orange trees almost died that winter too, but Lady Lynden rallied from her grief long enough to save most. She worked hard that year, with the gardeners' help. That was before she married Lord Lynden."

"The gardeners had to be let go after that," Cook said quietly. She stared at the steam rising from her bowl. "Master couldn't afford to keep them on. Nor most of the others." She glanced at Bessie. "We were the lucky ones. We got to stay."

"Aye," Bessie said sadly. "The master was kind and took pity on us. We three were too old to get work elsewhere you see. We knew no other way except how it was at Stoneleigh. He's the kindest master is Mr. Farley. The very best."

They both bowed their heads, their voices hushed. It was as if Farley were already dead. Perhaps the old man was more ill than he appeared.

"I have a question that's been nagging at me ever since I arrived at Stoneleigh," he said. "It's a little personal and if you think I'm prying..." He left the sentence hanging. In his experience, people liked to gossip about their betters. It made gathering information from servants his favorite method of investigation.

"Go on," said Cook. "We've nothing to hide." But she glanced at the back door leading to the kitchen garden and the outbuildings where Hendricks had gone.

"Lady Lynden is a widow and her husband was the brother to the current master of Sutton Hall?"

"Cousin," Bessie said. "It's coming up to twelve months since the previous Lord Lynden left us."

"How did he die?"

Cook shrugged. "Weak heart the coroner said."

"A coroner was called?" Usually a coroner was only sent for when a death was thought to be suspicious.

"Aye. Lord Lynden was young and his death sudden. A waste of time if you ask me. Course he died of natural causes. Anyone who saw the body would know that."

"Really? What did he look like?"

She looked at him like he was a simpleton. "Like he was dead."

"You saw him?"

"No, but I know others who did."

Orlando didn't ask the rest of his questions. He didn't want to raise her suspicions, and he suspected she wasn't the right person to ask anyway. He needed to find someone who'd seen the body. Preferably the coroner himself.

"Lady Lynden must have been heartbroken," he said instead.

The ensuing silence and furtive glances told him more than words ever could. Lady Lynden wasn't heartbroken in the least.

"He was her second husband, was he not?"

"Aye," Bessie said with another glance at Cook.

"How'd you know about that?" Cook asked, dropping her spoon with a clunk in the bowl.

"I asked at the village." Orlando held up his hands in surrender, spoon and all. "I confess I wanted to find out who would be in need of my services the most. The innkeeper at The Plough told me some of Lady Lynden's history."

"Bloody Milner," Cook mumbled. "Can't keep his mouth shut, that one."

"I'm sorry I pried," Orlando said. "But I admit, Lady Lynden intrigues me."

Bessie sighed. "She intrigues all the men," she said. "That's the problem."

"Problem?"

Cook pointed her spoon at him. She seemed to do a lot of implement pointing. "She's not for the likes of you, young man. She's a gentlewoman so keep your hands to yourself."

Hendricks re-entered the kitchen with a scowl that gouged deep grooves across his forehead. "And if you don't, you might find yourself carved up in the middle of the night."

Bessie and Cook stared at him, but Hendricks had his back to them, ladling broth into a bowl from the cauldron. They were still staring when he sat next to Cook.

"Just letting our young gardener know how things lie here at Stoneleigh," Hendricks said cheerfully, scooping up a spoonful of broth.

"That's enough, Mr. Hendricks," Cook said. "He means no harm."

The air in the kitchen suddenly seemed as oppressive and charged as a summer thunderstorm. Orlando decided to leave his question about Lady Lynden's poverty and ask a more pressing, but no less provocative, one. "Indeed I don't," he said. "Poor Lady Lynden is only young and yet twice widowed. That happened to my sister by the time she was eight and twenty." He had a thousand questions for the people who'd known Susanna all her life, but there was one burning above all others to be asked. He had to approach it carefully, with stealth, so as not to fuel their suspicions. "In my sister's case, her husbands both died in the same manner too. It was very sad. People began to suspect her of doing something to bring about their deaths."

"What are you implying?" Cook blustered.

Orlando shrugged. "Only that my poor innocent sister had to suffer through suspicion from certain quarters for a time. It was unfortunate."

"It was," Bessie said, reaching for the bread and the marmalade jar.

"But that's all it is," Hendricks said. "Unfortunate. There's nothing more to the deaths. Understand?"

"Of course." He understood. He understood that it was quite a coincidence that both of Susanna's husbands died from the same cause, one that was difficult to diagnose.

CHAPTER 3

*S*usanna supervised Holt all morning, directing him how to thin out the central unproductive branches on the orange trees to allow the light through. "Like you do on any fruit tree."

"We didn't have fruit trees at Collier Dean," he said.

"Not even an orchard?"

"No. The garden was ornamental. It was designed to look pretty from the upper floors and the viewing mount overlooking it from either end. The kitchen had an herb garden though."

"Didn't the kitchen maids take care of that?"

"We gardeners helped. A lot."

He worked without rest until the dinner bell rang and received scratches across the face and arms for his efforts. Gloves protected his hands but not the sturdy gardening kind Susanna used. His were made of softer leather, the sort worn for riding and everyday wear. He said he didn't own a pair of gardening gloves. His last pair belonged to the master of Collier Dean and he'd had to leave them behind. It seemed like a strange arrangement to Susanna. Most gardeners she knew kept their own. Gloves were such a personal item and Holt had such big hands it was difficult to imagine his gloves fitting anyone else.

He gathered up some of the branches scattered on the ground and she noticed the tip of one finger poking through a hole in the leather. "Bessie can repair those for you," she said.

"Never mind. I'll work without them this afternoon."

"But you have the afternoons off."

He shot her a smile and the two dimples appeared in his cheeks. "I haven't forgotten."

"So why do more than you need to?"

He dumped the branches in a pile near the box of tools. "What else have I got to do? I know no one in the village, I have no money, and I've done enough walking in recent days to make a gentle stroll seem like a chore." He straightened and flashed those dimples again. "Besides, I enjoy your company."

Good lord, is that how he coaxed kisses from the young maids at Collier Dean? The sentiment was pleasing enough but much too trite for her taste. On the other hand, it probably wasn't the unsophisticated words that made the women swoon. More likely it was the blue eyes focusing so intently on the one he addressed, the quick smile, and boyishly handsome face.

"Why are you looking at me like that, m'lady?" Those eyes she'd been admiring shone with merriment. He was laughing at her.

A pox on him! "I'm trying to get the measure of you," she said, quite honestly.

"Oh? How so?"

"Well, since you want to remain here when I've given you leave, it makes it seem as if you enjoy being ordered about by a woman."

He laughed, a deep, resonant sound that filled the garden and made the pit of her stomach flip. "Guided, not ordered, m'lady," he said when he'd recovered. "You've been very gentle with me considering my inexperience with orange trees. Thank you." He added a little bow that tipped his hat awry.

"First day introduction," she said, bending over the tool box and rummaging through it for twine. "Tomorrow will be different." She glanced at him over her shoulder and caught him looking at her rear.

He had the good sense to redden and stumble over his next words. "I, uh, let me do that." He took the twine and squatted beside her, bumping her with his shoulder. She lost her balance and put a hand out to brace herself but he caught her before she toppled.

"Steady," he said, his fingers circling her arm at her elbow. His other hand gripped her shoulder even though she was perfectly stable again, and his thumb rubbed the leather of her jerkin. "Are you all right, Susanna?"

He spoke her name in a whisper, and it drifted on the air like a warm breeze. Her stomach flipped again and an invisible string tugged at her heart. She knew that feeling.

She jerked away and rose. "Once again you get above yourself, Mr. Holt. It's 'mistress' or 'my lady' to you."

He bowed his head and removed his hat. After a moment, he replaced it and stood too, slowly, like it was an effort. "My apologies," he said without quite looking her in the eyes. "Where would you like these branches?" He crouched again and tied the bundle of branches together.

"The stables for now. Once they've dried they can be used for firewood."

"Not the barn?"

"The barn roof leaks. The only dry space in it is kept for my gardening equipment. There should be enough room at the far end of the stables."

She watched as he tied another bundle of branches with the twine and carried them out of the garden to the stables, one on each wide shoulder. It was so easily done, as if they weighed nothing.

He disappeared into the stables and, as an afterthought, she followed him. She hesitated at the entrance and watched him set the branches down then take in all the crates of marmalades and succades stacked in the stalls. He moved on to the next stall and Silver, Susanna's mare, popped her head over the barrier. Holt seemed surprised to see her there. He rubbed Silver's nose, murmuring in her ear the entire time. Silver seemed to be enjoying herself, nuzzling his shoulder in an attempt to get closer.

Susanna cleared her throat to let him know she was there and he looked up. He smiled. "I didn't know you had a horse," he said.

"Silver's a placid old girl but can pull the cart when necessary."

"She must be lonely in here all by herself."

"Mr. Holt, if we could afford another horse, don't you think we'd have one?"

He merely shrugged and fell into step beside her as they left the stables. "And what are all those jars and crates for?"

"Are you this nosy everywhere you go?"

He smiled. "Everywhere."

"And do you usually get answers?"

"Almost always."

"I see." She watched him out of the corner of her eye but found it difficult to get his measure even when he thought he wasn't being watched. He seemed like the calmest, most amiable man she'd ever met. It had to be false, a ruse to win her confidence. The other calm, amiable men she'd known had used those traits to cover up a more sinister side. Perhaps Holt's sinister side was that he was a thief, one who thought she had something to steal. Well, if he was, the marmalades and succades stored in the jars and crates in the stables would be of little interest to someone with no means of transporting them. He couldn't fit enough in his pack to make a decent amount of money selling them at market.

Besides, Susanna didn't think he was a thief—a thief would have gone to the wealthier Sutton Hall—but she couldn't be entirely sure yet.

"The products made from the oranges are in those jars," she said.

"I see." He showed not the least interest in finding out more.

They washed up and went into the kitchen for dinner where Cook and Bessie had set the table for five. In the middle of the table was a loaf of dark bread, bowl of peas, turnips, and slices of beef.

When Hendricks joined them, having delivered her father's dinner to him, Susanna bid them all to sit. "How is Father today?" she asked.

"Well enough," Hendricks said. "He seems in good spirits lately." His face knotted in thought. "Very good spirits. It's as if his troubles have ceased."

"Remarkable," Cook said.

"It's the Lord's doing."

And with that, they bowed their heads and gave thanks for their meal.

Susanna watched Holt surreptitiously through lowered lashes. He talked comfortably with the other servants, his manner friendly and open, although Hendricks scowled more than usual. It seemed she wasn't the only one who didn't quite trust Holt. It wasn't just that he was *too* friendly. It was also the way he'd unsettled her with his touch in the garden. It had been such an innocent gesture, yet not. Not the way she'd responded—like something dormant inside her had come to life.

He looked up suddenly and his lips curved into a wicked half-smile, as if he knew exactly what she was thinking. "Can you pass the bread, m'lady?" he asked. She did. "And is there any more of that marmalade from last night's supper? It was delicious."

Cook and Bessie chuckled and Hendricks snorted. "Aye," the manservant said, "there's plenty more marmalade." Susanna couldn't help smiling along with them.

Holt cocked his head to the side, his questioning gaze settling on her. "Is something amusing?"

"No," she said before anyone else could answer. "It's just that we all love marmalade at Stoneleigh, and there's always a jar or two available."

"I'll get it," he said when Cook rose. "Is it in the pantry?"

"Should be," she said, settling her bulk back on the chair and winking at Susanna. "If not, try the stables."

"You keep your preserves in the stables?" he said from the doorway to the pantry.

"Aye."

He emerged from the pantry holding a jar which he turned round and round in his hands. "Now I understand," he said to Susanna, holding up the jar. "This marmalade is made from your orange trees."

"It is," she said.

"And you store the rest of it in the stables."

"We do."

He set it on the table then spread some of the preserve over his bread and took a bite. It wasn't long before the whole piece was gone. "It's delicious." Holt licked his fingers. "Are all those jars and crates in the stables filled with orange marmalade?"

"As well as succades made from the peel," Cook said before Susanna could steer the conversation away. Just in case he was prying for nefarious reasons.

"I love succades," he said, then fell suddenly silent.

"You've tasted succades before?"

"No. I've confused succades with...something else." He cleared his throat and concentrated on his food. Susanna watched him, mentally adding another layer to the story of Mr. Holt. Succades were a luxury. She would not have thought a simple gardener would be able to afford the sugared fruit. Mr. Holt was turning into quite the mystery.

"We still need to find a buyer for them," Bessie said. She sounded quite disheartened, but when she caught Susanna's frown, she turned on a sweet smile.

Susanna didn't fall for that trick. She knew Bessie better than she'd known her own mother. The maid had been her nurse since Susanna was a babe and became her governess and lady's maid as she grew up. She was clearly worried.

Indeed, all three of her servants seemed cast down. They must have known how perilous their situation was. If Susanna could not find a merchant to buy her marmalades and succades, there would be no money to pay her beloved servants, no money to fix Stoneleigh. She thought she would have heard back from the

London merchants by now. Those letters had been sent months ago. If she didn't secure one of them soon, the situation would become dire. There was only enough money to last the winter. After that, she would have to do something drastic.

She would have to marry again.

A dark, cold mass seeped through to her bones. She shuddered violently and set her knife carefully on her plate. She was no longer hungry, not even for marmalade.

"Are you all right?" Holt asked, half-rising.

"Of course I am." She regretted her harsh tone immediately. Holt had been a great help to her, more than she could have hoped for. Her ill-feeling toward him was best pushed to one side and forgotten. No doubt it was merely a product of her suspicious nature when it came to charming men.

If Holt felt the barb of her words, he didn't show it. "You're not selling the marmalades at the village market?" he asked.

"We sell a few jars," Cook said. "Oranges are a rare luxury, see, and the locals cannot afford the fruit or the products, and we cannot afford to sell them for less than their worth."

"Only the highest of the nobility can truly appreciate oranges," Hendricks said with an imperial tilt of his chin. When he did that, his accent changed, so there was none of the country in it at all, but sounded as condescending as Jeffrey's. "Our succades are fit for the queen herself."

Cook snorted. "You're a toss-pot, Hendricks."

"Leave him," Bessie scolded gently. "He's right. Our oranges are the nation's best."

"We have the nation's *only* oranges," Cook said. "Aside from Sir Francis Carew's." She leaned closer to Holt at her side. "Don't mind Hendricks. He thinks Stoneleigh is the most noble country estate in all the kingdom."

"It may be," Hendricks said defensively. "The Farleys have owned it for hundreds of years, and they arrived with William the Conqueror himself."

"Unfortunately, it's not the *richest* estate," Bessie said then flushed and dipped her head. "At least, not right now."

"Hush, Bessie," Hendricks said. "The lad doesn't need to know our business."

"It's all right," Susanna said. "I doubt she's telling Mr. Holt something he doesn't already know."

"Aye, true." Hendricks stabbed a slice of beef with his knife more viciously than necessary. "Mr. Holt here does seem to have a way of finding out information about Stoneleigh."

Susanna's heart stilled. "What do you mean?"

Holt cleared his throat. "Mr. Hendricks is referring to the village innkeeper's gossiping. I asked him a few questions about the estates around about, and he told me more than I needed to know."

"He's got a loose tongue, has Milner," Bessie said.

"Ignore Hendricks," Cook said, shooting a glare at the servant across the table. "We do."

An uneasy silence settled around the small group. It was something Susanna wasn't used to. Her three servants always got along so well. There were never any harsh words exchanged between them, never charged silences.

"Is there any more marmalade?" Holt asked, tearing off another hunk of bread.

"Here you go," Cook said, passing him the jar. "Eat up. It soothes the stomach, you know."

"Helps with wind too," Bessie said. "Just ask Mr. Hendricks."

Everyone burst into laughter, all except poor Hendricks, who gave Bessie his most withering scowl.

"Lo! Lady Lynden?" Farmer Cowdrey's loud, gruff voice came from outside.

"In the kitchen," Susanna called back. She rose to greet him but it wasn't just Cowdrey's bulk that filled the doorway. It was his sister's much more slender form too, holding a basket.

"What a lovely surprise to see you both," Susanna said. "Margaret, how are you? Fully recovered I hope?"

Margaret Cowdrey's pretty features lifted in an unconvincing smile. "Yes, thank you." She handed over the basket. "Thank you for the marmalades and bread, but I assure you, it's not necessary. Unfortunately the bread went stale, but you'll find your marmalades just the same as when you gave them to Walter."

"Oh, you didn't need to give them back. They were for you. A get-well gift from Father and I."

"Thank you, but as I explained to Walter when he brought them home, we didn't need anything." Her brother blushed to the roots of his red-brown hair and studiously stared down at his boots. "My servants are capable of making preserves and bread, and you need them more than us."

Susanna took the basket. It was indeed still filled with the two jars of marmalade she'd sent to her ill neighbor. Margaret's pettiness grew worse and worse. Susanna felt a twinge of guilt at her unkind thoughts toward a woman she'd once called friend. They'd known each other their entire lives and played together as children, yet Margaret, the older by a year, had become distant as they grew up. When Susanna was fifteen, Margaret had gone so far as to turn her back as Susanna approached her after church. She'd offered no explanation then or since. Susanna had married and moved away a year later but upon her return, she'd discovered Margaret's feelings had not changed. Susanna eventually gave up trying to find out what the problem was and the two women successfully avoided each other most of the time.

It must gall Margaret that her brother had asked Susanna to marry him. That's if she knew. When Susanna had asked Walter what Margaret had thought after his first proposal, he'd simply shrugged and said he hadn't told her yet. She didn't ask him after the second and third. It no longer seemed to matter.

"What was your illness again? Your brother didn't quite know."

Walter Cowdrey shuffled his feet. "A fever," Margaret said. "I'm still a little weak from it, so do not expect to see me much." Indeed her face did seem paler than usual, the freckles more vibrant across her nose. She was a handsome woman with alluring gray eyes and a neat figure, yet she had failed to secure herself a husband. Perhaps it was because of all the bitterness running through her. The entire village knew to watch out if Margaret Cowdrey was in one of her tempers.

"Have you eaten yet?" Susanna asked.

"Aye," said Walter. "In The Plough just now, thank you, m'lady."

Out of the corner of her eye, Susanna saw Margaret wince, but she didn't know why. Perhaps it was because she hated the way her brother blinked his lashes at Susanna or the way he massaged the brim of his hat with his big hands as if it were Susanna's hand. Actually, the thought made her wince too. Having any part of her massaged by Walter made her want to run in the opposite direction.

Now if it were Holt doing the massaging...

"Please finish your dinner, Lady Lynden, and don't mind us," Walter said. "I'll just wait until you're done." He nodded at Hendricks, Bessie, and Cook, then his gaze fell on Holt.

Holt rose and Susanna introduced them. Holt smiled in greeting and Cowdrey almost did. One side of his mouth twitched and all! Farmer Cowdrey wasn't known for his joviality. Not that he was sour like his sister, he simply wasn't one of life's happy souls with a ready smile. Not like Orlando Holt.

A few years older than Margaret, Walter and his father before him were good neighbors. The Cowdreys had been luckier than her father and not lost their entire harvest to bad weather several years in a row. Or perhaps it wasn't luck but better management. Susanna was under no illusion that her father made a good farmer. A good gentleman perhaps, but he'd been sent away to live with his aunt in London at an early age and so had not received the same farm education that his older brother, the heir, had. He wasn't supposed to have inherited Stoneleigh at all.

"Sit. Eat," Walter said.

"I'm finished," Susanna said. She wasn't, but she couldn't eat while guests in her house did not, and especially with Margaret looking down her snub nose at the servants. "Is something the matter?"

"No." Walter's hands worked harder on his hat, crushing it even more. There was dirt under his overlong fingernails, and the skin around the knuckles looked dry and worn, much like his face. While not as haggard as Hendricks, Farmer Cowdrey had a comfortable face, rather like a well-worn pair of gloves. Permanent wrinkles fanned out from the corners of his eyes and bracketed his mouth. He didn't need to smile to make them appear. He looked far older than his thirty years. "I heard in the village that you'd hired a gardener." His gaze traveled to Holt and Holt nodded once more. He was still standing. "I told Margaret we had to come and find out more. Can't have you being taken advantage of, Susanna."

The use of her name caught her unawares, and the soft way in which he spoke it made her face redden. He almost always used the more formal Lady Lynden, unlike Margaret, and this new intimacy worried her. Could he possibly be working up to another proposal?

"I have, on a temporary basis only," Susanna said. "Mr. Holt is passing through and needed the work. Since I needed help, we came to a mutual arrangement." She saw no reason to discuss the particulars with Walter and Margaret. The entire parish didn't need to know how dire her father's financial situation was, although everyone had to know by now. Her lack of staff, horses, and land were a sign even the most dull-witted could see.

Walter took a step closer to her and lowered his head. Dark red strands of hair flopped over his face. "You could have asked me, Susanna. I would have spared a man for you at no cost. Still can."

"Walter!" Margaret said through a jaw so tight it must ache. "You're very noble, but have you forgotten how hard everyone is working at this time of year? I'm sure Susanna understands that we simply cannot spare anyone."

"Thank you anyway," Susanna said, giving Walter a sympathetic smile, "but I'm happy with Holt."

Margaret cleared her throat but said nothing. She clasped her hands in front of her skirts and tilted her chin, a rather insidious smile on her lips. There was no doubt in Susanna's mind what she was implying, but her brother seemed not to understand. He simply shifted his weight and watched Holt from beneath the curtain of hair. "Milner at The Plough said he's a stranger to these parts." He spoke quietly, but everyone in the kitchen would have heard.

Holt had still not sat down. There was no smile on his lips now, no friendly greeting in his eyes. He stood like a tightly coiled rope.

"He is," she said. "As I said, he's passing through."

"Where you from?" Walter asked Holt.

"Sussex."

"Where in Sussex?"

"A manor called Collier Dean."

"Never heard of it."

Holt shrugged. "I'd never heard of Stoneleigh, Sutton Hall, or Cowdrey Farm until I passed through the village. Doesn't mean they don't exist." He smiled, but it lacked the brightness Susanna had come to expect.

Walter's mouth worked as if he were chewing an invisible piece of straw. "You should have come to me, Susanna," he said, low. "We're neighbors. I don't like strangers here in our valley. Too many of them lately." He slapped his hat on his head, nodded at Susanna, and stormed out.

Margaret stared after them, her mouth agape like a dead fish. Slowly, a blush crept up her throat, over her cheeks to her hairline. "I, uh... Farewell." She left without a glance back.

Susanna watched them go, bewildered and a little annoyed. Like Jeffrey, Walter Cowdrey thought she was incapable of managing Stoneleigh on her own. It was nice of them to be concerned but honestly! She wasn't a child anymore and she had a father still living. She didn't need another parental figure, or another husband for that matter. How many times would she have to say no to their marriage proposals and offers of help before it would sink into their thick-headed male skulls?

"Please continue eating," she said to Holt and the others.

"Odd man," Cook muttered, slathering marmalade over her bread. "Always thought that."

"He's not odd," Bessie said. "He's just not as comfortable around people as most."

"Not as odd as his sister."

"At least they're locals," Hendricks said, saluting his cup at Holt. "We've known the Cowdreys forever, and they've always come to Stoneleigh's aid when we needed them."

Susanna had always been happy to accept their offers, but not now. Not since she'd turned down Walter's proposals. Any dealings she now had with him had become too awkward to endure. This was simply the latest, and the oddest.

* * *

SUSANNA LAY in bed and stared up at the tester, her mind awhirl. Usually she fell asleep as soon as her head hit the pillow, but not tonight. Tonight she couldn't stop marveling at how much work Orlando Holt had achieved in such a short time. The trees were pruned and the stakes in place for the canvas covering. He was a good worker, he never complained, and he rarely stopped, despite her insistence that he ought to. Indeed, the man always seemed to be smiling or jesting or flirting. She found herself liking him despite her instincts screaming at her to be wary, to not trust him.

She sighed and rolled over, pulling the blanket up to her chin, but still she couldn't sleep. Her stomach rumbled, a sure sign sleep wasn't going to claim her. She got out of bed and put on a warm housecoat and soft slippers then grabbed the candle and used the embers in the fireplace to light it.

She crept quietly out to the landing, not wanting to wake her father, and down the stairs. Halfway down, she stopped. Listened.

All was silent. Yet she was sure she'd heard something. The click of a door opening or closing perhaps.

"Father?" she whispered loudly. "Is that you?"

Nothing. She went back up to the first floor and opened her father's study door. "Father?" Nothing, and the door to his bedchamber beyond was closed. She checked the other unoccupied chambers, but they too were empty, silent.

With a shrug, she returned to the stairs and went down to the kitchen. It was still warm thanks to the glowing logs in the fireplace and she stood at the big hearth for a moment until the chill had left her bones. Another growl of her stomach forced her to investigate the pantry. She found bread and cheese and set them on the table. She was about to sit when Holt wandered in, yawning.

He smothered it when he saw her. "I didn't know you were in here, m'lady. My apologies for disturbing your late night supper."

"No need to apologize, Mr. Holt. I assume you couldn't sleep either, and your stomach led you here."

He slid onto the bench seat at the table and chuckled. The flame on her candle wobbled before straightening again. It wasn't until that moment that she realized he didn't have a light of his own. How had he seen his way in the dark?

"You have my measure, m'lady. I often wake with hunger in the middle of the night and can't sleep until I eat. You may soon regret your offer of board *and* food."

She slid the bread across to him. "A body as big as yours must take some fueling."

He looked down at himself. He was dressed in breeches and a shirt but not shoes. His feet must be freezing on the cold flagstone floor. "I am not *that* big."

"You certainly are, Mr. Holt. Not fat, mind, just tall and strongly built."

"Made for gardening," he said and laughed.

"You achieved a lot today. Thank you," she added and meant it.

She may not like the man, but he'd worked hard for little reward and deserved some thanks.

He lifted one shoulder. "I did no more than any other gardener would."

She shook her head. "I've had gardeners before and they weren't nearly as hard-working as you."

He balanced a slice of cheese on the top of his bread and regarded her. "So you don't regret refusing Lord Lynden's and Farmer Cowdrey's offers?"

"Not in the least. Their offers are not unconditional," she said without thinking. Perhaps she should be more careful—Holt was a stranger after all, and her business was none of his.

He was also just a gardener and she the mistress of the house. The likes of Jeffrey would be shocked to learn she and Holt shared a meal in the kitchen late at night.

"Oh?" he asked, watching her intently. "What do you mean?"

"Nothing." She bit into her bread to stop herself saying more.

He watched her a moment longer, and she was almost undone by the look of concern in his eyes, but then he blinked rapidly and shook his head, just a little, as if shaking off a thought. The curious movement intrigued her. What had he been thinking?

But she knew the answer to that. It was what all men thought about, particularly late at night, alone with a woman. She'd best remember that.

She returned her bread to the trencher and pushed it away, no longer hungry. "Good night, Mr. Holt," she said, her voice brittle.

"You're going?"

"I must." She had to get away from him. In quiet moments like this, she could feel her wariness dissolving, her defenses lowering. "Do you need the candle to light your way back to the servants' wing?"

He stood too. "No, thank you." He sounded distracted. "Is everything all right? You seem a little upset all of a sudden."

"I'm tired. That's all." She used her flame to light one of the candle stubs on the mantelpiece. "Take it," she said, holding it out to him. "I insist."

"I can see. There's enough moonlight coming through the windows."

"Take it." She shoved it into his hands. "I don't want you tripping and hurting yourself."

"Too valuable, am I?" Candlelight twinkled in his eyes and shadows played around his smiling mouth. Good lord but he was the most handsome man she'd seen. Much, much too handsome and too charming. There must be an entire county of heartbroken women left behind in Sussex.

"Ha! You're a gardener with no knowledge of fruit trees, Mr. Holt, I hardly call that valuable."

"Ouch."

She ignored him and nodded at the food still on the table. "Please eat your fill. There's always plenty of bread, cheese, and marmalade at Stoneleigh." The wheat for the bread came from Sutton Hall lands and the cheese from Cowdrey Farm, all reminders that she didn't need to be beholden to those men any more than she already was.

"I've finished anyway," he said. "Good night, mistress. You go to bed and I'll tidy up."

She paused at the door as a thought occurred to her. A thought that troubled her more than his flirting did. "Did you come straight from the servants' wing?"

"Of course. Why?"

"Nothing. It doesn't matter."

He came up to her and took her elbow for an instant before dropping his hand to his side. "Tell me, m'lady. What's wrong?"

"I thought I heard a noise upstairs near Father's study." She waved her hand in dismissal, but worry gnawed at her. She couldn't tell if he was lying. Indeed, his type were experts at lies, and she had no way of knowing when and if he spoke the truth.

"I'll check for you."

She was about to tell him no but decided to let him accompany her. Perhaps it hadn't been him. Perhaps there was someone else... Oh God. "Very well."

Together they returned the bread and cheese to the pantry and, each carrying a candle, climbed the stairs to the main private chambers. He kept very close, a solid presence at her side that was both a comfort and distraction. Being near him made her heart race and her skin hot as if she suffered from a fever. Indeed, thinking clearly had suddenly become very difficult. She'd been close to him before, out in the garden, and that was distracting enough, but in the dark and quiet house, it was heady and thrilling. A small voice told her she shouldn't be doing this with a strong man she hardly knew, but she didn't think she could tell him to leave. Not a single part of her wanted him to go, and all of her wanted him to stay. To move closer, to hold her so she could press her lips to his throat, his shoulder, his mouth.

She heaved in a ragged breath. Her self-control hung by a thread.

"Where did you hear the noise?" he asked.

She blew out the breath slowly, calming her nerves a little. "Near Father's study." She pointed to a door. "I thought I heard it open or close."

"Is it locked?"

"No."

"May I go in to check that no one is hiding inside?"

She nodded. Her heart hammered as she watched him look around the study, under the desk, inside the large trunks. When he finished, she opened the door leading to her father's bedchamber. He was asleep in bed, softly snoring. Safe. She closed the door and almost laughed at her silliness. No one had been sneaking around Stoneleigh. Who would do that and why? She and her father had very little to steal and no secrets. Even Mr. Holt, the only stranger in their midst, must realize that.

She watched him closely for any sign of guilt but saw none. Either he was a good liar, or he hadn't been there at all earlier.

Indeed, she'd begun to doubt her own hearing. A small *click* could be anything or nothing.

If he was lying and he *had* crept through the house, he would have discovered her father kept no money in his study. What little they had she kept well hidden in the outbuildings.

"Thank you," she said out on the landing. "Everything seemed in its right order."

"Good. I'm glad."

"Good night, Mr. Holt."

He suddenly caught her hand and before she could withdraw it, he'd pressed it to his lips. Her sharp intake of breath was as much from shock as desire. Both shot through her like a lightning bolt, catching her unawares. She did not remove her hand.

His mouth lingered, warm and soft, until all of a sudden he dropped her hand as if it had burned him. "I, uh...hell." He raked his fingers through his dark hair, making it stick out at distressed angles, and he looked to the beams overhead. "I'm sorry. I...you..." He completed the sentence with a shake of his head. "I'm sorry," he muttered again. "I'd better go."

She nodded, not trusting her voice. Her entire body shook with barely contained emotion, but her mind shut down, went numb. She backed away until she came up against her bedchamber door. She fumbled for the handle and opened it. Without saying another word, she stumbled inside and leaned against the closed door.

Breathe.

Thank God she'd got away before she did something foolish. If she had not...

The thought dangled like a tempting morsel within reach, so close yet too dangerous to even entertain it.

Later, when she was once more tossing and turning in bed, she congratulated herself on not making yet another mistake with yet another charming man.

* * *

ORLANDO SLIPPED AWAY DOWN the stairs, although his mind was still back up on the landing. He couldn't think straight, and he got lost on his way to the servants' wing. Somehow he ended up in the kitchen again.

He sat on a chair and lowered his head into his hands. Christ. He wanted her. Wanted to kiss her and take her in his arms. And bed her. He definitely wanted to do that. Not a good idea if she turned out to be a murderer. When he first met her he'd thought he could bed a woman for amusement then kill her if he had to. Now, he wasn't so sure. Susanna had gotten under his skin. Beauty and vulnerability had a way of doing that. The combination turned strong men into weak fools. Orlando thought he was strong enough, that his training had shut down the part of him that cared. Clearly it needed more work.

He breathed in deeply then, feeling better, stood and padded to the pantry. Since he was alone once more, he might as well continue his search. He didn't expect to find anything in the kitchen area, but he didn't dare return to the private chambers tonight. If Susanna felt as frustrated as he did, she would be awake for some time. He couldn't risk her discovering him sneaking about. She was already suspicious enough.

It had been a close call earlier. He thought she'd been asleep when he entered her father's apartments. If she had gone through to the adjoining bedchamber upon first hearing him, he would have been discovered. As it was, all he'd done was frighten her, something he regretted deeply.

Bah! He shook off the sentimental notion. There was no room for sentimentality. There was no room for the feelings that flared whenever he was near Lady Lynden. There was his job and that was all. It was his life. It gave him a purpose, a sense that he was achieving something by bringing justice into unjust world, but it was also a means of staving off boredom. Drudgery turned him into a person he despised and brought danger to the door of his loved ones.

Now there was only the Assassins Guild and its other two

remaining members, Hughe and Cole, his friends. His *brothers*, closer to him than his actual one. The likes of Orlando could hope for nothing more.

He held up the candle to throw as much light as possible around the large but mostly empty pantry. There were a few sacks of grain on the floor, several jars of differing sizes on the dresser, bread, and a wheel of cheese inside separate boxes. There had to be something to implicate or exonerate Susanna once and for all, and he was going to find it.

At least he now knew where her chambers were. He suspected what he needed to find would be located in there. All he had to do was get inside without making her suspicious and—

A scream rent the night apart.

Susanna!

He ran.

CHAPTER 4

*O*rlando burst through the door to Susanna's bedchamber. There was enough moonlight coming through the window for him to see her standing at the side of the bed. Alone, thank God.

"Out there!" she cried. "Quick, he's escaping!" She pointed a brass candlestick at the open casement window but did not move from the bedside.

He leaned on the sill and looked down. A cloaked figure sprinted along the path away from the house toward a horse teth-ered to a bush. *Bloody hell.* Orlando couldn't reach the intruder in time before he mounted, and raising a hue and cry would be useless with old Hendricks being the only able bodied man within earshot, and the able bodied part was debatable anyway.

Orlando thumped the window frame and the glass panes rattled. Like many things at Stoneleigh, it needed repairing.

"He's gone," he said, as the rider rode off. "He must have used the vines to climb up and down." They were one floor up and ivy covered the wall and part of the window itself. Using the vines as a ladder wasn't a method many would choose to enter the upper floors, nor was it something easily done. The intruder was agile and courageous. Or foolish and desperate. "Did you see him?"

When she didn't answer, he closed the window and returned to her. She still held the candlestick in both hands with the unlit wick pointed at the window. A weapon. He gently took her shoulders. She trembled.

"Susanna? Are you hurt?"

She shook her head.

He pried the heavy candlestick from her grip and placed it on the table beside the bed. She looked at him through wide eyes brimming with fear. He stepped forward, just as she too moved closer, and folded her in his arms. She didn't cry, but her body shuddered, and he held her harder, tighter, careful not to crush her but enough to let her know she was safe. Her cheek pressed against his chest and her head tucked under his chin. He'd expected her to smell of the earth but instead she smelled of something sweet. It must be the scent she'd added to her water but he couldn't place the aroma. Whatever it was, it smelled intoxicating and it scrambled his senses.

She drew in a long, ragged breath that pillowed her breasts against him and made the waterfall of her hair ripple over his bare forearms. He reached one hand up to massage the back of her neck, marveling at the way the soft strands slid through his fingers. Like the finest silk. Finer. He could tease it and hold her all night and not grow tired of the feel of her. His groin ached and his skin grew hot, tight. He wanted her more than he'd wanted any woman. To hear her soft moans in his ear, feel her flesh against his—

"Unhand her!" growled Hendricks from the doorway.

Susanna pulled away. Orlando sighed and wished he had a few moments more of the sweet torture.

"It's all right, Hendricks," she said. "Mr. Holt was...protecting me."

The shadowy form of the servant entered the bedchamber. He wore nothing but a nightshirt and cap. The poor fellow must be cold and indeed, the hand holding the dagger shook, but that could have been from age or from the exertion of running up the stairs.

"Oh, my lady!" said Bessie, crowding in behind Hendricks. "Oh my dear girl, what's happened? Has he hurt you?"

"It wasn't me," Orlando said, hands up in surrender. "There was an intruder."

"An intruder!" Bessie pushed past Hendricks and enveloped Susanna in her arms, but Susanna was the one who uttered soothing words of comfort to the maid.

"It's all right now. He's gone," she said, rubbing Bessie's back.

"You sure it wasn't this fellow?" Hendricks jerked the knife at Orlando.

"I'm sure." Susanna glanced at Orlando quickly then away. "I didn't see the intruder's face, but he went out the window the instant before Mr. Holt came through the door upon hearing my scream. It couldn't have been he."

"Upon hearing you scream, eh?" Hendricks said, frowning. "He came all the way from the servants' wing in an *instant*?"

"Not the servants' wing, from the kitchen." Orlando gave Susanna a shrug. "I was still hungry."

"Hendricks, please lower the knife," she said. "I can assure you, it was not Mr. Holt."

Hendricks obeyed. His frown didn't disappear but became more uncertain, as if he was thinking something through. He said nothing, however, just continued to glare at Orlando.

"Oh, my poor baby," Bessie said, "you could have been hurt." She held Susanna at arm's length. "Look at you in your nightgown. You must be freezing. Get back in bed."

"I'm all right, Bessie." She looked over the little maid's head as Cook rolled through the door, breathing hard. She pressed a hand to her bosom and held her candle high.

"What happened?" she asked. "What's going on?"

"An intruder," Hendricks said.

"An intruder!"

"Mr. Holt scared him away," Bessie said.

"Everyone's all right," Susanna added. "Now, please go back to bed. Nothing more can be done."

"Not yet," Bessie said. "He might come back."

Was Orlando the only one who could see the sheen of fear in Susanna's eyes again? He ached to comfort her. Alone. In her bed.

Later.

"I'll check the master." Hendricks shuffled off, apparently no longer thinking Orlando was a threat. If he only knew...

"And I'll warm up some milk," Cook said. "You used to like warm milk whenever you had nightmares as a girl." Instead of leaving, she leaned a shoulder against the door frame. "Just let me catch my breath first."

Bessie pulled back the covers on the bed and patted the mattress. "Hop in before you catch your death, m'lady."

Susanna glanced at Orlando. There was enough light to see that she struggled to control her emotions, but whether those emotions were fear, embarrassment, or desire he couldn't tell. He really hoped it was desire.

"Mr. Holt," she said, "thank you for coming to my aid. I appreciate it."

"You don't need to thank me. Rescuing damsels in distress is a hobby of mine. It's something I do when I'm not gardening." He said it to lighten the mood and it almost worked. A hint of a smile played around her lips. If they'd been alone, he would have touched her mouth to tease it out again, but both maids were staring at him and he could hear Hendricks's footsteps returning along the landing.

"The master's still asleep," the servant said from the doorway. "He can't have heard anything."

Susanna rubbed her temple. "Good. Now, off to bed everyone. There's no need for us all to be tired tomorrow."

"Not yet," Orlando said. "I have some questions."

"*You* have some questions for the mistress?" Hendricks's jaw went slack with disbelief. "She has ordered you to leave. I think you should listen to her."

"It's all right, Hendricks," Susanna said. "Ask away, Mr. Holt. If you think your questions will shed some light on this incident, then please go ahead. I would like to know who would do such a thing."

Orlando thanked her. "You said you didn't see the intruder, is that right?"

"I didn't."

"Not even a little?"

"He wore a hood and it was dark."

"He? Are you sure it was a man?"

The notion that it could have been a woman seemed to surprise her. "I, well, I don't know." She shook her head. "It's difficult to gauge size from the bed and he or she was only half way through the window when I screamed. I wasn't fully asleep so I heard it open."

"Did the intruder say anything?"

"No."

"Make any sound at all? Something that could identify him or her?"

"Nothing." She folded her arms over her chest and rubbed her shoulders.

"I think that's enough questions for now, Mr. Holt," Bessie said, circling her arm around Susanna's waist. "Maybe she'll think of something else overnight."

"Be sure to tell me if you do."

"Aye, and then we'll tell Lord Lynden too."

"Lynden?"

"He's the justice of the peace for the parish," Susanna said. "He needs to know if someone tried to steal from us."

What would a fool like Lynden do? The man didn't look capable of holding a sword properly let alone actually wielding it to apprehend someone. His lace cuffs would get in the way. Yet Orlando knew appearances could be deceptive. Hughe was the best swordsman he'd met, and he wore a ruff and an attitude of apathy to rival Lynden's.

As the justice of the peace, Lynden didn't have to exert himself anyway, he could send others to make an arrest—but first he needed to know who was guilty.

"I'll sleep with you tonight, m'lady," Bessie said, pulling back the covers on the far side of the large bed. "Cook, I'll have a cup of that warm milk too, if you don't mind."

"I don't mind, but Hendricks here'll have to bring it up. Those stairs will be the death of me. Don't know how you do it, Bessie," Cook muttered as she left.

Orlando followed Cook and Hendricks out of the bedchamber. He didn't look back at Susanna. He didn't want to see the fear in her eyes again. It unsettled him more than her beauty, and he had an inexplicable urge to banish it.

"If it's all right with you," he said to the two servants when the door was closed, "I'll sleep here for the rest of the night."

"What, in my lady's parlor?" Cook asked.

"Yes."

"On the floor?"

"It's dry and not crawling with lice—what more do I need?"

She huffed. "All right then. Hendricks, fetch Mr. Holt a mattress and blankets."

Hendricks did as he was told, but only after giving Orlando a glare that was as blunt and hard as a hammer blow.

"It might be a good idea not to mention this to Lady Lynden," Orlando told them when the manservant returned. "She may not want me here, so close to her bedchamber."

"She's not the only one," Hendricks muttered.

Later, sitting on the mattress with his back against the paneled parlor wall, Orlando sipped his warm cup of milk and tried to push aside his emotional reaction to Susanna's fear and think about the intruder.

Who would come into her room like that, and why? A thief who didn't know she had nothing to steal? A kidnapper?

Or an assassin?

If it was the latter, who aside from himself had been hired to kill Lady Lynden? And even more importantly, how hard were they willing to investigate her before performing the deed?

He got no sleep for the rest of the night.

* * *

SUSANNA MANAGED to keep her distance from Holt in the garden the next morning. It was easy enough to do the weeding at one end while he did the other, her back to him most of the time. Some of the weeds and grass reached to her thighs, but the work was relaxing and satisfying if a little tiring. Unfortunately it also let her mind wander—straight to the intruder.

Holt had asked more questions as soon as they were alone in the garden but none that she hadn't already tried to answer herself as she lay awake beside a softly snoring Bessie. Who would break into Stoneleigh and why? It didn't make sense. They had nothing to steal except for their marmalades and succades, and they needed a cart and horse to move them. Besides, the jars were in the stables and any thief would search the outbuildings first before venturing into the house. So it had to be someone who didn't know the situation at Stoneleigh. A stranger. She'd told Holt so. He'd simply nodded and set to work.

Holt. Orlando. He'd woken something within her last night outside her bedchamber, something she'd thought dormant. His simple kiss of her hand made her skin feel like it was on fire. Her heart had never thumped so hard or so loud. Then later, after the intruder left, she'd wanted to sink into Holt's strength and feel it envelop her, keep her safe. To be held by such a man...to make love to him...

She shuddered despite the warmth of the sun on her back. The emotions he'd triggered alarmed her. She'd tried so hard to bury that side of herself. In the light of day, she thanked God she'd been strong enough to walk away from Holt despite every part of her body begging for him. He was not a man she wanted to know intimately.

He suddenly looked up as if he knew she was watching. He didn't smile, didn't wink or do any of those flirtatious things she'd come to expect from him, but simply looked, as if he was trying to see into her.

She wrenched a particularly tough weed out and threw it onto the growing pile of uprooted ones. She forced herself to think about something other than Holt or the intruder, and planned the formal garden directly in front of the house instead. Come spring, she could plant lavender and roses. They smelled divine when in bloom and their flowers were so pretty. The formal garden had been neglected since her father let the gardeners go but Susanna wanted to restore it to its former beauty. Hopefully she would soon secure a buyer for the succades and marmalades and there'd be money to spare for plants.

"Let me help you with that," said Holt.

At first Susanna thought he was speaking to her, but when she turned, she saw him approach Hendricks who struggled with a heavy chair.

"Mr. Farley wishes to sit in the sun and watch you work," Hendricks said to Susanna, ignoring Holt even as the gardener took the chair off him.

"Set it near the oranges," she said. "That's his favorite spot."

"How will he get out here?" Holt asked, setting the chair down.

"I'll help him walk," Hendricks said.

"Allow me."

"I can do it."

"You both can," Susanna said. Honestly, men were worse than children sometimes.

They left together, and she continued weeding until they brought her father into the garden. He limped heavily and had one arm around Holt while Hendricks carried a blanket and cushion. The servant looked unhappy and took great pains to plump the cushion and arrange it on the chair.

"Ah," her father said, sitting. "The fresh air pleases me."

"The air is certainly fresh out here," Susanna said, placing the blanket across his lap. "Tell me when you get cold, and Mr. Holt will take you back inside."

He waved off her concern. "The sun is out. The sky is blue. It's a perfect autumn day."

Susanna glanced first at Holt then at Hendricks. They'd all agreed not to trouble her father about the intruder. There was no point upsetting him.

He fingered one of the orange tree leaves hanging near his head. "I do look forward to spring, my dear. It's my favorite time to sit here with the scent of the blossoms in the air to remind me of your mother. She always smelled of orange blossom." Longing clouded his eyes. He missed her mother. Theirs had been a love match. Being the second son and not meant to inherit, he'd been allowed more freedom than his older brother and chosen his own bride.

"What do orange blossoms smell like?" The deep, velvety tones of Holt's voice drew her attention.

"Like Heaven," her father murmured.

Holt regarded him with a curious expression.

"My mother added dried blossoms to her bathing water," Susanna said. "The scent is not like anything you've smelled before, I can assure you."

"You have a jar of dried blossoms, don't you?" her father asked. "To use for special occasions."

"I have. Not that I attend many special occasions these days." She dipped her head and hoped they didn't see her blush. She'd added the blossoms to her bathing water the night before because she missed their lovely scent. It had nothing to do with wanting to smell nice *for* anyone.

"You would attend events if you accepted more invitations," Farley grumbled.

Holt forked an eyebrow at her. She ignored him and tried to walk off but her father caught her hand. "Why don't you accept Lynden's invitations to dine? He's a good man. Not at all like his cousin."

Out of the corner of her eye, she saw Holt's other eyebrow join its mate. He watched her intently, waiting. Beside him, Hendricks shifted awkwardly and glanced from her father to Holt to her. The poor man wasn't sure what to do or say.

"I have no desire to travel all the way to Sutton Hall in the middle of the day," she said. "I have too much to do here and I'd rather stay with you."

"You don't dine with me," Farley said huffily, "you eat with the servants. Now that you have Holt to help, you can take some time away from the garden to pay your respects to Lynden. He's our neighbor and your kin by marriage, and we are dependent on his goodwill to a certain extent, and that of Cowdrey. Indeed I urge you most insistently to pay attention to Farmer Cowdrey. He may not be as witty as...other men, but he too is a good man and earnest."

At times like these, she thought there was nothing wrong with her father's mind. It could be as sharp as ever. He knew exactly how desperate their situation was or he would not be suggesting she encourage Walter Cowdrey in his attentions. He knew she didn't want to marry again, and he'd told her he respected her choice, but it was clear that he didn't *like* it. Just how much he was prepared to argue with her over it was not something she wanted to discover in front of the servants.

"Father, can we discuss this another time please. When we're alone."

He waved a hand at Holt and Hendricks. "Back to work, both of you."

Hendricks left and Holt returned to his pocket of garden but stole glances at Susanna. She knew because she faced him and couldn't stop looking up from her task of weeding. His mouth tilted in a lazy smile but she knew his mind was mulling over the conversation she'd had with her father. No doubt he was wondering why the mistress of Stoneleigh refused to court Cowdrey when she was still of childbearing age. Walter might be a step or two down in status for a baroness, but his wealth made up for his lack of position in the eyes of the world.

Let him wonder. It was none of Holt's business. And she hated talking about the past anyway. Her marriages in all their disastrous glory were buried along with her husbands, and that's how she wanted it to stay.

"There'll be a good crop this year," her father said some time later. Susanna thought he'd fallen asleep but he seemed lucid and alert. "Is everything in place for the shelter? If it stays this clear you'll need to secure the canvases over the trees tonight."

She smiled at him. He still loved the trees, still cared for them. He would until the day he died, if only because his wife had loved them so. "You're right," she said, coming to stand beside him. She pressed her hand to her aching back and stretched. "If you're here for supper, Mr. Holt, perhaps you can help me throw the canvases over the trees. It's not an easy job to do on my own."

"I'll be here," he said, carrying a box filled with weeds over to them. "I think I'll head into the village this afternoon, if that's all right with you, m'lady."

"Of course. I told you to take the afternoons off. Indeed, I feel guilty if you don't. We're not paying you enough to stay here and work all day."

"Why aren't we paying him?" her father asked, blinking up at her. He looked tired. It was time to return him inside for his dinner and a nap.

"We can't afford to," she said.

"Oh. Pity." He indicated the patch Holt had weeded. It was clean and much larger than her own. "I hope you can stay until the spring, Holt. There's so much to do in the spring, isn't there, my dear."

"Yes, Father. Now, I think it's time for you to go inside. Mr. Holt, do you mind?"

Holt put the box of weeds down and, instead of helping her father to stand, picked him up bodily and carried him out of the garden. Susanna tried to pick up the chair, but it was large and awkward and far too heavy for her to carry all the way back to the house. She packed away the gardening things and a few minutes later Holt returned and took the chair.

"Tell me more about Sir Francis Carew's orange trees," he said suddenly. Of all the things she'd expected him to say, that was not one of them. "You said he builds a structure over them to protect them. How big is it? What's it made of?"

"It's like a small barn, I suppose, but it can be removed in the warmer months. Three of its walls are wooden and the fourth is the brick wall of the garden. The top is open except on cold nights and wintry days when he covers them with a wooden roof. He followed a design drawn up by our French supplier. I sent off for it too but haven't built it yet. You see, orange trees can go without sunlight for some time, so it doesn't matter if they are protected in this way for several days during particularly bad weather."

He nodded. "It sounds like a good method."

She sighed. "It's the best we have."

"Is it not good enough?"

"A milder climate would be better, particularly as we get more trees. That wall is the best spot for them, but I can't fit many more plants along it."

"I can't do anything about the weather," he said, chuckling.

"Or the wall."

"Where will you get more trees? Buy them?"

"I can't afford to buy more. I want to graft them. It's easy enough to do, according to the Frenchman who sold Mama and Sir Francis the saplings. But I have nowhere to shelter them. I need to build something out here to protect them. It's the bane of enterprise, Mr. Holt. You cannot be prosperous unless you have a lot of product to sell, but you won't get a lot of product if you can't afford to invest in them. Does that make sense?"

His smile set off his two boyish dimples. "I think my poor gardener's brain can wrap around the concept."

She winced. "I'm sorry. I didn't mean to imply you're dull-witted." He may be a servant and ignorant about orange trees, but she shouldn't have assumed he was stupid. Her other three servants certainly weren't.

He hefted the chair and she tried not to stare at the way his muscles in his arms bulged. "Why can't you build a moveable barn like Carew? You said you have the plans."

"We have no money for materials or labor."

"What about me? I can build it."

"You'll be leaving soon. A structure big enough to cover all the orange trees would take weeks to build."

"Hmm," he said, and together they went into the house.

* * *

ACCORDING to the Plough Inn's innkeeper, a stranger had arrived a few days earlier in the village of Sutton Grange. He told Orlando he'd find the man at Sutton Hall, so that's where he headed. The manor house was situated amidst wide green fields a mile from the village. The house itself was much grander than Stoneleigh with wide wings and dozens of chimney pots reaching like fingers into the sky. It was also in better repair. It looked fresh and new, a virgin compared to an old hag.

He avoided the house itself and sought out the stables where he found a scrawny lad leaning on his broom handle, gazing across the countryside.

"Lo," Orlando hailed him.

The lad almost fell over in his haste to get back to work mucking out the first stall.

"Don't mind me," Orlando said. "Keep doing what you were doing. I just want to know if the land steward's here."

"No," the groom said. "He's ridden out with the master."

Good. Orlando didn't want to happen upon either of them or any servant of authority. The person he really wanted to speak to was right in front of him. A stable boy. A maid would have been better—more prone to gossip, and they responded well to his questioning techniques—but the chances of getting inside and not raising suspicions were nil.

"Maybe you can help me," Orlando said, patting the nose of an inquisitive horse over one of the low stall doors. There were seven stalls, all but three of them occupied. The stables were clean and the smell of leather hung in the air so either the lad didn't day dream all of the time or he had help. "I'm the gardener over at Stoneleigh. Lady Lynden needs some timber for building, and I thought a place like this one would have some to spare. Can you help her?"

The lad's mouth twisted as he leaned on the broom again. He was about sixteen and wore ill-fitting and faded livery. "There might be some left over from the second barn. It was built last spring after your mistress sold her inheritance back to my master."

"She sold her widow's rights to him?"

"Aye, in a manner." The lad gave a sigh of strained patience. "I don't know if it was all official, but they made some sort of agreement where Lord Lynden bought her inheritance back. She needed the money to fix up Stoneleigh, see. It was in a right bad state a year ago with half the roof gone."

That explained a lot. Orlando had wondered why Farley and Susanna were so poor. As a widow, she was entitled to a portion of the income generated from her late husband's lands. By all accounts, Sutton Hall was a profitable estate. But if she had sold those rights back to Jeffrey and used the money to fix up Stoneleigh, then it was no wonder she had little left to pay for servants. A new roof alone would have cost a fortune.

"So there's timber left over from the barn?" Orlando asked.

"Aye, I think so. Umberly could tell you more when he gets back. That's the land steward. I'm sure my lord could come up with a fair price for your mistress to get it off his hands, them being related and all."

"The only fair price I can think of would be nothing. Their being related and all."

"Nothing?" The lad snorted and started sweeping again. "The master don't care for his relations *that* much."

Then Orlando would just have to find a way to make him care. It hadn't been his intention to ask about building materials for Susanna's orange tree shelter. It had simply been a good way to start a friendly conversation with the lad, but since Orlando would probably be around for a few more days, he might as well start building the structure. Just start it, mind, not go on with it. She would have to find someone else to do that job after he left.

If she lived.

His stomach clenched and the breath suddenly left his body. Hell. It was *not* the sort of reaction he should have when thinking about doing his job. Hughe would remove him immediately if he knew he had doubts about assassinating Susanna.

"He doesn't want to care for the widow of his cousin?" Orlando asked, laying a steadying hand on the stall door. "Just think, to have two husbands die in the same manner...very unfortunate." He shook his head, warming to his subject as he had done with the Stoneleigh servants the first time he'd met them.

The lad seemed intrigued too. He was leaning on his broom again, having accomplished little so far. The stable floor was as filthy as when Orlando entered it. "Never thought about it like that. I didn't know they died the same way. Did they?"

Orlando shrugged. If there weren't any rumors about it, he certainly didn't want to start any. The fact there were no rumors was what he wanted to establish. Milner from The Plough also hadn't mentioned the coincidence, and he seemed like a fellow who liked to gossip. So no one seemed to think Susanna guilty, yet someone had anonymously employed Hughe to assassinate her because she was a murderess. Interesting.

"Perhaps I'm mistaken," he said. "How did the previous Lord Lynden die?"

"His heart stopped, so they say."

"And how did they know his heart just stopped? Was someone with him at the time?"

69

"He was asleep. His man found him in bed the next morning. Sad business. He wasn't a bad master. Course, all the maids wept into their aprons for weeks after. The village girls too." He sniggered and gave Orlando a wink.

Orlando was an expert at schooling his reactions, but this time he had to call on all his experience and training. While it wasn't unusual for a man of Lynden's station to have mistresses, Orlando couldn't believe that someone married to Susanna would need to stray. Not only was she beautiful, but she was passionate too. He didn't need to bed her to know that, he could see it in the way she trembled at his touch, the way her face heated and her breath quickened.

Lord Phillip Lynden had been a bloody fool.

"Did his man tell you how he found him?" Orlando asked. "How he looked? Was there anything unusual about his skin or his eyes?"

"He was dead. Sounds unusual enough to me."

The conversation was going nowhere. If Orlando wanted to find out if the body showed signs of poisoning he would need to speak to the manservant himself, or someone else who studied the body.

"Was a coroner called?"

"Widow Dawson was sent for first. She's the village wise woman, and the parish pay her to look over the dead too. She said the coroner should be fetched on account of the master being young and strong. Took him three days to get here."

Orlando made to walk off but stopped at the entrance. "One more thing. Where can I find the stranger who arrived here three days ago?"

"You can find me right here."

CHAPTER 5

*O*rlando nodded a greeting to the man standing near the stable entrance. The stranger nodded back without taking his cool gray gaze off Orlando.

"My name's Holt," Orlando said. "I'm the gardener at Stoneleigh across the way."

"Monk," the stranger said.

"That a name or a description?"

"Whatever you want it to be." He sounded bored, as if he'd heard the jest a thousand times and given the same response. He was a tall, lean man with brown hair and the sort of face women looked twice at if he passed them. His clothes were that of a country gentleman, well-tailored to his broad-shouldered frame but not as ostentatious as Lynden. The ruff was small and there was no lace in sight.

"So why does the gardener at Stoneleigh want to speak to me? I wouldn't know an apple tree from a cherry, so I doubt it's for advice." Monk smiled and Orlando smiled back, despite his unease. Monk's stance was deceptively casual. Most observers would think him simply a man enjoying a conversation with another, but Orlando knew differently. One hand rested on his hip near the sword strapped there, his other was at his side, the fingers flexed.

He stood with his weight evenly balanced on both feet, blocking the exit.

So Monk was defensive and prepared to fight. That meant he had something to hide.

Orlando held up his hands. Perhaps it was foolish to take them away from the dagger tucked into his belt, but he was playing the role of a simple, unthreatening gardener. "My apologies, it's nothing personal, but I was told by Milner at The Plough that you and I were the only strangers to come to the village lately."

"So?"

The *swish* of the broom behind him stilled. The lad was listening too. "There was an intruder at Stoneleigh last night," Orlando said.

The stable boy gasped then swore softly. Monk blinked and a small line appeared between his brows. "And you think I am that intruder."

Orlando shrugged one shoulder. "As strangers passing through, we are always the first to be accused of such crimes. It was not me, however."

"Why not report it to Lord Lynden? He is the justice of the peace, is he not?"

"Aye," the lad said, "he is."

"Lady Lynden plans on doing just that," Orlando said. "Perhaps she has already been here."

"Perhaps she has," Monk said. "I've been out riding, so I wouldn't know."

"If Lord Lynden or one of the servants can vouch for your whereabouts then all is well. One of the maids perhaps? It was late at night."

The gray eyes turned as cold and hard as flint. "Lord Lynden will tell you I was with him. We were up late talking. The servants were all asleep. Ask him."

"No need," Orlando said cheerfully. "I'm sure he'll say the same thing." Whether it was true or not didn't matter. Lynden would vouch for Monk, or Monk wouldn't have spoken with such certainty. "So what is the nature of your business here at Sutton Hall?"

That got a bigger reaction from Monk than anything so far. He actually laughed and looked genuinely amused. "*You're* asking me what *my* business here is?"

"There are few servants at Stoneleigh and none of them are young. Mr. Farley is aged and Lady Lynden is unwed. I've taken it upon myself to find out what I can about the intruder."

"Think yourself her champion, do you?" Monk's laughter vanished, replaced with a sneering lift of his top lip. "I hear she's very beautiful."

Could Orlando hit him before the other man drew his sword? He would like to thump that smirk off his face.

"Your business here...?" Orlando prompted.

"Is not your business, Mr. Holt. It's between Lord Lynden and myself. Now, I suggest you return to your lovely mistress before she discards you in favor of another...gardener."

Orlando smiled when all he felt was a simmering anger welling inside. "You sound like a man who's suffered at the hands of a beautiful woman before. But don't fear on my account," he said lightly, "I've never been discarded in favor of another. I think you'll find it's always the other way around."

He touched the brim of his hat in farewell and pushed past Monk. Most men would step in front of him at such a juncture or give a challenging punch to his shoulder, but Monk did not. Orlando may have only spoken to him briefly, but he already knew Monk was not so petty as that.

Orlando did, however, feel the intense gray gaze slicing into his back like needles of ice.

* * *

"You should have reported it to Lord Lynden," Cook said, grinding the cloves with so much force Susanna was worried the pestle would crack under the pressure.

73

"I didn't see the point," she said. "We have no clues as to who it was. Besides, Jeffrey would only worry."

Hendricks snorted as he handed a tray to Susanna. "Only in that he'd be worried the intruder would take it upon himself to break into the Hall next."

Bessie clicked her tongue as she set the table where Holt sat listening and watching. It wasn't like him to be so quiet. Susanna had grown used to his friendly chatter, his easy laughter, and flirting. Something was on his mind, something to do with where he'd gone that afternoon. He'd only been back a short time and together they had covered the orange trees for the night before coming inside. She'd gone straight upstairs with Bessie to wash up for supper and returned to the kitchen to see him sitting at the table, saying little and apparently lost in thought.

She'd assumed he'd gone into the village but hadn't asked. He could do as he wished in the afternoons. Curiosity gnawed at her nevertheless. Curiosity and a dull ache. Most likely he'd gone to see a woman. Men like Holt always had women waiting for them somewhere. They seemed to attract them like bees to lavender.

The ache turned to a wrenching twist and she turned her back to him lest he notice her staring. No matter how much she tried *not* looking at him, her gaze always wandered there when he was nearby.

"You're unkind, Hendricks," Bessie said. "Lord Lynden would be concerned for his kinswoman and you know it."

"I s'pose so." Hendricks peered over Cook's shoulder and sighed. "But I'm not sure he could do much to help, as the mistress says. What can he do when we don't know who it was?"

"It should still be reported," Cook said with a grunt as she pounded.

"Are you trying to turn those cloves to dust?" Hendricks asked. "They look ready to me. Come on, put 'em in, I'm starving."

Cook shook the pestle at him. "Don't tell me how to do my job, Mr. Hendricks. I don't tell you how to do yours, do I?"

"Yes, you do."

Cook humphed and scraped the cloves into the pot simmering over the fire. "A few more minutes to let the flavor seep through then we're ready."

"He'll probably come to see you tomorrow," Holt said, rising.

"Who?" the servants all said as one.

Susanna knew the answer. "You were up at the Hall?"

He nodded and came to stand beside her. There was an extra intensity about him tonight that hadn't been there before, as if something troubled him. She didn't like it. She missed her amiable gardener. Could the intruder be worrying him? Or something else?

Something to do with the desire that had passed between them?

"You spoke to Jeffrey about last night?" she asked.

"Not him, no. I spoke to a stable hand and another man there. I'm sure it won't take long before Lynden comes to speak to you. I mentioned the intruder to Milner at The Plough."

"You did what?" Hendricks whipped around so fast the spoon in his bowl did a full swivel around the rim before settling back into place. "You fool! Now everyone will know. Cowdrey will—" He caught Susanna's glare and stopped.

"Leave Farmer Cowdrey to me," she said. "Anyway, I'm sure Mr. Holt had good reason to tell Milner."

"Two reasons," Holt said, addressing Hendricks. She applauded him for that. Hendricks, bless him, was as protective of her as her own father, perhaps more so since her father's health had begun to fade. Holt may never win the servant over before he left, but treating him with as much respect as he would the master of the house was a good start. Particularly as it didn't feel like he was treating her with any *less* respect by doing it. Indeed, she felt as if his words were directed at her, meant for her ears only.

"First," he said, "Milner is the quickest way to get word out about the intruder. Once word is out, it's less likely to happen again. The village will be on edge, watchful. Anyone who was away from their home last night will come under suspicion. I think it's

75

the best way to ensure it won't happen again, if the intruder was a local."

"And if he wasn't?" Bessie asked in a soft voice.

"And if he wasn't, I know who it might be. That's my second reason for speaking to Milner. He told me about a stranger to the village, other than myself. The stranger asked directions to Sutton Hall, so I went there after leaving The Plough. That's when I spoke to the stable lad and the stranger himself."

"And?" Cook prompted, her attention as focused on Holt as the rest, her cooking forgotten.

"His name is Monk. He claims he was at the Hall last night talking to Lynden."

"So it can't be him," Bessie said, satisfied. "His lordship will vouch for him."

"Aye," Hendricks said. "Did you ask him?"

Holt shook his head and turned to Susanna. She saw the unspoken words in his eyes. He didn't want to ask Jeffrey because he didn't trust him to tell the truth.

But that was absurd. Jeffrey had no reason to send a man to climb through her window. Why would he? Of all people, he knew they had nothing worth stealing.

"Of course it may not be someone who went into the village at all," Cook said, ladling broth into a bowl from the pot. "There could be someone hiding in the woods." She stopped ladling and gasped. "Oh my."

Bessie clasped Hendricks's arm. "Do you think it's possible?"

A shiver slithered down Susanna's spine and she found her hand safely enclosed in Holt's big one. The pad of his thumb rubbed her knuckles, the movement soothing, sending a different kind of shiver through her. A warm one that made her heart lurch in her chest. His gaze locked with hers, reassuring. Comforting. She felt utterly safe with this man beside her.

Yet that was absurd. Orlando Holt was a mystery and she needed to remember that. What sort of gardener needed direction for even the basic tasks, and didn't have his own gardening gloves?

What sort of servant worked for no pay when much wealthier manors were within walking distance?

She could not trust him with all her secrets. Not yet.

"No one is hiding out in the woods," Hendricks said, patting Bessie's hand. "It's much too cold tonight. There's frost in the air already. Anyway, I'll protect you." His wrinkles bent into a reassuring smile meant only for the maid. She smiled back, but it lacked assurance.

Cook handed a bowl to him and he had to let go of Bessie's hand to take it. "No offense, Mr. Hendricks, but I'll sleep with my sharpest knife under my pillow tonight, just in case. Unless Mr. Holt wants to sleep outside *my* door?"

"Hush, Cook," Bessie scolded, lowering her head but stealing a glance at Holt.

Susanna removed her hand from his. "What do you mean?"

"I slept in your parlor last night after we scared the intruder away."

"You did? On the floor?"

"Yes. It's surprisingly comfortable and the rushes smelled pleasing."

"I always have clean rushes," Bessie said. "But I hope it wasn't too uncomfortable."

"He had a mattress," Hendricks snapped.

Susanna hardly heard either of them. Blood pounded between her ears, deafening her to almost everything else. He had watched over her. Knowing such a strong and handsome man had spent hours outside her bedchamber door was a heady thing. But not as heady as knowing he'd done it to ensure her safety and not for more base reasons.

Her gardener may be a mystery, but he had just endeared himself to her in a way that his flirting never could.

"Why did no one tell me?" she asked but not harshly. She did not want Holt or the others to think her ungrateful.

Bessie, Hendricks, and Cook exchanged worried glances as they passed bowls between each other. "We didn't want to alarm you, m'lady," Bessie said. She handed Susanna a bowl of the steaming broth. "You'd had quite an ordeal and, well, we weren't sure if you'd welcome Mr. Holt sleeping so near."

"Oh. Yes. Of course." She placed the bowl on the tray to take up to her father. "It's unconventional, true, but I must be told everything that occurs in this house."

"Yes, m'lady," Bessie said, passing over another bowl which Susanna set next to the first on the tray.

"In that case," Orlando said. "I should tell you that I plan on sleeping in the parlor again tonight."

"I don't think that's necessary. As Hendricks said, the intruder is unlikely to return tonight."

"Protest all you like, madam, but I *will* be sleeping on the parlor floor again."

The nerve of him! She was about to tell him he should mind his place but bit her lip to stop herself. Holt sported a devastating smile. He knew precisely what she'd been about to say.

"Shouldn't you be asking me and not ordering me?" she said instead.

He cocked his head to the side and she almost laughed at the cheekiness of his stance and the impish gleam in his eyes. He was certainly a man used to breaking a tense mood with his charm. "In that case, *may* I sleep on your parlor floor tonight, m'lady?"

"No," she said, just to see his reaction.

"Not the right answer." When she began to protest, he added, "You told me to ask so I did. You mentioned nothing about obeying."

"Are you this impertinent with all your employers?"

"Always, but they couldn't help but like me anyway."

"Are you sure they didn't simply tolerate you? Perhaps they were short of strong backs in the garden."

He pressed a hand to his chest. "You wound me, dear lady."

She chuckled despite herself and shook her head. He was incorrigible.

"I'll let you make it up to me by allowing me to sleep on the parlor floor," he said.

"Not the floor, a mattress," Hendricks grumbled. "From the most comfortable guest bed, mind."

Susanna picked up the tray with the bowls of broth for both her father and herself. "Good night, everyone."

"Good night, m'lady," Bessie, Hendricks, and Cook intoned.

Orlando merely gave her a wicked smile.

* * *

SUSANNA DISMISSED Bessie from her bedchamber and watched her leave through the adjoining parlor where Holt was laying a blanket over the mattress he'd carried in moments before. Hendricks wasn't so easy to remove. He hovered in the doorway, a stern expression giving his wrinkles extra depth.

"Good night, Hendricks," she said. "You may go now."

But it was Holt who walked out. "Forgot the pillow," he said, heading to the guest bedchamber.

Hendricks crossed his arms. "I'll wait here awhile, m'lady. Just until he's asleep."

She sighed. "Hendricks, it's all right. Mr. Holt has proved himself trustworthy. If he wanted to harm me, he'd have done so when we were alone in the garden."

"I'm not worried about him harming you," he muttered.

Nor was she. She suspected she was in more danger of being seduced than harmed.

She squeezed his arm. "Go now. Blow out the lamps on the landing on your way down."

He didn't move for several beats, but eventually he bid her good night, followed by a loud huff directed at Holt as they passed on the landing.

"Should I be worried that he'll stab me in my sleep?" Holt asked, throwing the pillow onto the mattress then squaring up to her.

Goodness, he was tall and solid. The muscles in his upper arms bulged beneath his shirt sleeves and his shoulders were so wide.

"I would lend you some of the old family armor for protection, but I'm afraid you'll find it uncomfortable for sleeping."

"Such unexpected kindness, thank you."

"Unexpected? I'll have you know I've been very kind to you so far. I gave you a job despite your lack of skill with orange trees and your impertinence, I allowed you to pull out my weeds, and I've let you sleep on my floor on the best guest mattress."

"It is a good mattress," he said, taking a step toward her in a move that reminded her of a predator stalking its prey. Deliberate. Stealthy. Primal.

Her housecoat suddenly felt too tight across her chest.

"And the rushes smell nice," she said, somewhat pathetically. She should move away. Should get out of his presence before she was sucked in.

Too late.

"Speaking of nice smelling things..." He breathed deeply.

"Are you sniffing me, Mr. Holt?"

"I prefer to think of it as drawing in the scent of you. Is that the orange blossoms I can smell?"

"Yes. I sometimes add dried ones to my bathing water."

"Interesting," he murmured, not sounding in the least bit interested. He took another step closer so that he was mere inches away, and regarded her with smoky, half-hooded eyes. "Delicious."

"I, uh... Pardon? What's delicious? The oranges?" Good lord, thinking had just become the most difficult activity. Thinking and breathing, quickly followed by talking. Those three things were greatly over-rated in her book. Much better to touch. And taste.

"I've never tasted oranges." His voice whispered across her skin, leaving a trail of devastation in its wake in the form of goosebumps.

"You should," she heard herself say. This brazen woman was not her, did not sound like her, could *not* be her. Not after everything she'd learned from her two husbands and swearing off men forever.

And yet...and yet...

He lifted his hand to her face but did not touch her. His fingers hovered near her cheek, as if he were too afraid to put skin on skin, as if he were unsure whether he wanted to set off the avalanche of emotions that would inevitably follow.

It wasn't clear who moved the fraction required to close the gap. Perhaps she leaned in, or he stretched his fingers. His touch sent a shock through her body, made every part of her hum with awareness of him, of his masculinity, his power and beauty. She'd thought he had an innocent, boyish look about him when they first met, but not now. Now she'd wager there was nothing innocent on his mind.

There was nothing innocent on hers either.

No matter how wrong, how foolish, she had to keep going. Had to. She could no more stop what was about to happen than she could hold back that avalanche with her bare hands. In the back of her mind, way back in a dark, cramped corner, she knew they were making a mistake. But there was no chance of that thought escaping its prison when he touched her with such delicacy and looked at her like she was something wondrous. Like he could see past her face and right *into* her heart.

His thumb brushed along her jaw to the corner of her mouth. His other hand cupped her cheek.

Then he kissed her. Softly, carefully, as if she were a skittish deer and he was afraid of startling her. She wasn't in the least startled. She was alive and on fire, utterly aware of every part of her body and of the nearness of his. She reached up and did something she'd wanted to do ever since he'd walked into her life—wrapped her fingers as far around his arms as they could go and relished the ripple of muscle and sinew.

Deep down, a knot unraveled inside her.

Then he broke the kiss.

No!

He groaned and stepped back, dropped into a crouch, and busied himself with the blanket. Then she heard it too. Footsteps coming up the stairs. She pulled her housecoat closer and scrambled to gather up her scattered wits to greet the servant who thought she needed rescuing.

It was Bessie, holding two cups in one hand and a candle in the other. She paused in the doorway and her jaw went slack as she regarded Susanna first then Holt. Her eyes widened and the cups tilted at a dangerous angle.

"I brought you both warm milk," she said. "I...we...we thought you might like some." She held out the cups. Susanna took hers, but Holt didn't look up from his task. Bessie set his cup down on a table near the door. "Is there anything else, m'lady?"

Susanna shook her head. She didn't quite trust her voice, and so Bessie left without hearing a word of thanks. When her footsteps had finally faded, Holt stopped his fussing. He turned and regarded her over his shoulder. She'd expected to see the remnants of smoldering desire in his eyes but instead his expression deadened her heartbeat. He looked like a hunted man.

Somehow, she found her voice. "We shouldn't have." It hurt to say the words, and they almost stuck in her throat, but she forced them out. It had to be said. Now that the first reckless flush of passion had faded and her mind was working again, the foolishness of their kiss became apparent. It had unleashed things inside her that should forever remain bound.

"I know," he said, heavily. He was still crouching, one hand on the rushes for balance.

"It was a mistake."

The incline of his head was so small she almost missed it. "I know."

She held her cup to her chest with both hands and returned to her bedchamber. As the door clicked closed behind her, she wondered what had happened to turn Orlando Holt from predator to prey in mere moments.

CHAPTER 6

Susanna found Holt in the stables after breakfast. He stood with his back to her, facing the crates filled with jars of marmalades and succades. He couldn't have failed to hear her footsteps crunching on the gravel as she approached, but he didn't turn around.

She took a moment to admire his strong, straight back and the width of his shoulders, and the way his unruly hair brushed the nape of his neck. Her face heated at the memory of his lips on hers, the way he'd looked at her as if she was something precious. Her nerve endings sizzled and the embers of desire stirred.

She threw cold water on them before they could flare again. Last night had been a mistake. They both agreed. Today...today was going to be awkward.

"Are you ready to get to work, Mr. Holt?"

He nodded but didn't turn. "All these things," he said, indicating the crates, "you're trying to find a buyer for them?"

"Yes. I've sent letters to several shopkeepers in London but have had no reply as yet." The lack of response was frustrating. She'd written the introductory letters in her father's name and even mentioned Sir Francis Carew to legitimize themselves. The letters had been delivered almost two months ago. She was relying on selling the products to pay the servants' wages and buy more jars for the next batch. If she didn't receive an answer soon, all their savings would dry up.

"Not just any shopkeeper I hope," he said.

"What do you mean?"

"Your products are rare, luxury items, particularly the succades. You want to sell them to the nobility and the wealthy. Most shops aren't frequented by their maids, only a select few. You want someone who specializes in the exotic and exclusive. Someone who attracts the right sort of shopper."

"And what do you know of selling orange marmalades and succades to the nobility, Mr. Holt?" Indeed, what *did* he know? From his confident tone, he was implying he knew much more than a simple country gardener ought.

He turned slowly, and she was struck by how tired he looked. Shadows rimmed his eyes and his usually smiling mouth was flat. "Nothing," he bit off. "I'm a fool." He pushed past her and she stood, swaying a little as the force of his bitter words struck her.

She stumbled after him. "I don't think you a fool." Her voice sounded weak, shaky, but he heard her.

He stopped and turned, shook his head, sending the blond locks tumbling over his forehead. "I know," he said, giving her one of his crooked smiles. It reassured her somewhat. "That was directed at myself."

She didn't ask for an explanation and she suspected she wouldn't have got one anyway. Somehow she knew he was referring to the previous night and their kiss. *Fool.* The word could easily describe her too.

They set to work in the walled garden under a cloudy sky, neither saying much as the morning wore on. Even with her back to him, Susanna knew precisely where Holt was and when his gaze landed on her.

As the hour of dinner approached, the heavy silence that hung between them was broken by the rapid *clip clop* of hooves on the gravel drive. Susanna and Holt both straightened at the same time, but he remained behind as she left the garden through the archway to investigate.

Jeffrey hailed her and dismounted. "Good morning, Cousin." His greeting was jovial but his expression was one of distaste as he took in her appearance. "You have dirt on your forehead again."

She wiped her forehead with the back of her hand.

He sighed and shook his head. "You made it worse." If it were any other gentleman, she would expect him to wipe the dirt off, but not Jeffrey. A union between them may be illegal, yet laws could not stop a man desiring a woman. It had not stopped her first husband's brother from trying to kiss her every moment they were alone. But not Jeffrey. He had never shown the least interest in her. It was refreshing, and she had to admit it was the reason she tolerated his interference.

"What can I do for you, Jeffrey? Or is this a social visit?" It wouldn't be. Jeffrey never made purely social calls. Everything he did had a purpose, and that purpose was to further himself or his estate.

"I heard about your intruder and came to see if you were all right. I see that you are, and I'm relieved."

"We are all fine, thank you. It was very kind of you to check on us. But please, if you see Father, don't tell him. There's no need for him to be alarmed."

"If you wish, but I do think he should know. It's his right."

"It may be his right, but I think it's for the best not to worry him unnecessarily. He's not well."

"*Is* it unnecessary though, Susanna? What if the intruder returns? What if he resides in the house this very moment in one of your unoccupied chambers?"

"I saw him run away from the house with my own eyes!"

"What if he came back? Or had an accomplice who managed to enter the house another way? Perhaps I should go and search the place myself." He strode off.

She ran after him and caught his arm. "Don't be absurd, Jeffrey.

Besides, my servants checked every nook thoroughly and found nothing and no one."

She let go and he flipped the edge of his cape back as if in protest at being manhandled. "Those relics can hardly walk up and down the stairs let alone see properly."

"My servants are perfectly able to search Stoneleigh and you know it."

"The gardener perhaps," he grumbled, looking over her head to the house.

"Speaking of Mr. Holt." She glanced toward the arch but couldn't see him. "He mentioned there is a stranger residing up at the Hall. I hope you don't mind me asking who he is and if you can trust him."

He flinched. "Of course you can trust him. I trust him and you trust me, don't you? Susanna, I'm deeply offended." He pressed a hand to his chest. His jerkin must have been padded there because he looked larger than usual. "Deeply."

"I'm sorry, Jeffrey, but he is the most obvious candidate since he couldn't possibly know the situation here at Stoneleigh."

"Who says he doesn't know?"

She frowned. "What have you told him?"

"Nothing, nothing." He tried to move past her but she blocked his way.

"Have you questioned him about that night?" she asked. "In your capacity as justice of the peace, I mean?"

"No need." He thrust a finger between his ruff and neck and scratched. "I was with him until late. We had business to discuss."

"Business? Interesting," she said lightly. "So the stranger is a man of trade?"

He sighed. "Dear Susanna, Mr. Monk is of good character. He won't harm you."

But would he climb through her window if he thought she had something to steal?

"You don't know how relieved I am to hear you say that," she said.

His lips pressed together and she could see he was trying to decide if she mocked him or not. Then he looked past her.

"Ah, perhaps *he* can convince you that the house must be thoroughly searched."

She turned to see Walter Cowdrey riding toward them. As he dismounted, Holt emerged from the garden. Walter ignored him and joined Susanna and Jeffrey. Holt came closer, near enough to hear but still apart.

"Lady Lynden!" Walter sounded breathless. "I came as soon as I heard." He grasped her hand between both of his rough ones. "Are you all right?"

"She looks all right, doesn't she?" Jeffrey said.

"I'm well, Mr. Cowdrey, thank you. As you can see."

Walter's gaze raked down her body. A short distance away, Holt crossed his arms. Walter increased the pressure on her hand. "Yes," he said, coloring a little. "Yes, I do see. You look...lovely." He licked his lips and cleared his throat. His grip became almost unbearable.

She tugged her hand and he released her. "How did you hear about the intruder?" she asked.

"I've been seein' to personal matters in the village just now and everyone's talkin' about the intruder at Stoneleigh the night before last." His gaze shifted to Holt. "Your gardener told Milner and now everyone knows."

"I've already thanked Mr. Holt for making enquiries on my behalf. He's been most helpful in this endeavor."

Jeffrey snorted.

"*I* could have made enquiries," Walter said. "It would be a pleasure and an honor."

His earnestness elicited another snort from Jeffrey.

"Thank you, Mr. Cowdrey, that's very kind," Susanna said.

"Next time, come to me. Understand? No need to involve the gardener."

"Let's hope there is no next time."

"Yes. Of course we hope that." Walter cleared his throat again. "The intruder hasn't come back?"

"No."

"But what about tonight? Then what?"

It was the same question that plagued Susanna and her servants. She dared a glance at Holt, but he was pretending to prune a hawthorn bush. By the way he snipped off the tips and not entire branches, she knew he wasn't concentrating on his task and was listening to the conversation instead.

"All the doors and windows are locked at night," she said. "And perhaps now that everyone in the village knows of the situation, the intruder won't dare come again."

"That don't sound like a good plan to me," Walter said, scratching his hair under his hat. "Think I'll stay tonight. Scare off anyone who might—"

"No!" The thought of having Walter in the next bedchamber made her skin clammy. "Mr. Cowdrey, please don't trouble yourself."

"No trouble. I insist." He gave her a closed mouth smile which was all he ever gave because he didn't like his crooked teeth.

"No, *I* insist," she said. "We are capable of taking care of ourselves at Stoneleigh."

He sniffed then wiped his nose with the back of his hand. "Your servants are old, Lady Lynden, they won't be much help."

"I have Mr. Holt."

Both Jeffrey and Walter looked to Holt at the same moment that he looked at them. Holt's expression remained bland as if he was completely disinterested.

"The gardener," Walter said flatly.

"You let him sleep in the house?" Jeffrey asked.

"Of course."

"Well he don't have to no more." Walter straightened to his full height. When he didn't stoop, he was actually quite tall. As tall as Holt, but not nearly as imposing. "Put him in the barn."

"He can't sleep in the barn," she said, "it's not weather tight."

"So?" He flicked dirt off her shoulder and his eyes softened.

"This is why you need to marry again, Susanna," he murmured so that only she could hear. "You need protectin'."

"I've told you before, I'm not ready to remarry."

"But—"

"Gentlemen," Holt said. He sauntered over, smiling like an amiable, innocent fool. She didn't believe it for one moment. "No one tried to break in last night," he said. "I think we're all safe now."

"I'm stayin'," Walter said.

"No, Mr. Cowdrey, you are not," Susanna said.

"You don't know what you're sayin'." Walter went to take her hand again but she folded her arms. "It's best if I come round and—"

"She said no." Holt's voice cut through the air like a brutal axe blow.

Walter's nostrils flared and his top lip curled. "Shouldn't you be doin' somethin' useful instead of wastin' Lady Lynden's time and money?"

"Mr. Cowdrey, there is no need for you to stay," Susanna said before Holt poured gunpowder on the fire. "Now, if you gentlemen don't mind, I have work to do."

Holt and Walter glared at each other, but it was Jeffrey who made the first move. However it wasn't to capitulate and leave. "I'm going to search the house," he said, striding off.

Walter followed him. "I'll help."

"What!" she bellowed at their backs.

Jeffrey stopped suddenly and faced up to Walter who almost slammed into him. "I don't need help, Cowdrey. Susanna is my cousin, and it is my responsibility to protect her."

"She was your cousin's *wife*," Walter said, "and the responsibility for her falls on all of us who care for her."

"Yes, well, everyone with eyes can see why *you* care for her." With that, Jeffrey stormed off, his nose in the air.

Walter trailed behind him like a small child following his mother.

Holt did not go after the others, but she knew that she just had to ask and he would do it. His presence buoyed her.

"Enough!" she shouted. Both men stopped up ahead. "Leave. I do not like my household being disrupted, and I do not appreciate you coming here and taking over as if you own Stoneleigh."

As if you own me.

Walter was the first to capitulate. He trudged back, casting a fierce glare at Holt the entire time. Jeffrey took longer. He glanced at the house, at her, then Holt, and once more at the house before sighing.

"We only care about you," he said.

Walter took her hand again without warning. "Forgive me, my dear lady. I only wished to help."

"Thank you," she said, removing her hand. "If I need your help, I'll ask."

He looked somewhat blankly at her, and, as if her dismissal had finally sunk in, nodded slowly. "I offended you, m'lady. My apologies." Shoulders stooped, he plodded back to his horse.

"Wait."

His face brightened. "Yes?"

"My letters. Are you sure your man took them to London back in September?"

"Of course. I would have told you if he hadn't."

"I'm sorry. I'm not doubting him or you. It's just that I haven't heard from any of the recipients and I expected to by now."

"P'haps they're not interested." Walter mounted his horse and pointed his considerable chin at the walled garden. "P'haps *quince* marmalade is good enough for *them*." He pulled hard on the reins and rode off. Mud flicked up from the hooves and splattered her cheek.

Holt came up beside her. "All right?" he murmured.

She wiped off the mud with her sleeve and nodded. But she was not all right. She'd offended Walter and he didn't deserve it. Her constant rejections of his marriage offers must sting, and now it sounded like she didn't trust him. She would have to make it up to him somehow.

"What a tiresome man," Jeffrey said with a sigh.

"Don't," Susanna said. "He doesn't deserve to be mocked."

Jeffrey merely shrugged. "Since I'm of little use here, I'll bid you good day. But do let me know if you change your mind about having a *gentleman* present in the house. I would be happy to stay the night and you know *my* motives are pure."

"I'm well aware what your motives are, Jeffrey. Thank you."

If he detected her sarcasm, he didn't show it. He bowed and walked off to his horse but Holt called after him. Jeffrey stopped and turned, frowning. Susanna, too, frowned. What was he up to?

"Yes?" Jeffrey asked, irritation dripping from the single word.

"Your stable lad told me you have spare materials left over from when you built your new barn. Lady Lynden is in need of some to build a structure around her orange trees."

Silence. Then, "And?"

"Can she have them?"

"Your gardener is bold, Susanna. I would shorten his leash if I were you, lest he bite."

It took seven beats of her heart before her anger was under control and she could trust herself to speak casually to him. "But you are not me, Jeffrey, and I do not treat my servants like dogs. Mr. Holt is also in a different situation than most in that I am not paying him. Indeed, he's not really a servant at all since he is doing me a favor and I him."

Jeffrey gave a short, derisive laugh.

"Well?" asked Holt. "Can she have the timber or not? She is your nearest relation after all."

"How do you know who my relations are?" Jeffrey snapped.

How indeed?

"Nearest in distance as far as I know," Holt said.

"That timber cost quite a lot."

"Not that you would want your cousin to reimburse you, I'm sure. After all, you are very considerate of her welfare."

Jeffrey's eyes narrowed and Susanna thought he might actually walk off without answering, but then, after much pursing of his lips, he said, "I will give you the timber, Susanna, if you do something for me in return."

She should have expected Jeffrey would not simply hand it over. "Go on."

"Let my man Monk help you build this structure."

Beside her, Holt went very still. "Why?"

"Why not? It will make your task easier." Jeffrey grinned, triumphant. Somehow he had just won, but Susanna didn't know what the contest had been about.

"I thought Mr. Monk was a man of trade, not a servant," she said.

Jeffrey shrugged. "He's working for me and will do as I direct. I am offering his services in exchange for my timber. I think that's fair since the expense is all mine. Don't you?"

"A moment ago you did not want to even give me the timber. Why the change of heart?"

He stiffened and blinked in surprise. "Susanna, my deepest apologies, I thought you understood why. I'm sorry for my rudeness earlier and I wish to make it up to you, that's all. Please don't be suspicious of my motives. They are innocent. As poor Phillip's widow, it's my duty and my honor to care for you. Please accept my offer."

There was not a hint of mocking in his tone and his face was all seriousness and concern. She felt contrite but not guilty. "Thank you, Jeffrey, but...do you trust this man Monk? He is very new to your acquaintance, isn't he?"

"I've known him a long time," he said as he moved off. "I'll send him down after dinner. Good day."

"Don't send him today," she said. "Mr. Holt has the afternoons off and I'll be heading into the village. Tomorrow morning will be better."

After a pause, Jeffrey said, "Very well. Tomorrow morning." He mounted and rode off.

"It must be almost time for dinner," she said, turning to Holt. She was surprised to see him looking at her. She thought he'd been watching Jeffrey leave.

He lifted his hand and skimmed her cheek with his thumb. She felt his touch all the way through to her bones where a sweet ache set up residence. "You missed a bit of mud," he said.

"Thank you, Mr. Holt. I appreciate everything you did today. I wish..." *...that I could kiss you and touch you and be held by you.* "I wish I could pay you what you're worth."

His chuckle was low. "There are some who would say I'm not worth what you're already paying me." His smile slipped and he looked away.

Who could possibly think this handsome, active, and friendly man was worthless? She almost asked but didn't. The hard planes of his face warned her not to pry.

She walked off and beckoned him to follow. "Help me put the garden tools away. It's time to go inside."

Together they returned to the walled garden and silently packed the tools in the box. Holt picked it up and joined her at the archway. "Does Lord Lynden often have visitors to stay? People he's known before he inherited, I mean."

"Hardly ever. He has some cousins I believe, but if he has any friends, he's never introduced me to them. I think Jeffrey is trying to distance himself from his old life as much as possible."

"To make better, higher friends, you mean?"

She nodded and they walked to the barn. "He travels frequently to London where no doubt he tries very hard to come to the notice of the court."

"Tries and fails, I'd wager. Someone ought to tell him he's wasting his time. The court aren't likely to notice someone as slow-witted as Lynden"

"Really?" And how did he know that?

He lengthened his strides. "So I assume."

She waited for him while he carried the box of tools into the barn. When he rejoined her, they headed for the kitchen garden.

"I'm driving into Sutton Grange later," she said. "There'll be room in the cart if you want to come."

"No, thank you. It's a nice day. I think I'll go for a walk."

She looked up at the sky. It was gray and threatened rain.

* * *

THE RAIN HELD off until Susanna reached the Sutton Grange chandler's shop. She could have sent Bessie to the village on her own but the maid didn't like driving the cart and Susanna wanted to greet some of her friends anyway. She'd had little opportunity to go into the village lately and missed them. With Holt helping in the garden, her workload had eased. She still couldn't believe he was going to build a more stable structure to protect her orange trees. Getting the timber for it, plus an extra pair of hands to help, was quite a triumph. She didn't think Jeffrey would acquiesce but he had. Thanks to Orlando Holt. Her gardener was worth every penny it cost her to feed him.

Heat rippled through her body, right down to her toes, warming her all over despite the cool air. It happened whenever she thought about Holt, about his kiss and the way he'd touched her. She knew she should push thoughts of him aside, knew that thinking about him in her bed would only lead to yet another mistake.

But it was impossible to ignore him. He was like the taste of an orange—the sweetness lingered long after the last bite. Running errands and chatting to friends was the only way to keep thoughts of him at bay.

In the chandler's shop, she purchased her candles on credit. "We know you'll pay." Anne Lane, the chandler's wife, handed the box packed with a mixture of wax and tallow candles to Bessie.

"In the meantime..." Susanna pulled out a jar of orange marmalade from the basket over Bessie's arm.

"Oh, delicious!" Anne cried, accepting it. "I hear you got some help over at Stoneleigh finally." A gleam danced in her soft brown eyes. She pushed aside a box she'd been packing candles into and leaned on the counter top. Her crossed arms propped up her large bosom. "Quite handsome help too."

"I suppose so," Susanna said, trying to control the heat rising to her face. "If you like dimples and boyish looks."

Anne chuckled. "Oh, I like 'em. So does every silly creature in the village. He and that other stranger, Mr. Monk, are all they talk about. Mind you, if the girls had to pick a favorite, I'd put your Mr. Holt ahead. That other fellow's not as amiable, so they say."

"He's not *my* Mr. Holt," Susanna said, pretending to be interested in a brass lamp hanging from the ceiling beam above her head. It dangled there among several others for sale, near enough to touch and inspect but not to bang one's head on.

The chandler's wife chuckled and returned to her task of packing the boxes. Susanna didn't mind her light teasing. Anne might have grown-up children of her own, but she'd been a flirt herself when she was younger apparently. She'd been a kind friend to Susanna's mother, as had most of the village women, and that friendship had naturally extended to Susanna. Her mother had always stopped to chat to the shopkeepers' and farmers' wives when she could. As with Susanna, they had been her only friends in the parish, and Farley hadn't minded his wife and daughter socializing with them. Indeed, he had many friends among the Sutton Grange inhabitants himself.

Phillip, however, had tried to end her friendships. The village women were beneath the wife of a country gentleman, he said. When she asked him who she was supposed to have for companionship he offered up Margaret Cowdrey. The Cowdreys weren't as gently born as the Lyndens and Farleys, but Phillip tolerated their friendship since the Cowdreys had become richer than both families in recent years.

Susanna had not ended her friendships, but it had been the cause of many arguments between her and Phillip. Arguments and, once, a slap. It had been that slap across her cheek that ended any lingering affection she'd harbored for her second husband. With that slap, he'd become just like her first husband and that marriage was not one she liked to think about. Ever.

But Phillip was gone and Susanna was a widow. She intended to take full advantage of her status this time and enjoy the relative freedom that came with it.

"What do you know of Mr. Monk?" Bessie asked, resting her basket on the counter.

"I haven't seen him, but I believe he's quite the handsome devil too," Anne said.

Bessie giggled. "I mean is he friendly? Can he be trusted?"

Anne shrugged. "As trusted as any man can be. Oh good," she said, looking past them and out the window to the street. "Here comes Mistress Cowdrey. I'm always sure of getting a sizeable order when she comes in. Pass me that lamp over there, Susanna. The big one." Susanna lifted the large brass oil lamp onto the counter. Anne picked up a cloth and began to polish it even though it shone brighter than any other in the shop.

The door opened and Margaret Cowdrey paused just inside. "Lady Lynden, I didn't know you were here."

"Mistress Cowdrey," the chandler's wife said, coming out from behind the counter. "Come in, come in. Is it still raining? Can I take your cloak and shake it out?"

Margaret waved her aside. "Thank you but don't trouble yourself, Anne. I'm here for candles."

"Then you've come to the right place."

Margaret rolled her eyes and laughed. It was as brittle as the woman herself but not unkind. Her dislike for Susanna didn't seem to extend to anyone else in the village. "Two dozen, if you please."

"Wax?"

"Of course." The Cowdreys did not need to economize and use the cheaper tallow like Susanna. Tallow stank, which was why she only used it sparingly in larger, airier rooms.

Anne bent to look under the counter where she stored extra

boxes and crates. "We were just discussing the newcomer up at Sutton Hall. Do you know anything about him?"

Margaret sidled in between Susanna and the counter, blocking Susanna out. "A newcomer up at the Hall?"

Anne straightened. "Aye, a Mr. Monk. You haven't heard about him then?"

"No. The only stranger I know of is Mr. Holt, your gardener," she said over her shoulder to Susanna. "How long has this Monk been here?"

"He arrived in the village on the same day as Mr. Holt."

"Did he? And what's the nature of his business?"

"No one knows. He asked for directions to the Hall and went there right away."

Margaret finally turned to Susanna, as if she'd just given permission for her to join the conversation. "Lord Lynden hasn't told you anything about him?"

"No," Susanna said. "He doesn't confide in me."

Margaret took the boxes of candles Anne handed to her. "How vexing for you."

Susanna was about to ask what she meant but refrained. No doubt Margaret would say something Susanna didn't want to hear, something bitter and sharp that was meant to wound. It was why Susanna avoided her. When they were younger, Margaret had been even crueler, telling Susanna that her mother loved her orange trees more than she loved her and that her father was a wastrel who didn't know how to manage his ancient family lands. She told Susanna her patched-up gowns were ugly, which they were, and that people only liked her because she was pretty and a Farley.

It had been awful at first. They'd been so close as little girls. Their mothers had been friends. They'd played together and swapped doll clothes. But then womanhood arrived and Margaret turned into a viper toward Susanna. At first she kept her barbs for when they were alone, but when Susanna returned to Stoneleigh after her first husband died, Margaret no longer bothered to keep her waspishness to herself. The entire village knew of her dislike for Susanna and many had offered an explanation—Susanna was the prettier of the two. She'd protested that Margaret was not ugly in the least and while all agreed with her, they said it wasn't enough. Not for Margaret. She was jealous, bitterly so. Susanna finally had to admit they may be right. She could think of no other reason why such hatred was directed at her and Margaret refused to discuss it.

"I saw your brother at The Plough talking to Farmer Digby the other day," Anne said. "I thought those two didn't get along."

If she was hoping to hear some gossip from Margaret on the subject, her attempt failed. A shadow darkened Margaret's brow but quickly cleared, and she simply shrugged in answer.

Anne didn't pursue the topic. She picked up her cloth and began polishing the lamp again. "Can I get you anything else, Mistress Cowdrey? This lovely piece just came in. The pattern in the brass here is pretty and the style elegant."

"It *is* lovely, thank you," Margaret said, hardly looking at it. "I'll take it." She turned to Susanna. "May I walk out with you?"

She was so surprised, it took Susanna a moment to gather her wits. "Of course." They waited until Anne finished packing the lantern in a box then left together.

Out the front, Bessie climbed into the cart and set the basket at her feet. Margaret pulled Susanna a little aside out of earshot.

"My brother returned home in a state earlier," she said. "Had he been to see you?" Her eyes, already slanted because of the tightness of her hairstyle beneath her hat, narrowed further. Her mouth was a mere slit.

"Did he say he had?" Susanna was not going to make it easy for her.

"No, but you are the only one who upsets him so."

"It wasn't intentional, I assure you."

"He's infatuated with you," she spat, as if the very notion disgusted her. "Until he comes to his senses I think it wise if you avoid him. Please," Margaret added quietly. "I don't ask much of you, Susanna, but I am asking this. It's important."

It must be if she was pleading. She had never asked anything of Susanna and certainly never begged. "Of course," Susanna said. "But I cannot stop him from coming to see me." Although she wished she could. Walter's visits always produced a stab of guilt in her chest. Every time she refused him, it twisted deeper. All she wanted was for him to leave her alone and treat her like a neighbor, not a potential wife.

Margaret said nothing. Her gaze skipped past Susanna to a point behind her. Susanna turned and saw what had taken her interest. Two strangers rode up to The Plough Inn on the opposite side of the street. One sported a portly belly and wore green livery. He was dark in appearance but whether from too much sun or an exotic heritage, it was difficult to tell. The other man was clearly a gentleman. He was slender compared to his servant and wore a crimson cap with a peacock plume shooting from the crown. The colorful eye at the top of the feather bobbed back and forth as the gentleman pulled his horse to a stop. The servant dismounted effortlessly despite his size, and his master bent to say something to him. When the gentleman straightened, he flipped his cape back, flashing the crimson lining of the elegant garment.

"More strangers," Susanna said. "I wonder why they're all attracted to Sutton Grange lately."

Margaret stared unblinking at her, her eyes like deep, still ponds. "Yes. I wonder."

CHAPTER 7

*I*t was late when Orlando returned to Stoneleigh, and supper had finished. Cook and Bessie were in the scullery washing pots and Hendricks was helping Farley into bed. Susanna had retreated to her rooms. Orlando knew because he'd seen light coming from her window and he thought he saw her face peering out but couldn't be sure.

"It's about time," Cook said when he entered the scullery. She wiped her hands on her apron and led him back to the kitchen. "It's been dark for hours. Supper's cold."

"I've had cold suppers before," Orlando said, pecking her on the cheek. "It's never stopped me from eating every last crumb."

Cook chuckled and whacked him lightly on the arm with a trencher before handing it to Bessie who'd followed them from the scullery.

Bessie forked slices of mutton onto it from a pot warming on the hearth. "We've been worried about you."

"Worried about me?" He laughed. "That's new."

"You never had anyone worry about you before?" Cook asked.

He thought about it. "My mother used to. She said I ought to keep my mouth shut more and do as I was told." Hughe and the others worried too of course, but only rarely and they never admitted it. They never fretted if he didn't return one night, but they would search for him if he failed to show at a designated meeting time and that in itself was a comfort.

"Seems her advice worked," Cook said, piling peas on his plate beside the mutton. "You always do as the mistress tells you."

"That's because she's a fair mistress." And ravishing and because he needed to work at Stoneleigh so he could investigate her. He took the trencher and sat down to eat.

"Aye, she is fair, but I'll warn you she's in a bit of a state tonight. Don't be surprised if she's harsh with you."

"Harsh with me? Why?"

"Because she was worried about you, fool." Cook chuckled and replaced the lid on the pot.

"She was?" Well, well. Could she possibly be thinking of him as much as he was thinking of her?

But his thoughts bent toward the carnal, not the emotional. The only reason he thought about Susanna was because he wanted to bed her, and once he'd done that, he could focus better on his job. There were too many distractions where she was concerned, and it was time to put a stop to them. Once he scratched that particular itch, the other thoughts that plagued him would go away.

He intended to scratch it tonight.

"We were all worried," Bessie added. "Don't stay out so late next time without telling us."

"Yes, ma'am."

Cook grunted and pointed a wooden spoon at him but then she broke into a smile. "Ah, you're the devil you are, with those dimples and blue eyes. I swear you just have to twinkle them at me and I'll believe everything you say. No wonder the girls in the village are all a-flutter over you."

"They are? I hadn't noticed."

"Course you haven't."

"Where were you today anyway?" Bessie asked.

"I went for a walk," he said.

"All afternoon and into the dark?"

"I got lost."

Both women seemed to accept his explanation, something for which he was grateful. He didn't like lying to them. It was akin to lying to his mother and although he'd done it easily enough as a young lad, after his father died, guilt stung his conscience every time he told her he was going to practice archery out at Finsbury Fields when instead he visited a girl or attended the theatre.

"I better go see if the mistress needs help," Bessie said. "Will you be sleeping in her parlor tonight, Mr. Holt?"

"No, he bloody well will not," growled Hendricks from the doorway.

Cook and Bessie both looked to Orlando. "I think that's up to the mistress to decide," he said, slicing his mutton.

"I protest! The mistress...she..."

"Don't worry, Mr. Hendricks. I didn't ravish her last night or the night before. What makes you think tonight will be any different?" God, he hoped it would be different. Another sleepless night with an aching groin and unwelcome thoughts about a more permanent arrangement between himself and Susanna would be too much. He put down his knife and regarded all three of the servants seriously. "I'm exhausted," he said, quite honestly. "I haven't slept properly for two nights. If you think me capable of doing much more than falling into a deep sleep, you over-estimate my manliness."

Bessie's eyes widened, and Cook let out a raucous laugh that made her whole body wobble. Only Hendricks continued to scowl. "If you are so exhausted, what use are you sleeping in her parlor? An intruder will walk right past you if what you say is true."

"Even in my deepest sleep, I'm always alert to unusual sounds. It's a skill that has served me well on my travels. I could not have survived without it."

Bessie covered a small squeal of horror and bustled out of the kitchen. Hendricks said nothing but he too walked off. Orlando exchanged a glance with Cook who shrugged, then he returned to his supper. He was starving. Spying on Monk all afternoon without being seen was tiring. The man was active, riding out with Lynden, walking around the gardens, chatting to the other servants. Unfortunately Orlando had learned nothing from his efforts. Monk was as much a mystery as ever.

* * *

Susanna didn't greet Orlando when he entered her parlor carrying the spare mattress. She merely dismissed Bessie from her bedchamber and closed the door on him. Much, much later, when the house was quiet and her nerves were completely shredded, she went to the door separating them.

She didn't open it. Instead, she leaned her forehead against the solid oak and sighed. There was no point opening it. No point in waking him and demanding he relieve her of the longing that gnawed at her bones. No point starting something that she would regret.

She walked back to the window and looked down. She could see the walled garden and her orange trees covered with the canvases as well as the eastern approach to the house. Holt had returned that way earlier in the evening. It had been dark and he carried neither torch nor lamp, but she'd known he was there as surely as she knew he was still in her private parlor now. She just knew.

A soft knock on the door made her jump. She hesitated a moment then answered it. Orlando stood there holding a candle, a sleepy smile curling his lips.

"You should be asleep," she said and winced at her pathetic attempt at light conversation.

"You disturbed me." His voice sounded rough.

"I was very quiet. I couldn't possibly have woken you."

"I didn't say I was asleep, just that you disturbed me."

Go back to bed, Mr. Holt. It's what she ought to have said. She opened the door wider.

He didn't move, and she stopped breathing. She must have read him wrong. He never wanted their flirtations to go this far. It was all a terrible, humiliating mistake.

But then he crossed the threshold. "Are you sure?" he asked.

"Yes," she whispered. "Are you?"

There was that smile again. Sensual. Wicked. "That's not usually a question I'm asked at moments like this." He held the candle up to her face and brushed his thumb across her lower lip. "I'm sure, Susanna."

Her name was a whisper of silk, a breath of air. She wanted to hear him say it again while he was inside her, but she managed to stop herself from grasping him by his shirt and dragging him to the bed. Just.

With a hand to his chest, she gently pushed. He straightened and frowned, confused. His gaze faltered, and she thought she'd ruined everything and he would storm out of her bedchamber. Or worse, out of Stoneleigh. A heavy weight pressed down on her at the thought and that alarmed her even more.

"Would you rather I called you, m'lady?"

Just like that, the tension between them burst like a bubble. She smiled, relieved. "Hearing you say my name was a bit of a shock, I'll admit."

"You're not going to tell me I get above myself, are you?"

"I should. Because you are."

"It won't change anything." He held the candle up to her face, illuminating his own at the same time. He no longer smiled, and his eyes were as inky as a moonlit night. "It won't change what I want to do to you in that bed," he murmured. "Or out of it, if you prefer."

She drew in a shuddering breath. "Anywhere. Everywhere." Her gaze focused on the triangle of bare skin revealed by his partially unlaced shirt. She wanted to lick him there. "But you need to know something first." It was an effort to talk, but she managed to reign in her galloping desire.

"There's nothing you can tell me that would persuade me to step back into your parlor and close the door. Unless it's 'no.'"

"It's not that." She thought she saw desire flicker in his eyes, but it could have been the reflection of the flame. "What happens here, tonight, stays in this room. You tell no one, and our arrangement remains the same."

He bent his head and kissed the spot just beneath her ear. Her blood throbbed in response.

"As you wish," Orlando murmured. Through the haze clouding his mind, he was aware of one clear thought: relief. Bedding Susanna was what he needed to do, right now, this moment. To hell with ignoring the desire between them—it had done nothing to alleviate the ache in his groin. The only way he could get her out of his every thought was to tumble her tonight. After that he could walk away or kill her if necessary. No regrets. No ties. No unnecessary emotions. It was the only way.

He set the candle down on a table and crossed the floor to the fire. He put on two more logs then, without further ado, picked her up bodily. She wrapped her slender arms around his neck and kissed him brutally. Her mouth was hungry, and he matched that hunger with his own. He'd never wanted to bed a woman as much as he wanted to ravish Susanna.

Without breaking the kiss, he set her down on the bed. She ran her hands through his hair, scrunching it in her fingers, making sure he didn't move.

He wasn't going anywhere.

She broke the kiss and fumbled with the laces on his shirt. In frustration, she tore it a little as she dragged it off his shoulders.

"Perfect," she murmured. Her teeth nipped his left shoulder and her lips followed it with light kisses. "I've been wanting to do that for days."

He chuckled. "Since we're playing out our fantasies..." He stretched alongside her and unlaced her nightshift. The sight of the deep V between her breasts made his mouth go dry and his pulse jump. He teased aside the cotton to reveal one plump nipple, ripe and ready. He closed his mouth over it and groaned as the taste of her orange-scented water and another aroma that was all Susanna teased his tongue.

She replied with a matching groan of her own and an arch of her back. "Yesssss," she murmured. "Orlando..."

God, but it was good to hear his name from her lips. She gripped his shoulders and hung on as if anchoring herself to him. He liked that. Liked it a lot.

He switched his attention to her other nipple, cupping her breast to push it up and out, into his mouth where he could lavish it with all the attention the morsel deserved. He rolled on top of her and hovered, careful not to crush her. Beneath him, she drew up her legs.

He leaned away, breaking the contact and she whimpered. "Come back," she said.

"I want to look at you first." The logs on the fire had caught, throwing more light into the bedchamber. She was everything he'd known she would be under the manly gardening clothes. Slender limbed, soft, round breasts topped with fat nipples, an elegant neck and the face of a goddess. Worthy of a master painter. And all his.

For tonight.

A blush crept up her throat and she drew the edges of her nightshift together. He stayed her hand with his own. "Don't. You're beautiful."

She winced. With pain? Disappointment? *Hell.* What had he said? Women liked to hear they looked beautiful. He should know, he'd told enough of them in just such a moment. None had looked as extraordinary as Susanna, though, and none had reacted like her.

Fear squeezed his insides. Fear that she would end this before it had begun. So he kissed her again. It wasn't as hungry, but it was just as urgent. Her long fingers pushed his hair off his face and kept his mouth right where he wanted it to be. On hers.

She hadn't changed her mind. Thank God.

But the kiss wasn't enough. He needed to see the rest of her, needed to feel her naked body sliding against his. He broke the kiss and stood, pulling her off the bed with him. Wordlessly, he undressed and reached for her to help her out of the nightshift, but she put a hand against his chest.

"My turn," she said, her voice throaty. She stepped back, crossed her arms and her gaze stroked him from head to toe and back up again, lingering on his cock. It jutted out, hard and pulsing for her touch.

She licked her lips and his mind fled. He went to her, but again she held up her hand.

He groaned. "Are you trying to torture me?"

With a devilish smile playing on her lips, she circled her finger in the air. He turned. Her hands on his shoulders stopped him when his back was to her. Slowly and somewhat painfully for his waiting cock, she traced his spine with her fingertip all the way to his arse. Both hands cupped his cheeks, and her thumbs stroked the curves of muscle slowly, deliberately, as if she were studying him and was fascinated by what she saw.

"Can I turn around?" he rasped.

"No."

"You really are torturing me."

Her fingers slipped down and he parted his legs so that she could toy with his balls. He bit down on his lip against the jolt spiking through him, centering on his groin. He tasted blood and didn't care. He could feel nothing except her fingers on his heavy sacks. Along his shaft. Up to the tip of his cock.

Everything in him tightened, like a trap poised to spring. A long, loud groan filled the room as he held the tide back. *Not yet. Not yet.* He reached up and grabbed the bed's tester to stop himself stumbling forward, to give himself something solid to hold in a room spinning out of control.

"Stop..." But he didn't want to stop and she knew that, the vixen. Her thumb circled the head of his cock, slick with his own juices, and he wanted to beg for release.

Then suddenly her hands were gone. His head fell forward and, unbalanced, he gripped the tester harder. "Susanna...?" he muttered. He couldn't form the question, his tongue wouldn't work.

The rustle of cotton behind him gave him all the answer he needed. Before he could turn, she wrapped her arms around him and leaned into his back. Her luscious, lovely breasts pressed against him. No way was he going to have her naked in his presence and not look at her.

He turned in her arms, and his cock throbbed at the sight of her. If he'd been capable of thinking and speaking, he might have said something poetic about her loveliness but he wasn't and he didn't know if she wanted to hear it anyway.

She reached for his member, but he moved away and shook his head. Another touch and he would explode. When he was certain she understood, he moved close again and, keeping his body a little apart, kissed her gently.

Her response was to grab his shoulders, pull him closer and deepen the kiss. He slipped his hand between them and cupped her sex. She was hot and wet, her nub swollen, and when he thrust his middle finger inside, she cried out. Another finger slid in easily and she broke the kiss to throw her head back. Her breathing came hard, fast, making her beautiful breasts quiver, begging him to take them in his mouth.

He did. His cock thickened and dripped. *Not yet. Not yet.*

His fingers set a slow, steady rhythm but with a moan of frustration, she thrust her hips and quickened the pace. He switched to her other breast, suckling, and her fingernails raked his shoulders in response.

"Now," she mumbled almost inaudibly. "Take me now."

Those were words he didn't need to hear twice. He pressed his cock to her opening then sank into her to the hilt. She gasped and thrust up to meet him.

He stopped. He wanted to stay there a moment. Feel her

wrapped around him and the throb deep inside her. Wanted to savor it lest it never happen again.

It lasted all of a second or two, and either she or he began to move against the other, or it might have been both together. She lifted one leg up until her knee touched his hip, allowing his cock to reach deeper. He kissed her, swallowing her cry, and picked her up, his hands supported her neat round arse. She wrapped her legs around him and hooked her feet at the small of his back. He felt like he was cocooned in her.

Just where he wanted to be.

He laid her on top of the bed and pounded into her, not wanting it to end but wanting so very much to feel that thrilling rush of climax.

It started with the heat. It spiraled inside him and he could feel it coming off her in waves. Then came the trickle of tingles, a teasing, sweet torture. It lasted but a moment until Susanna stiffened in his arms and only her thighs and hips moved, jerking involuntarily.

"Orlando!" she cried, arching into him.

There was no hope for him after that. The flood came and he rushed to pull himself out of her, to spurt his seed on the floor, but she pressed her feet into his arse, holding him there.

"No need," she gasped.

He stayed and exploded into her. His body shuddered violently and he pressed his face into her shoulder as every last drop was milked from him.

They stayed like that for several furious heartbeats until their breathing calmed, and then he rolled off her.

It was over. They should part. He should return to the mattress on the parlor floor. But he didn't want to go and she didn't tell him to leave. Indeed, she rested her cheek on his chest. Her fingers stroked his arm.

"Lie with me," she said. "So that when I wake I don't have to fetch you."

He laughed softly and she snuggled beside him, her head

resting on the pillow of his arm, one leg over his. The curves of her body fit neatly into his side. He kissed the top of her head and drifted off to sleep.

Sometime later, he awoke. She was watching him. The fire had died down again and the candle had gone out but despite the dark, he could see her eyes glistening. He wondered if it had anything to do with what she'd said earlier when he'd tried not to spurt his seed into her.

No need.

The note of sadness had been small, but he'd heard it, despite his preoccupation. She'd been married twice, and yet there were no children. It was likely she was barren, and that pained her.

He touched her cheek and she turned her face into his palm, kissing it. That simple gesture set his heart racing again and his cock hardened.

"Susanna," he said, levelly, "I want you."

She looked at him. Her eyes seemed full but there was a firm, determined set to her mouth. "I want you too."

They made love again, slower, taking their time, exploring each other. He found she liked to be licked, everywhere, and she discovered that his nipples were as sensitive as hers.

Afterward, she lay with her hand on his chest, her fingers teasing the hairs there. "Whatever happens next," she said, "I want you to know I'm glad we had this night together." She stopped twirling and spread her fingers out, over his heart.

He kissed her forehead. He wanted to say something, reassure her that he agreed.

But he couldn't.

He wasn't glad or satisfied or reassured. Making love to her was supposed to ease the longing that dragged at his limbs.

But it hadn't. It had only made it worse.

He closed his eyes and willed himself to be still, his mind to be silent. But it didn't obey and wandered down paths he did not want it to tread. Could not allow it to tread.

She yawned, oblivious to his turmoil. "Orlando, where did you go this afternoon? And don't tell me you went for a walk."

The question came from nowhere and slapped him out of his melancholy. He was so grateful he decided to answer her directly. "I went to Sutton Hall to find out more about Mr. Monk. I want to make sure he's not our intruder before we allow him to work here."

"That's very good of you." She yawned again. "And did you find out anything useful?"

"No. It might have been him, or it might not. Considering he's the only stranger to the area aside from me, I'd wager it was Monk though."

"Not necessarily." She shifted so that her head rested on her own pillow, but her leg remained draped over him and her hand still rested on his chest, over his heart. "I forgot to tell you earlier. Two more strangers arrived in Sutton Grange today."

"Two strangers? What did they look like?"

"Like a pampered gentleman and his fat servant." Her eyes fluttered closed and she smothered another yawn. "But it couldn't have been them here that night. They only arrived today."

He stared up at the bed's canopy and listened to the silence of the night as Susanna drifted off to sleep. Eventually he slept too, but only lightly. The *whoo whoo* of an owl woke him some time before dawn. He sat up, careful not to wake Susanna, blissfully asleep with a small smile on her lips and her tousled hair covering half her face. He gently brushed it back and his cock stirred at the sight. Her lips curved into a pout and the hard edge of her jaw had softened as sleep relieved her of the day's burdens. His hand hovered at her cheek but he decided against touching her. Outside, another *whoo whoo* sounded.

He dressed quickly and silently went downstairs to meet Hughe and Cole.

CHAPTER 8

*T*here was no owl of course. It was Cole, using the call the Guild members had perfected for their nocturnal meetings. Orlando found Cole and Hughe at the edge of the woods. Or rather, they found him. Dressed in black, they were almost impossible to differentiate from the trees.

"Finally!" Hughe stepped away from the trunk of a massive oak to reveal himself, while Cole did the same on the other side. "You took your time."

"I was busy," Orlando said.

"Sure you were." Hughe's voice held a smirk in it.

"You're always *busy*," Cole, the third member of their band, said. He gripped Orlando's arm in greeting. "Nice to see you enjoying your work." He wasn't fat like Susanna described him, just broad across the shoulders. He must have removed the padding strapped to his stomach for his disguise to make the journey to Stoneleigh's wood. Orlando couldn't see or hear horses, so they must have walked.

"Come to check up on me?" Orlando asked, flipping the hood off his head. He'd worn it to hide his blond hair as he crossed the open grounds of Stoneleigh. It would have acted like a beacon if the moon came out.

Hughe removed his hood too. Cole didn't have one.

"I needed to escape London," Hughe said. "The dowager countess has arrived for the winter." Orlando didn't need to see his friend's face to know he'd screwed it up in distaste. The dowager countess was Hughe's mother, and her favorite pastime was parading potential wives in front of her son. There were many and they were all silly or grasping, so Hughe said. Orlando supposed that was the price of being one of the richest earls in the kingdom. Better to be a nobody and free than a nobleman and hobbled to a wife, estate, and duty. He could think of nothing duller.

He glanced over his shoulder toward Stoneleigh. At that moment the moon came out from behind a cloud and illuminated the vine-covered walls, the steeply pitched roof and windows. He thought he saw a light in Susanna's bedchamber, but he couldn't be sure. Hopefully she was still sleeping and wouldn't realize he'd left her until the morning. Perhaps by then he would know what to say.

"It's going to be a bleak winter for you in that case," he said, turning back to Hughe.

"Aye. And a long one. I think I'll have urgent business in other parts for most of it."

"You won't get far. The roads are poor enough already. Another month or two and they'll be unusable."

"I only need to get as far as the nearest inn," Hughe said.

"And the nearest warm bed," Cole said.

Hughe and Orlando laughed. Cole did not. He never laughed. Their dark, serious friend had a bleak, black streak through him that ran deep and cold. Orlando had not been able to find out why, although he suspected Hughe knew. Bloody Hughe knew everything.

"How goes the investigation into Lady Lynden?" Hughe asked. "We saw her yesterday in the village."

"She saw you too," Orlando said. "She thought your hat was ridiculous by the way." She'd said no such thing, but Orlando knew the sort of hat Hughe usually wore when he was playing the part of the fop and they were always elaborate and impractical.

"That was my best hat."

"She's very beautiful," Cole said, unexpectedly. He never noticed beautiful things, not even women. Or if he did, he never commented. For him to say Susanna was a beauty meant he'd certainly noticed.

"So?" Orlando snapped.

"So I was expecting a murderess to look more...bitter. Shrewish."

Orlando's head began to pound inside his skull. "Perhaps she's not a murderess then," he heard himself say.

"If she isn't," Hughe said lightly, "I wonder if she'd agree to become the next Lady Oxley. I wouldn't mind that slender body wrapped around my—" He slammed back into a tree trunk and his muttered *oomph* echoed through the woods.

Orlando shook out his hand. It hurt, but it felt bloody good shutting Hughe up. It wasn't often he caught him unawares like that.

"I win," Cole said.

Hughe rubbed his jaw and grunted. "That wasn't a wager I wanted to lose."

It took a moment for their words to sink in. It was like a hive of bees had taken up residence in Orlando's head, and their buzzing was making it hard to think. "What are you talking about?"

"We had a wager after the innkeeper pointed out Lady Lynden to us in the village," Cole said. "I told Hughe you'll go the same way as Rafe."

Rafe? What did their friend have to do with any of this? Then it fell into place. Rafe had left the Assassin's Guild and fallen in love barely two months ago. According to Hughe, the only one who'd seen him since, Rafe was besotted. The thought of ruthless Rafe Fletcher falling in love had made Orlando laugh when he'd first heard it. Now...now it bothered him. No, it *angered* him. Their friend had abandoned them for a pretty face and someone to keep his house. It was true that he'd left the Guild before he fell in love, but he would have come back when he was ready. Now he couldn't. He was tied to that life and that woman forever. Orlando hoped for the wife's sake that boredom didn't do to Rafe what it did to him.

"You're fools," he said. "Both of you. Rafe might be happy to lose his freedom, but I'm not." He glanced at Stoneleigh, but the moon had been swallowed up by the clouds again and it was shrouded in darkness. "Settling down isn't for the likes of me," he said, quieter.

"That's what I said." Hughe opened his jaw wide as if to see that it still worked. "It would take more than a pretty face to tempt you."

"He just hit you for insulting her!" Cole said. "What more proof do you need?"

"He's a champion of the female species, that's all. Doesn't mean he's developed a foolish attachment to one of them. Does it, Holt?"

The edge in Hughe's voice wasn't lost on Orlando. He could feel both men watching him, trying to gauge his feelings on the matter despite the darkness. "Indeed."

Hughe grunted and rifled through a pack nestled against the base of a nearby tree. He pulled out something and put it to his lips. A flask. He handed it to Orlando and he too sipped. Aqua vitae burned his throat and blazed a path down to his stomach. He hadn't realized how cold he was. Frost clung to the air like an icy blanket and stung his nose and ears. He drank again and handed the flask to Cole.

"So what say you, Orlando?" Hughe asked. "Is she a murderess?"

Tingling warmth spread through Orlando's limbs and dissolved some of his tension. "It's unlikely," he said. "There are no rumors in the village, and everyone seems to like her."

Hughe's hesitation was small, but it was there. "You know as well as I that that means nothing at all."

"You've always trusted me, Hughe. Always."

"You have good instincts, both of you do. I wouldn't have hired you otherwise." He didn't need to add 'but' for Orlando to hear it.

"I don't think she's capable of murdering anyone. I have no proof, but I *will* get it."

Hughe returned the stopper to the flask and took his time putting it back in the pack. Somewhere in the distance, a real owl called. "You'd better."

"And if I don't?"

"You know what. If we can't prove guilt or innocence with any assurance, we leave her alone, but that won't mean someone else won't be hired instead. And if guilt *is* proven, we'll dispense justice accordingly. If you can't do it, Cole will."

Orlando had no doubt about that. Cole never flicked an eyelash when he undertook his job, no matter who or what the circumstances. *He'd* killed women before.

"What if she did kill her husbands but had good reason?" Orlando asked. "You can't go ahead with it then."

"We'll cross that bridge when we come to it," Hughe said.

"No," Cole said and his deep, rumbling voice commanded they listen. "If they were deserving, then we leave her be."

Hughe stood very still. It wasn't often his men defied him. Only one man had dared, and he was buried in a grave somewhere in London after Rafe was forced to eliminate him upon Hughe's order.

"I'm not killing anyone who had no choice," Cole went on.

"She's not like the others," Orlando said quickly, sensing an opportunity to press his case. The murderers they'd been hired to kill in the past were all cruel, vicious madmen who needed to be stopped. Their crimes were heinous, their victims often innocents, and their positions powerful so that the authorities could be bribed. Moreover, there was never any doubt as to their guilt. Most even gloated to their assassin's face before their throats were slit.

"As I said," ground out Hughe, "we'll decide when we know for sure."

Orlando could punch him again to get his point across, but he suspected Hughe was ready for it this time. He doubted it would make any difference anyway. Hughe respected facts and witness accounts, not emotions or suppositions.

"Did you find out anything about the client?" Orlando asked. "If Susanna is innocent, then someone is trying to implicate her because they dislike her."

"Or they want her out of the way," Cole said. He still stood with his arms crossed and his feet apart, as much a part of the woods as any of the massive trees.

"The letter I received was unsigned," Hughe said, "and the casket containing the money has no identifying markings on it. Whoever it was has taken great pains to remain anonymous. I don't even know where it originated from."

Only the members of the Guild knew that Hughe was its leader. The rest of the world thought Lord Oxley was a dandy who split his days between the playhouses, baudy houses, and court. Work filtered through to them via a network of inns across the country and the Continent. Whenever someone came to the innkeepers or serving wenches with a problem that required the Guild justice, they would send the information on to an abandoned building in London. The building, owned by Hughe under another name, was checked often by one of the band in disguise. All were experts in going about undetected or knowing when they were being followed. Only once had Hughe needed to change the house where the messages were sent when an innkeeper had been forced to reveal its location. The innkeeper had found himself dropped out of the network after that, as much for his own safety as that of the Guild members.

It wasn't often Hughe didn't know his client's name, but he always found out one way or another. Until now.

"Keep asking your contacts," Orlando said.

"Thank you, Holt," Hughe ground out, "I wasn't sure what to do next, but you've enlightened me. I knew I employed you for more than your pretty face."

"Ha."

Cole grunted, but that was as much humor as he was capable of showing.

"So we speak to the coroners next," Orlando said. "Did you find out their names?"

Hughe sighed. "There wasn't one for John Bullen, her first husband. He was much older, and his humors tended to be overly sanguine apparently. His death didn't come as a surprise so no coroner was called. It was entered into the parish books as a failure of the heart. Phillip Lynden, however, was different."

"I know," Orlando said. "The parish wise woman sent for the coroner because she thought he was too young and healthy to die suddenly. But the coroner found no suspicious markings on the body. I'd still like to question him."

"He's dead. Died a few months ago from a fever."

Orlando swore. "I'll need to speak to the wise woman then, without trying to raise suspicions somehow." His list of people to talk to was growing. Right at the top was Mr. Monk. "That's not all. There are strange happenings at Stoneleigh. Someone tried to climb through Susanna's window, but I don't think they were trying to steal anything since there is very little to steal and the entire village knows it."

"So what do you think he was doing?" Hughe asked.

"Attempting to kill her."

"Bloody hell," Hughe murmured. "Someone's trying to take our business."

"That wasn't my first concern."

"You're right. If she's innocent, then we have a problem. She'll need protecting until the intruder is discovered, and her guilt or innocence proven."

"Do you know who it might have been?" Cole asked. "Could it be the same person who commissioned us?"

"There's only one other stranger to Sutton Grange and he's living up at Sutton Hall. His name's Monk. Whether he's connected to our client or not, I don't know. It's likely."

"Sutton Hall," Hughe mused. "You think Lord Lynden hired this Monk to kill his cousin?"

"Possibly. He covets what little remaining land Farley has. But...I don't know. I don't think he is greedy enough to kill her for it."

"What about others? Who else do you think may want her dead?"

It felt strange discussing Susanna's life and death so coolly with men he'd watched kill others in the name of justice. Orlando was surprised at how level he sounded, how unaffected. Inside, his stomach churned. She didn't deserve this and certainly didn't deserve to die. If she killed her husbands, she would have had good reason. She was a good soul. He was absolutely certain of it now.

"I don't know. Cowdrey is her nearest neighbor on the other side and has already purchased a lot of land from Farley in lean times. But he wants to wed Susanna, not kill her."

"Are they going to marry?" Hughe asked.

"She's refused him."

"Then he might want revenge. He's angry at being rejected, and he wants her punished for humiliating him..."

"Or he doesn't want anyone else to have her," said Cole.

An icy shiver tore up Orlando's spine.

"What about enemies?" Hughe asked. "And don't tell me she doesn't have any. A woman as beautiful as that always stirs up jealousy among the plainer ones. Milner from The Plough told me most of the unwed girls are afraid she'll dazzle all the bachelors now that she's a widow again. They're worried none will look elsewhere until she's safely remarried."

"You enquired about her?"

"Of course. I asked who the beautiful woman outside the chandler's shop was and if she was available. I didn't know it was her at the time."

"As subtle as ever I see."

"Are you going to hit me again?"

"Don't tempt me."

"Or me," Cole chimed in. "I'm often tempted. Very, very tempted."

"He's not used to playing a servant," Hughe said with a laugh. "It's been a long few days. For both of us."

Cole simply grunted.

"Are you staying in Sutton Grange?" Orlando asked.

"Only another day then we'll travel to Harveston to make enquiries about John Bullen's death. You remain here and continue investigating husband number two's death until we return. Be subtle."

"Of course. Cole's the one who couldn't be subtle to save his skin."

"Subtle is the size of a brick and just as hard, is it not?" Cole said.

"Light and dark, you two, and not just in appearance," Hughe said, shaking his head. "Not sure where I'd be without you both."

"Working harder," Cole said.

"Getting your hands dirtier," Orlando chimed in.

Hughe clamped one of those hands around Orlando's arm and squeezed. "Just make sure neither of you get yourselves killed nor follow Rafe's path."

"Same thing," Orlando said, grim. Being a good, reliable, and faithful husband was not for him. He needed open spaces, adventure, and freedom to go where he wanted. Being tied to one place would drive him to boredom and boredom sat like a canker on his shoulders. After their father died, he went to work for his brother in the family merchant business. It had slowly sucked the life out of him. Day in and day out of paperwork and counting—counting yards of cloth, barrels of wine, jars of spices and money. At the end of the day his eye twitched and his legs felt restless. He needed to *do* something. So he drank too much, fought too often, and made love to all the wrong sort of women.

When one of those women turned out to be wed to a thug with big friends and sharp knives, he'd left. He'd had to. They'd already slashed his brother, Thomas, across the face and promised to come back for his wife May if he didn't pay compensation. He paid, of course, but Thomas had asked him to leave London. So he had, despite wanting to stay and work harder. He owed Thomas. His brother bore the scar of Orlando's actions. The least he could do was give him everything he was capable of giving.

But then, if he'd stayed, what's to say he wouldn't have spiraled down that path again? He couldn't afford to test his own resolve. Not at the expense of Thomas and May.

Orlando would not shackle a woman he cared about to a man who turned into an amoral arse when he grew restless.

"I don't think you need to fear either of us following Rafe's path," Cole said and Orlando could feel his friend's gaze on him even though he couldn't quite see it in the darkness. Was Cole testing him, questioning him, or something else altogether?

"Good," said Hughe, flipping up his hood. "Come on, Cole, time to go. It's starting to rain."

Cole sighed and snatched the pack off the ground. "It always rains when we've got to walk."

"If you hold the pack over your head, you won't get your pretty hair wet," Orlando said.

"Or I could borrow your cloak. It has a hood."

"I know. That's why I have it."

"Swap with me. It's only a short distance to the house. If you run, you'll avoid most of the raindrops."

Orlando gave him a withering glare, but it would have got lost in the dark. With a sigh, he removed his cloak and accepted Cole's in return.

"Take care," Hughe said, grasping Orlando's arm. "We'll call on you when we return from Harveston."

The damp leaves deadened their footsteps as they walked off and soon even their shadowy figures were swallowed up by the trees and the night. Orlando trudged back to Stoneleigh just as the first golden rays of dawn peeped shyly over the horizon.

He didn't run like Cole suggested, but walked to give himself time to think. He knew what he had to do next and it had nothing to do with making enquiries into Phillip's death and everything to do with the base urge to see Susanna's naked body again.

* * *

ORLANDO's naked body felt cool against Susanna's back, and his hair damp as it brushed her shoulder. She'd kept her eyes closed as he returned to her bedchamber and her bed, but feigning sleep was the coward's way so she opened them. She liked to think she was no longer that fearful young girl who'd gone into her first marriage with eyes just as tightly shut. Figuratively anyway.

"Where did you go?" she asked, rolling over, ensuring a few inches of distance remained between them. Orlando closed the gap quickly, squishing her breasts against his chest. The urge to wrap her arms and legs around him to warm him was strong, but she resisted. Let him stay cold. Unless he had a good explanation for his wanderings...

No, even then she would not curl up to him. Dawn had arrived and that heralded a return to their previous arrangement of mistress and servant. The role of lovers would have to wait until nightfall.

"I thought you were asleep," Orlando said, his smoky eyes watching her. His fingers circled her breast lazily.

Perhaps they could be lovers for a few minutes more. Dawn was slowly spreading its glow through the room but Bessie wouldn't come upstairs for some time.

"I awoke when you left," she said, nuzzling closer despite a small voice in her head warning her to stay away.

"And here I thought I'd been quiet."

He had been extremely quiet. It wasn't that she'd heard him leave, or felt the absence of his body next to her, it was more a sensation that had washed over her in her dreams. She'd felt the loss of him keenly in her sleep, only to find it was because he'd left her in the waking world.

"You haven't answered my question," she said, determined to

get an answer no matter what he did with his fingers and lips. "Where did you go?"

Those lips nibbled her ear, her throat, and a little sigh escaped her. Oh, he was good. He was very, very good. He knew just the right spot to draw a gasp from her and set her body tingling. She put her hands to the sides of his face...

...and pushed him away.

"A fair attempt to distract me, Mr. Holt, but it won't work."

He gave her a wounded look. "What happened to calling me Orlando?"

"It's time to return to being Lady Lynden and Mr. Holt again."

"I'll call you whatever you want, and you can call me anything you like, but don't banish me yet. Please. It's still early and I want to linger in your arms awhile longer." He sidled closer and she could feel just how much he wanted to linger. His member prodded her thigh, thick and hard.

"It's a very bad idea. Bessie—" All words and thoughts about how much of a bad idea it was, ended when his hand cupped her sex. He gently rubbed, and she sucked in air through her teeth.

Oh!

Yesssss. There. There.

His quick, long fingers brought her close to climax, but he stopped too soon. Cruel man! She gave a small sound of protest, but he smothered it with his mouth. His hungry kiss devoured her, made everything else fade from her mind except their bodies and the pool of desire welling up inside her. He flipped her onto her back and rose above her, not breaking the kiss. His chest rubbed against her nipples, teasing them to tender, aching points. He kissed one and entered her.

She cried out as he slid all the way in. She was dimly aware that she should keep quiet and not alert the household, but the servants were so far away and Orlando was not. He was inside her, setting a methodic, deep rhythm that had her body singing.

"More." She dug her fingers into his shoulders and held on as he brought her higher, closer to the edge.

His thrusts became faster, his breathing rapid and ragged. "I have to...now..."

She felt him pull away so she pressed her feet to his buttocks and held him inside her. "Stay," she whispered between gasps.

He groaned, the low, keening sound vibrating through her body, tipping her over the edge and launching her into free-falling nothingness.

He exploded into her. The muscles in his body trembled and his eyes screwed shut. The look on his face, of sheer pleasure and fulfillment, made her climax linger.

They lay together, both breathing hard, legs and arms entwined so that it was difficult to tell where one ended and the other began. She could feel every aftershock rocking him, feel every twitch of his muscles as if they were her own.

He kissed her throat near her ear. "I like being inside you to the very end," he murmured.

She liked it too. Very much. But not enough to take away the pain behind the reason *why* it was safe to spill his seed inside her—she was barren. It was such a familiar pain now, but different. It wasn't as sharp as it once was, but its aching heaviness pressed down on her heart still.

It hadn't always been so. She'd not fallen pregnant to John, her first husband, but with Phillip she'd lost a babe soon after they wed. She'd only told Phillip, her father, and Bessie who'd come to be her maidservant at Sutton Hall. She'd not even called for the wise woman. Bessie assured her that losing a babe so early happened to many women, and that she shouldn't worry.

Yet Susanna had grieved for that unborn child. It had been her first.

Her second, however, was much worse. Again, few knew she was in that state as it was very early. Phillip, however, knew. That's why his actions had been particularly shocking. He'd slapped her during their argument over her refusal to relinquish her friendships in the village. Although it hadn't been hard enough to leave a permanent mark on her cheek, she'd lost her balance and tripped over a small coffer near her feet. She'd fallen heavily to the floor. Phillip had simply walked out.

She'd gone to bed that night with a pain in her womb. The next morning, she'd woken up covered in blood. This time the wise woman had been called, but she only told Susanna what she already knew. The baby was lost. She cried for weeks and refused to see anyone, most of all Phillip. He'd only asked to visit her once, but she'd sent him away with vicious words of anger and accusation.

It was three months before he tried again. He begged forgiveness, promised not to touch her except in loving embrace. She'd allowed him into her bed because she wanted a child so much, but there had been no pleasure in the act. He'd torn her heart to shreds, and it was too late to gather up the pieces and mend it.

Despite their attempts, she remained childless until his death. Losing her second babe must have damaged her womb irreparably.

"Thank you for warming me up." Orlando's voice startled her.

She shook off her melancholy and touched his cheek. He smiled at her, a sweet, uncomplicated smile that buoyed her spirits but got her thinking again. "Thank you for reminding me," she said. "You've been avoiding my question. Where did you go?"

"Not avoiding, my suspicious little baroness." He kissed the end of her nose and rolled out of bed. He picked up the shirt he'd dropped on the rushes and pulled it over his head. "I was hungry. I went down to the kitchen."

"In your boots?" She propped herself up on an elbow and watched him.

"I didn't want my feet to get cold."

"How did they get damp?"

He picked up a boot and studied it. "I suppose they haven't dried from my afternoon walk yet." He set the boot down but instead of getting dressed, cocked his head to the side and regarded her with a curious expression. "Why the questions?"

Her gaze faltered and she pulled the coverlet up to her chin. "I...I don't know. I suppose with the intruder the other night, and now all these strangers appearing in Sutton Grange, I'm on edge."

"Susanna." He sat on the bed, causing the shirt to ride up and reveal his powerful thigh. She stared at it because it was better than staring at his eyes. Orlando's eyes had a way of pulling her into their depths and making her forget her convictions. "I had nothing to do with the person at your window the other night. I know you're frightened, but we'll find him." He smoothed the hair off her forehead and tucked it behind her ear. Her heart lurched in her chest. His touch was so gentle, his crooked smile so honest. "Don't be afraid."

She reached out and clasped his hand in her own. "I'm not. Thank you, Orlando."

He kissed her forehead and stood. "Now, I'd better go before Bessie arrives and boxes my ears."

Susanna grinned and watched as he dressed, enjoying the performance immensely although the one where he removed his clothes was better. Once his boots were on, he picked up his cloak and draped it over his arm.

"Until later, fair maiden." He bowed elaborately and backed out of her bedchamber into the parlor beyond.

Susanna lay very still, staring at the closed door between them. Her heart had stopped in her chest and her fingers curled into the coverlet, holding on.

He had a different cloak.

The liar.

CHAPTER 9

"Your cloak," Susanna said, opening the door to her private parlor. She'd hurriedly dressed in her gardening clothes to confront Orlando. Some things shouldn't be done while naked. "It's different. Your other one was a darker gray and had a hood."

The blue of his eyes flared briefly before flattening again. "I have two."

He couldn't have two. His pack wasn't big enough and men like him—men who traveled and earned little—didn't own two cloaks. They owned one. One pair of boots, one pair of gloves, one cloak.

So where had he got it? More importantly, whom did he meet? He must have switched cloaks with someone.

"Why are you lying to me?" Her voice sounded small, but she might as well have shouted, it had such a visible impact on him. He stepped back and his mouth fell open but he quickly gathered himself.

He came to her and rested his hands on her shoulders. He dipped his head lower and caught her gaze with his own. She couldn't look away. "Susanna..." His gaze faltered for the smallest of beats, then connected again. "Susanna, my goddess." He leaned in and kissed her mouth, light as air but full of promise and desire.

She pushed him away. "Do not avoid the question."

"I'm not avoiding it."

She cocked her head to the side and crossed her arms. He would not distract her with his kisses and wide, blue eyes. "Answer me then. You're lying to me about the cloak and I want to know why. Whose cloak is that?"

He scrubbed a hand through his hair. "It belongs to my friend. The stranger you saw yesterday in Sutton Grange."

"The gentleman?"

"His servant." He took her hand and gazed down at it as he circled his thumb over the knuckles. "We are old friends and haven't seen each other in years. I ran into him yesterday in the village, quite by coincidence. We didn't know the other was here. His master never lets him out of his sight, so we decided to meet up in the woods last night. We wanted to talk, exchange news, that sort of thing. He used to have an affection for my sister."

"He wanted to speak to you in the cold and damp of night?"

He shrugged. "It was the only way. His master would not have let him go otherwise."

"Why is his master in Sutton Grange at all?"

"My friend didn't know."

She removed her hand and he finally glanced up at her. Desire still smoldered in the depths of his eyes. And something else—a raw, plaintive plea to be believed. If he was feeding her falsehoods, he was an extremely good liar.

"It began to rain while we were talking," he said, his gaze now locked with hers. "His cloak didn't have a hood and because he had to walk back to the village and I only needed to return to the house, we swapped." He dipped his head but still looked at her. Impish. "There. Happy now?"

She nodded. Yet doubt lingered. He sounded honest enough, but the coincidence of meeting his friend in Sutton Grange was great, and the notion that someone would come to the wood near Stoneleigh on a late November night just to exchange news seemed equally unlikely.

A knock at the door banished any further questions. "Come in," she said. Orlando stepped back to the mattress but still his gaze remained on her.

The door opened on Hendricks. He stepped aside to let Bessie through, carrying a tray. She set it down on the table.

Hendricks pointed at Orlando. "Breakfast is in the kitchen for you, not here." He bowed at Susanna. "Good morning, m'lady. Did you sleep well?"

Susanna hoped her face didn't give her away. "Yes, thank you. Is Father awake?"

"Aye. I just took in his breakfast now."

"I'll go and say good morning." She left without looking back but could hear Hendricks ordering Orlando to return the mattress and bedcovers to the guest bedchamber.

Orlando responded with a good-natured, "Aye, sir. I had a good night's sleep too, if you were wondering. Best one since I arrived here."

Susanna hoped Hendricks and Bessie didn't detect the note of satisfaction in his voice.

* * *

A TALL, strongly built man was inspecting the makeshift canvas structure over the orange trees when Susanna and Orlando arrived in the walled garden. He looked around as they approached and Susanna was struck by a set of shrewd gray eyes that took in her appearance with a swift sweep. He gave no indication what he thought of her but removed his hat and bowed. His hair was short and brown, his face clean-shaved and the jawline firm. She could see why the chandler's wife said all the village women were talking about him in the same breath as Orlando. He was handsome, not in the striking and obvious manner of Orlando but more like a classic statue.

"Good morning," Susanna said. "Mr. Monk, I assume?"

He nodded and Orlando introduced them. A strange darkness

threaded through his voice as he did so. She glanced at him sharply. His passive face gave nothing away. That in itself was odd. Orlando almost always had a friendliness about him.

"Ready?" Monk asked.

"Where's the timber?" Orlando said.

"It's being loaded onto a cart now. Lord Lynden will send someone to deliver it later."

"We have to remove the canvases first," Orlando said. "You do that end. I'll start with this."

"Wouldn't it be better if we both worked at the same end?"

"Why? Can't you reach the top?"

Monk's mouth twisted in a wry smile. "You may have an inch on me, but don't underestimate me, Holt."

"Enough," Susanna said with a shake of her head. They had the decency to look sheepish at least. "I thought I employed men, not boys."

"My apologies, Lady Lynden, I should explain. Holt here thinks I may be hiding something from him and as such, he's decided he doesn't like me."

"I don't trust you," Orlando said.

"You don't need to trust him," she said, "you need to work alongside him. Nothing will get done while you two stand around and beat your chests."

Monk threw his head back and laughed. It transformed him from austere to affable, and Susanna couldn't help smiling along with him.

Orlando stormed off to the other end of the line of orange trees.

"I think I'd better help him," Monk said, speaking in low conspiratorial tones. He touched the brim of his hat and strolled after Orlando.

Susanna watched them, still smiling, a sense of satisfaction rolling through her like a warm wave. She couldn't identify the reason, but she knew it had something to do with Orlando's reaction to Monk's presence.

The men worked together to remove the canvases and the wooden stakes from the temporary structure. They spoke to each other only to give directions, and those were curt. The morning was cool and the air damp, but it wasn't raining. The men wore jerkins over their doublets and shirts, the sleeves rolled up to keep them clean. By the time they finished, they'd both discarded their jerkins. Orlando threw his over a hawthorn bush to keep it off the muddy ground but Monk dropped his onto a leather pack he'd left on the gravel path.

"Where do you want the canvases?" Monk asked, rolling up one of the large coverings.

"The stables, in the far corner," she said. "I'll show you."

"No," both men said.

"I'll show him," Orlando said.

"No need." Monk walked toward the arch, the rolled canvas slung over his shoulder.

To her surprise, Orlando neither argued nor tried to go with him. Once Monk was gone, he strode over to the pack. "Watch for him returning."

"What are you doing?"

"Looking for clues as to the real reason he's here."

"Jeffrey already told us. He has business with Mr. Monk. You don't believe him?"

He regarded her from his squatting position, the pack in his hand. "You do?"

She felt the sting of his disbelief across her face. It was as if he were disappointed in her for thinking Monk and Jeffrey told the truth. "I...I don't know." *That* was the truth. Jeffrey had no reason to lie to her, and yet he'd not explained Monk's presence to her satisfaction.

Orlando, however, *had* lied. He'd lied about his new cloak.

Despite her reservations, she stood by the arch. Orlando was intent on searching Monk's pack. Twice she turned to see if he'd found something, but he continued to rummage through the contents, checking each item thoroughly before placing it to one side. On her third glance, he'd stopped rummaging and his nimble fingers skimmed across seams, along the leather straps.

"Ah." The word was so soft she almost missed it.

"You found something?"

He pointed at the arch. "Keep watching."

She did but had to grind her teeth from telling him it was not his place to order her about. Her ears strained to listen but she could only hear the wind rustling the leaves.

"He's coming," she hissed when Monk emerged from the stables.

"Stay there if he's seen you," Orlando said. "If you move now, he'll grow suspicious."

"I don't like this," she said. "I wish we'd left him alone."

"I'm glad we didn't." He was right beside her, his voice soft in her ear. He stood near the wall so that Monk wouldn't be able to see him until he was through the arch. Orlando's hand touched her hip, reassuringly heavy.

"Why? What did you find?"

But he moved away and returned to the canvases dumped on the ground.

Monk smiled at Susanna as he neared the arch. "Your stables are interesting," he said. At her quizzical look, his smile widened. "It has only one horse but a lot of crates and boxes. I hope you don't mind, but I looked in one. Will you satisfy a simple man's curiosity and tell me what's in the jars?"

Simple? Mr. Monk was not simple. Everything about him was a puzzle. He spoke with a cultured, educated accent yet occasionally a word slipped through that made him sound like a stable hand. Like Orlando, he wasn't afraid to work hard and get dirty, something she found most of the upper classes didn't want to do. And when he smiled, it didn't quite reach his eyes. There was a faraway sadness amid their determined depths but only when he thought no one was looking.

It seemed she had two mysterious men on her hands.

"Most of it is orange marmalade," she said. "Cook and I make it from the fruit harvested from those trees." She nodded at the orange trees where Orlando worked. He lifted his head and frowned. She could tell he was warring with himself over approaching them. It must be torture standing there, wondering what they were saying. Yet he stayed.

"*Orange* marmalade," Monk said. "So that's what those trees are. I wondered why you were going to great lengths to protect them. It's fortunate you have help." He nodded at Orlando. "Those canvases are awkward."

"Very fortunate," she said, quietly.

"Forgive me, Lady Lynden, but I need to ask...where is your man from?"

"Why do you *need* to ask, Mr. Monk?"

"Because the distrust goes both ways, I assure you."

"You don't trust him? Why not?" She wasn't sure she wanted an answer, but she felt compelled to hear Monk's reasoning.

Trusting Orlando had just become one of the most difficult things to do, yet the most important. She wanted to trust him, desperately. When she lay in his arms she'd had no doubts. Not a single one. How could a man lie to a woman after he'd looked into her eyes with such intensity as he entered her? There'd been a raw openness in his gaze, and she knew with every piece of soul that their lovemaking had affected him as much as it had affected her. She would have staked Stoneleigh on it.

But in the light of day, the shadows of his lie and his nocturnal wanderings had remained when the shadows of night had fled. The feeling that she'd been manipulated would not leave.

"He seems too good to be true," Monk explained.

She had to laugh at that. In a way, it was the essence of her own reasoning. How could such a handsome, clever man with a dazzling wit and powerful presence be a mere gardener? Surely the Maker had something more in mind for him. "He worked in a manor house called Collier Dean in Sussex," she said, careful not to look at Orlando as she spoke.

"Where was he born? Who was his father?"

She tensed. "I was satisfied with his credentials and his terms of employment, and didn't ask. I don't find it necessary to pry."

"My apologies, I didn't mean to offend you. But...Lady Lynden, I urge you to ask more questions about his background. The credentials you speak of came from his lips, I assume. Did he have a letter of introduction from his master at Collier Dean?"

"That is not your concern, Mr. Monk." It was a pathetic response, but she could think of no other.

"You're right, and it's not. However, you shouldn't employ someone you know little about."

"Like you, you mean?"

He nodded his head once, conceding her point. "All I'm suggesting is that if I were a woman alone I would not trust any pretty face that presents himself."

"Come now, Mr. Monk, I would hardly call yourself pretty. Handsome, yes."

He laughed. "Quick of wit *and* beautiful, I see."

Her face heated and she looked away.

"My apologies, I didn't mean to embarrass you."

"Thank you for your concern about Mr. Holt, but it's unfounded."

"You have reason to trust him? I'm glad to hear it."

She *wished* she had a reason to believe Orlando. There was, however, one thing she knew he was not guilty of. "No doubt you heard about the intruder here the other night and think Mr. Holt is to blame."

He lifted one shoulder. "I suppose so."

"Then you're mistaken. Mr. Holt could not have been the intruder. He was at my side as the man ran away. He could not possibly be in two places at once."

"No, of course not." He gave a perfunctory bow. "My apologies, I can see you are a formidable woman. But if you find your gardener is...not what he seems, you know where to find me." He walked off before she could ask what he meant.

Susanna followed him and received a loaded glare from

Orlando when he looked up from the canvas he was rolling. A blankness quickly closed over his face and he threw the canvas at Monk. "Think you can carry two?"

Monk held out both arms, the canvas balanced on top of them. "Pile on another. I'll need to rearrange them in the stables, and make more space. Could take awhile."

"Take your time."

Monk left the garden carrying both of the heavy canvases as if they weighed nothing.

"What were you two talking about?" Orlando asked her when he was out of earshot.

"That's between Mr. Monk and myself."

He took a step closer and she swallowed. The look in his eyes was primal. The boyish humor had vanished, the dimples too. She shivered and rubbed her arms. But it wasn't fear that rippled through her, it was passion. Bold, fierce. Raw.

He was looking at her the same way. As if he would take her right there, on the damp ground, and stake his claim.

God help her, she would have let him too. She wanted him like she'd never wanted any man. But just as quickly as the change had come over him, it vanished. He stepped back, the storm clouds chased from his eyes as he stared at her in dazed confusion. It was as if he'd been in a trance or a dream and suddenly woken.

He turned and strode to the last orange tree where he remained, his back to her.

Orlando tried to breathe. It wasn't easy. His chest felt too tight to contain his wildly beating heart and his skin felt hot all over, especially at his groin. He closed his eyes, but all he could see in the darkness was Susanna touching Monk's arm and the cur laughing at something she said.

Hell. He wasn't supposed to feel like this.

"Will you come to me tonight?" she murmured in his ear.

He opened his eyes and drew the cold, sharp air into his chest. "Do you still want me to?"

"Of course."

"Then I will." There'd never been any doubt on that score. Not on his part. His relief at hearing the eagerness in her voice was immeasurable.

"He'll be back soon," she said. "What did you find in his pack?"

"There was a letter of introduction addressed to Lord Lynden from Lord Whipple slipped inside a partially opened seam."

"Lord Whipple? Monk's previous employer?"

"Possibly."

"Did it contain anything of note about Mr. Monk? Anything that may allude to him being untrustworthy?"

The last traces of the fog that had engulfed Orlando lifted. He finally remembered where he'd heard Lord Whipple's name before. A chill prickled his scalp and made the hairs on the back of his neck rise. "The letter contained very little of use, but it did reveal a prior connection between Monk and Lynden. It seems they knew each other years ago, but Whipple informed Lynden that Monk had changed in that time. He then urged Lynden to employ Monk. He said he was very good at his job." *Very good. Urge.* Neither were the precise words contained within the letter.

Lord Whipple hadn't *urged* Lynden to employ Monk, he'd forced him to do it by way of thinly-veiled threats to his person and property. And Monk wasn't *very good* at his job, apparently he was 'the best'. Unfortunately, the letter had not explained what he was best at, or what Monk was supposed to do for Lynden. There must have been earlier correspondence between the gentlemen.

Orlando didn't like it. Lord Whipple was a Catholic, suspected by the queen's spymaster of being behind several attempts to replace their Protestant monarch with a Catholic one. Orlando knew this because the Guild had been commissioned by the spymaster to watch him. When they'd not found enough evidence linking Whipple to any uprisings or plots, they had let him live.

If Whipple was indeed embroiled in something treasonous, how was Lynden connected? Why the need for Monk, a man Whipple described as deviously clever and single-minded?

And what did it all have to do with Susanna?

"How odd," she said. "I'll have to confront Jeffrey about it."

"Not yet." Hell, he'd already told her too much. She was not the sort to sit idly aside when something was afoot, yet that's precisely what she needed to do for the time being. "Susanna." He took her shoulders and locked his gaze with hers. "This is important. You mustn't confront Lynden or Monk. I have reason to believe you may be in danger—"

"What!" Despite her defiant outburst, he felt her shiver.

"I think Monk was our intruder the other night, and until we know his reason for climbing through your bedchamber window, we must assume the worst."

She shook him off. "Are you suggesting he wants to harm me? That Jeffrey employed him to..." Another shiver wracked her, but this one was more visible, more violent.

"It's a possibility we must consider."

"Don't be absurd." She began to pace, four strides to the left, turn and back again. "Jeffrey is my cousin by marriage. I cannot think of any reason he'd want me..." She stopped pacing. "No. It's not possible. There is absolutely no gain to him if I were not here. None whatsoever."

"He could buy Stoneleigh at a good price. Who would inherit it if you were to...?" He couldn't finish the thought let alone the sentence. In five short days, he'd gone from being prepared to assassinate her to not being able to think of her death let alone speak of it.

She didn't look at him, and he knew she was considering whether Lynden was greedy enough to go to such lengths. In the end, she shook her head. Her panic seemed to have eased and her mind taken back control. She was thinking more clearly now. Good for her. He took her hand and squeezed. She squeezed back.

"I find it so hard to believe that Jeffrey would think like that. He's not a malicious man, nor violent. In fact, I think he abhors it. I once saw him turn away from a fight that broke out at The Plough. He'd gone quite green at the first spray of blood."

"Which would explain the need for Monk."

Her nostrils flared and he felt her tense. It was as if she was holding herself together, trying hard not to show fear or make a sound. "You think he..." Her words were barely a whisper.

"I don't know." Yet it would explain much. Monk's presence for one thing, his ability to stealthily approach the stables the first time they met, the unsettling feeling Orlando got whenever he was near.

However, it didn't explain why Orlando had never heard of him. Hughe made it his business to know the names of the other assassins operating on English soil. There was no Monk. He could be new, or he could be so good that he'd escaped their notice until now.

"Do not be frightened." He rested a hand on her shoulder, close to the small ruff she wore, and rubbed his thumb along her jawline. "I'm going to protect you, but be vigilant, my goddess."

She swallowed hard. Nodded.

"I'll go in search of him, see what he's up to."

He found Monk coming out of the brewery. The strong smell of fermenting malt leeched from the small building and hung on the air like an invisible fog.

"What were you doing in there?" Orlando asked, stepping in front of Monk.

"Looking for a drink. I was thirsty."

"You can go to the kitchen for that."

Monk shrugged one shoulder and made to walk around Orlando. Orlando stepped into his path once more. Monk raised a lazy eyebrow and smiled.

"Is there a problem, Mr. Holt?"

"What were you doing in the brewery?"

"I told you. Getting a drink. Ah, here's the building materials just arriving. Excuse me, I have work to do."

Orlando let him pass then followed even though he needed to investigate the brewery himself to see what had been disturbed.

He would not leave Monk alone with Susanna.

But as he passed by the entrance to the kitchen garden, Cook beckoned him from the doorway with a hiss and a crook of her stubby finger. "Did you see him coming out of the brewery just now?" she asked when he was close.

"Yes."

"Well, that's not the only place he went." She clutched Orlando's arm and pulled him closer. She was amazingly strong. "He was in the bakehouse before that."

The bakehouse stood next to the brewery. Like the stables, barn, and the main house itself, both buildings needed repair. Someone had fixed them up enough so they could be used, but all needed more work. The brewery in particular looked like a strong wind might blow it away.

"No one is to enter either the bakehouse or brewery until I've gone through them first," he said. "Understand?"

"But I've got to make the bread!"

"I'll do it immediately after we dine. Can the bread wait until then?"

"Aye, I suppose." Cook looked to Monk where he stood near the walled garden, giving directions to the men who'd delivered the timber. She frowned and the spidery lines across her cheeks reddened. "I don't trust him. It's those eyes. Too many shadows in them, like he's...haunted. He's hiding something, mark my words."

"I agree." Orlando went to join Monk and Susanna and hoped that Cook didn't see the shadows in his eyes.

CHAPTER 10

"Nothing out of the ordinary that I can see," Orlando said from the brewery attic.

Susanna agreed. The brewery was as neat as when she'd filled up a jug the evening before from the ale keg. It wasn't a large brewery, certainly not as big as the ones at Sutton Hall and Cowdrey Farm, but it didn't need to be. Hendricks made the ale and beer because Cook was too busy helping Susanna make the succades and marmalades, and he was very particular about keeping the barrels clean and the place tidy.

If Monk had disturbed anything, he'd put it all back before he left. It had been the same in the bakehouse. Susanna and Orlando looked everywhere for signs of what Monk was up to but found nothing amiss.

Orlando swung down from the attic by hanging one-handed from a beam and dropping to the packed earth floor with a soft thud.

"You could have taken the ladder," Susanna said.

"Not as much fun." He pecked her lightly on the nose, but the impulsive gesture seemed to catch him unawares as much as it did her. He stalked off.

"Any thoughts on what Mr. Monk was doing in here?" she

140

asked, catching up to him as he headed out of the brewery. She had to step quickly to keep up with his long purposeful strides.

"None."

"What do you mean, 'none'? Surely you have some thoughts?"

His hesitation was slight, but she noticed it. "No."

"You do. I can hear it in your voice. You have *some* thoughts, yet you don't wish to share them with me."

"*Hmph.*"

"That is not an answer."

"I wasn't aware you'd asked a question."

Why was he being so difficult? "Is it because I'm a woman and you think our sex incapable of keeping a secret?"

He stopped suddenly and regarded her. "No. It's because I'm not sure what any of this means. I need to think about it awhile." He stepped closer and touched her fingers, just the tips. He bent his head and whispered, "Thinking about it in your arms may help. We could return to the bakehouse and...think in there. It's nice and warm."

"Cook will be baking soon." She stepped back, otherwise she might find herself agreeing to his scheme. When it came to making love to Orlando Holt, the word no seemed to have vanished from her vocabulary.

"In the stables then. Not as warm but there is all that lovely soft straw."

"Straw is not soft."

One eyebrow shot up and those wicked dimples appeared. "Oh? And how does the lady of the manor know that?"

She turned away. "I'm going to the village with Bessie and Hendricks to visit an ill friend I didn't get to yesterday. What are you doing this fine afternoon, Mr. Holt?"

He fell into step beside her. "I prefer Orlando when we're in private."

"We're not in private." She nodded at the kitchen door visible over the top of the low wall surrounding the herb garden.

Hendricks stood there like a faithful hound, the folds of his wrinkles practically trembling in indignation as he watched Susanna and Orlando approach together. All he needed were fangs and a snarl.

"How goes it, Mr. Hendricks?" Orlando asked.

"Everything all right, m'lady?" the servant said, ignoring him.

Poor man, he was quite out of his depth when it came to Orlando. Not that she was any better. Her gardener was like no man she'd met before, yet in some ways he was just the same. His ability to charm her into bed, for example. Both John and Phillip had been like that during their courtship, hence her understanding of the ways straw could poke tender places.

"Everything is well, Mr. Hendricks," she said, "however, if you have any suggestions as to why Mr. Monk was looking through our bakehouse and brewery, I would welcome them."

He shook his head. "None, madam. All I can say is he was looking around for something to steal."

"Steal what? Bread and ale?" She clasped Hendricks's arm. "I'm sorry. I didn't mean to speak harshly. I'm concerned and more than a little confused."

Beside her, Orlando shifted. She wondered if he wanted to touch her and comfort her as much as she wished he would.

"Come, Hendricks, let's go into the village as planned." She turned to Orlando. "What about you, Mr. Holt? What are you going to do this afternoon?"

He grinned. "Come with you."

ORLANDO DIDN'T MIND BEING RELEGATED to the back of the cart with Hendricks while Susanna and Bessie rode on the seat. He'd offered to drive and, to his surprise, Hendricks had been an ally and agreed to the arrangement since he thought women not strong enough and his own eyesight was poor. Susanna had declined Orlando's offer and brooked no opposing argument.

It was market day and Sutton Grange was busy. Orlando

remained vigilant for Lynden or Monk but neither seemed to be in the vicinity of the Green. That didn't mean they weren't there, blending into the crowds purchasing goods from carts and makeshift stalls set up in rows across the Green. Or perhaps they were in one of the permanent shops, waiting for Susanna to arrive, or The Plough inn.

He would not let her out of his sight while so much uncertainty surrounded Monk, and certainly not when so many people occupied the village.

"It's late and some have packed up and already left," Bessie said as the cart pulled to the side of the road. "But we should be able to get what Cook needs. Oh look, there's William Frate the grocer. Why don't you speak to him today, m'lady?"

"I'll give the London merchants more time to respond," Susanna said, setting the reins down. "I don't think Mr. Frate will know what to do with orange marmalade any more than Mr. Goody, our regular village grocer," she added for Orlando's benefit.

He was about to ask her which merchants she'd sent enquiries to but remembered he wasn't supposed to be from London let alone know any merchants so kept his mouth shut. He jumped down and helped Bessie then Susanna to climb off. He offered his hand to Hendricks but the old servant declined with a brusque flick of his hand. He stepped cautiously from the back of the cart onto the slippery, muddy road.

"There still seems like many sellers here to me," Orlando said. The Green was a hive of enterprise. Farmers tried to out-do each other, announcing their wares in their loudest voices. Since it was already afternoon, many had lowered their prices and the competition to attract customers was fierce. Added to the din was the cluck of hens, the snorting of pigs, and the honks of geese. Women walked from cart to cart, baskets over their arms, and men stood in clusters discussing events. Everyone seemed to be ignoring the children who no doubt liked that arrangement very much. Younger ones played in the dirt and fallen leaves while older ones skipped or threw a ball. A group of about seven youngsters ran past, two of them holding a stick topped with a sticky ball covered in seeds and nuts. Their squeals of laughter lingered long after they disappeared around the corner.

"Market day is always busy," Susanna said, her gaze on a small child sitting by herself, intent on the rag doll in her lap. Susanna's eyes shone and a wistful smile slowly appeared, but it remained small, distant. Forlorn.

"Draws the farmers from all around here," Bessie said. "See there, that's Farmer Cowdrey's men tending to his carts. He always has the most to sell. He doesn't come himself anymore. Doesn't like crowds much."

"Doesn't like people much," Hendricks muttered. "A word of advice, Holt," he said. "Don't try to get a drink in The Plough today, Milner will be run off his feet. Course it won't stop his mouth. Might just make it go faster, actually, what with all the extra ears to hear him."

Orlando laughed again. "You're witty when you want to be."

Hendricks glared at him. "I'm not trying to be witty, Mr. Holt."

"So what will you do while we visit my friend and do some marketing?" Susanna asked Orlando.

"I'm coming with you," he said.

Her lips formed a perfect O. It would seem she didn't understand the extent of the danger she could be in. "Then we'd better go. If you're coming along, you might as well put those big arms to use and carry the basket."

Away from the market, the village was a quiet collection of crooked houses pushed up against each other, rather like in London. Unlike London, most of the houses were only two stories high with attic windows peeping from beneath the steeply pitched roofs. The village itself was small and the short, narrow streets radiating off the High Street disappeared into the countryside or simply ended. Susanna's friend lived in a wooden house with a dangerous lean to it. If it hadn't been propped up by the house next door, it probably would have fallen over.

"Joan's a widow," Susanna said, "with four children to care for.

She recently became ill and I need to make sure she's not lacking anything."

Orlando lifted the cloth covering the basket and peeked inside. Susanna was a generous friend since she could ill afford to give much away. The basket was packed with jars. Some of them he knew contained her orange marmalade, plus brown bread, dried fruits, vegetables, and a pie.

"Bessie, would you mind visiting Widow Dawson for some cure-all." Susanna untied the pouch from her girdle—she'd changed into women's clothes for the journey into the village— and handed it to her maid. Coin jangled.

"Widow Dawson is the wise woman?" Orlando couldn't believe his luck. The wise woman had studied Phillip's body and had been the one to call for the coroner. With the coroner dead, she was the best person to tell Orlando what the body looked like after death. "Is her house nearby?"

"Just across the road." She nodded at a thin building opposite.

Perfect. He could keep watch on Susanna's friend's house from the front window and speak to the wise woman at the same time without raising suspicions.

"I'll buy the cure-all," he said, holding out his hand for the pouch.

Bessie glanced at Susanna who shrugged and the maid passed him the pouch.

Hendricks snatched it away. "We can't give him money! What if he runs off with it all?"

"Mr. Hendricks," Susanna said on a sigh, "if Mr. Holt wanted to steal from us, he would have done so already. Besides, there's hardly enough in there for a hearty meal. Give him the pouch."

Grumbling, Hendricks reluctantly handed it over. "Why are you so eager to go see Widow Dawson anyway? Got an ailment you're not telling us about?"

"Hendricks!" Bessie and Susanna cried.

"That's none of our business," Bessie said.

"Course it's our business," he said. "What if we catch it?"

"I don't have anything contagious," Orlando said, tying the coin pouch to his belt.

"Are you sure?"

"Quite sure. My ailment is..." He glanced at Susanna. She looked beautiful dressed in women's clothes. Hell, she looked beautiful all the time. "My ailment is of a personal nature. It's not something you'll catch." Although it was debilitating. Utterly. Perhaps Widow Dawson could give him something to expel it. He didn't like feeling this way about one woman. Nor could he afford to.

He crossed the road and knocked on the door. The leather and cloth pouches filled with sweet smelling herbs nailed to the wood shook. Above the door was a sprig of rosemary for warding off evil spirits, illness, or perhaps both. Orlando didn't have much faith in most of the concoctions sold by apothecaries and used by wise woman and physician alike. What was sold in the shops wasn't always what they'd bought from his brother's imported stock. Unicorn's horn, a valuable ingredient in many medicines, was more likely to be the teeth of a cow and although the snake skin might be genuine, he'd never seen any benefit come from consuming it, wearing it, or smoking it.

The door opened and the pouches jiggled as it swung. A young girl of about ten stared up at him, eyes wide with alarm. She shrank back behind the door.

"Is Widow Dawson at home?" he asked, employing a smile he knew would soften the girl's fear of his size. "I've been sent on an errand by Lady Lynden to fetch a cure-all."

The girl stepped away from the door but it was Susanna's name that had done the trick, not his smile. "Come in, sir. Ma's in the kitchen."

He followed her through the parlor and into the kitchen beyond. It was small compared to the one at Stoneleigh and cramped. The large central table left little room for anything else and the herbs hanging from the beams made the ceiling seem lower. Orlando had already removed his hat but he still needed to stoop or the dried leaves would comb his hair. A mix of strong smells filled the room, their scents difficult to distinguish although he detected rue above all else.

An attractive woman of middling age with golden eyes and brown hair sat on a stool at the table, grinding something with a pestle. She glanced up at him and continued grinding as her gaze lingered on Orlando.

"You must be one of the handsome strangers I keep hearin' 'bout," she said, eyes bright with amusement. "So question is, are you the one workin' for Lord Lynden or the one helpin' out Lady Lynden?"

"The latter. My name's Orlando Holt. I'm her gardener, but I'm running an errand today. She needs a cure-all for her friend across the way." He glanced back through the open kitchen door, through the parlor's window to the street beyond. Joan's house was clearly visible. He stayed there where he could see anyone coming or going.

"Aye, I can see the dimples now that you smile. They said you had dimples a woman could lose herself in." Her laugh was throaty and rich.

"They?"

"Aye, and don't play the innocent with me. Men like you know all the women have eyes for you." She half-turned. "Bel, keep stir-rin' or it'll burn."

The girl, Bel, obediently sat on the stool near the hearth and swept her skirts aside to keep them clear of the coals. She picked up the stick lying across the cauldron that was suspended from the rod above the fire and began to stir slowly.

"A cure-all, you say." Widow Dawson shook her head. "She needs somethin' more spific to her ailment. Too phlegmatic, Joan is. I been waitin' for someone to come to me and buy her a medi-cine. She's a friend, but I can't give my cures away for nothin', can I?" As she spoke, she rose and walked into an adjoining room. She emerged carrying a lidded jug. "Course I knew Lady Lynden would come round soon enough. She's a good friend and most would agree with that."

"Most?"

She set the jug on the table, removed the lid and sniffed the contents. "There's some say she needs to get herself another husband, or she'll grow too headstrong. Looks like it's too late for that if you ask me." She laughed her throaty laugh again. "She runs Stoneleigh now that Mr. Farley's health's gone and does all right for a chit of a thing. Course, she's not been able to sell her orange stuffs yet, but she will. She's got a good head on her, not just a pretty one." She returned to the storage room and came out cradling several small earthen jars to her chest. "There's those in this village that think only men should do the thinkin', and not all of them that say it are the men neither." She shook her head. "Those silly fools are the ones who won't know what to do when their menfolk die. They're the ones who'll need charity from the likes of Lady Lynden. We're a different kind of woman, she and I. We've got heads for trade and that'll see us by in the lean times."

"So you don't think she should wed again?"

"What do I care if she does or doesn't? Means nothin' to me. Course, she prob'ly won't."

"Why not?"

"Well, she's barren ain't she? She lost a babe once, and it must have ruined her. She hasn't carried another since. What man'd want a barren wife?" She paused, still holding some of the jars, the rest she'd set on the table. "Less he's already got brats of his own from a first wife and don't need more. That'll be her best chance, if she wants it."

A strange sensation crept into Orlando's chest, like a clawing of his vitals. Susanna knew she would never bear children and the knowledge ached deep within her. He'd suspected it, but hearing the wise woman confirm it made it seem more real, and explained so much about Susanna. The wistfulness in her eyes when she watched children playing, the hitching of her voice when she told him there was "no need" to waste his seed.

The clawing became a squeezing.

"And are there any men like that in Sutton Grange?" he asked.

"Any men worthy of the daughter of Mr. Farley and the widow of Lord Phillip Lynden, I mean?"

"Not one that's already got his own children. Farmer Cowdrey *thinks* he's worthy, but he's just a farmer, no matter how rich he is now. Course, she may not get too many other offers. Don't get many newcomers to Sutton Grange, 'specially not of her class. That gentleman what was here yesterday was the best that's come through in an age, but he left." She chuckled. "A bit too foppish for our Susanna Lynden anyway. He didn't look like he'd want to get dirt under his fingernails, and Lady Lynden likes to be out in the garden. Course that might make the perfect marriage, eh? They wouldn't have to see each other 'cept in the marital bed." Her raucous laughter echoed around the kitchen. The girl, Bel, grinned as she stirred.

Orlando laughed too, but hopefully Widow Dawson couldn't hear the strain. If Susanna knew that Hughe cared not a whit whether his hands were dirty, she might be interested. Yet Hughe would not. She wasn't high enough to earn his mother's approval and her barrenness would be a problem for Hughe. The earldom of Oxley would end with him if he had no legitimate children and Orlando knew he didn't want that.

"How did Lord Lynden die? Phillip, that is," he asked, trying to set aside his dark thoughts. He was here to find out one thing and that was whether Susanna killed her husband. Everything else was unnecessary to his work and his reason for getting close to Susanna in the first place.

"Natural causes, so the coroner said. They called me up to the Hall first, didn't they, Bel, and it was me that told 'em to send for the coroner."

The girl nodded. "Ma went in the morning and I got to go too," she said, proudly. "I'm her 'sistant, see. Well, he was cold as ice, weren't he, Ma? Stiff as a plank too." She sounded amazed, not horrified. Perhaps she'd seen many gruesome things as her Ma's "sistant".

"Aye, that's death for you. Bein' a gen'leman don't change nothin'."

"So you agree with the coroner's findings?" Orlando asked.

"Course I agree. Who am I not to?"

"What did the body look like when you saw it?"

"Stiff," Bel said. "I told you that."

"Hush, foolish child, Mr. Holt wants a profesh'nal 'pinion." Widow Dawson folded her arms and furrowed her brow. "Well, let's see now. It was some time ago, but I remember him all right." She paused. "Why do you want to know, anyway? What's it to do with you?"

He shrugged. "I have an interest in health and medicine. I probably would have become a barber surgeon if my father had let me make my own decisions."

Although he'd never wanted to be barber surgeon, Orlando hadn't lied about his father. Decisions, both great and small, had rarely been his to make. The only choice he'd had was whether to count the goods as they entered and exited the warehouse, or cultivate more customers and tend to existing ones. He chose the customers, but that decision was retracted when his brother took control. It was the warehouse and paperwork for Orlando with boredom, disaster, and banishment soon following. The first choice he'd made after leaving London was to get into a fight in a Southwark inn where he'd come to the notice of Hughe. His choices had been getting better ever since.

"Well then, I s'pose it's no odder an interest than any other," Widow Dawson said. "So let's see." She frowned hard. "Oh yes, there was no blood on the body, no cuts that I could see, and no markings or colorings on his skin or fingernails. I only sent for the coroner because Lord Phillip was in his prime. I'd seen old men dead from heart failure but not a young one." She shrugged. "Anyway, that's what it was, so the coroner said."

He wasn't poisoned then, or stabbed. Indeed, the signs, or lack of them, seemed perfectly consistent with a man whose heart simply stopped. Even more telling, the wise woman had not once suggested Susanna or anyone else might have killed Phillip. Clearly the coroner's verdict satisfied her.

Any lingering doubts Orlando had over Susanna being a murderer were finally quashed. He rubbed a hand over his face in an effort to hide his relief. He knew it would clearly show on his face because he felt it through to his core.

Susanna was innocent. He didn't need Hughe and Cole to return from Harveston to confirm it.

But the question remained: who hated Susanna enough to want her dead but didn't want to perform the act themselves?

"Thank you," he said and turned to go.

"Wait," she said. "The medicine." Widow Dawson surveyed her collection of jars. With a small shake of her head, she picked up the lidded jug and handed it to Orlando. "Take it all. Tell Joan I'll check on her in three days and if she's better, I'll take the unused amount back. It'll rebalance her humors and loosen the phlegm. She's to swallow one mouthful every time she feels it build up on her chest." She held out her palm. "Tuppence."

He handed over the coin and bowed to the little girl, Bel. She giggled beneath her hand and for some reason, Orlando found that funny. He grinned back.

"Thank you, ladies. Widow Dawson, you are the wisest wise woman I have ever had the pleasure of meeting."

"And you, sir, are a terrible flirt. Be off with you."

Bel's giggle and her mother's laughter followed him all the way to the front door and out to the street. It wasn't until they were all in the cart some time later, their marketing done, that he realized he'd forgotten to ask Widow Dawson for a remedy to dampen his desire for Susanna.

Ah well, he could always return another day.

* * *

ORLANDO SEEMED to be in an excessively good mood. Granted he smiled, laughed, and flirted often, but the humor didn't always reach his eyes. Something Susanna had only just come to realize. The man helping her down from the cart outside Sutton Hall oozed happiness from every part of him, but it was his eyes she noticed most. They sparkled. What had Widow Dawson said to him? Or, more appropriately, what had she given him?

"Did you eat anything at the wise woman's house?" she asked. Her face heated when he kissed the back of her hand, his warm lips lingering longer than was decent.

Hendricks cleared his throat and Orlando stopped kissing and bowed deeply to him. "Forgive me, Mr. Hendricks, but don't you think she is particularly beautiful today?"

"You ought to stop looking, Mr. Holt, if that's all you see."

"You're right," Orlando said. "Consider me chastised. Lady Lynden, to answer your question, I ate nothing at Widow Dawson's. Nor did I drink anything." He lifted Bessie down from the cart, swinging her to the ground as if she were a child.

"Oh my," Bessie said, pressing the backs of her hands to her flushed cheeks.

"Was she brewing something?" Susanna asked. "That could account for it."

"Account for what?" he asked.

"For the way you're acting," Hendricks said.

"How am I acting?"

"Like a toss-pot."

"Mr. Hendricks!" Bessie cried. "Leave him be. Perhaps it's just natural," she said to Susanna. "Perhaps there's no explaining it."

"Explaining what?" Orlando shook his head, confused.

"Why you're smiling like you just found something you thought lost?" Susanna said.

His smile vanished, and she wished she'd kept quiet. She liked that he was in such a good mood. It lifted her own somewhat troubled one.

"Wait for me here. I won't be a moment," she said and began the walk up the drive to the house.

"No," Orlando said. The word was spoken quietly enough, but

the underlying note of command halted her. She did not return to him but remained halfway between the grand steps leading up to the front door and the cart. He came to her instead. All good humor had vanished and his eyes were dark, flat. "Until we know more about Monk's intentions," he said, voice rumbling like thunder, "you remain within my sight."

"You did not follow me into Joan's."

"I could see her house from Widow Dawson's." One corner of his mouth twitched up. "I adore the way you thrust your chin out when you're annoyed with me." They were out of earshot from Hendricks and Bessie, but that didn't stop Susanna from blushing or Hendricks from scowling.

"Stop it. Be serious. We are at Sutton Hall. What could happen to me here? The place is crawling with servants and I'll be with Jeffrey the entire time."

"The man who hired Monk. I'm coming in with you."

"Don't be ridiculous."

He pressed a hand to his heart and tilted his head to the side like an adorable puppy. "You mean I'm not good enough to go in the front entrance with Lady Lynden? I'm wounded. I may be a mere gardener in occupation, but I'm a prince on the inside."

His words were spoken in jest, but they cut her to the bone.

"Stop it," she snapped. "Please." She wrapped her arms around herself, but it was too late. Her 'mere gardener' had got under her skin and there he'd set up camp.

"Ah, so it bothers you, eh?" His eyes still sparkled, damn him. "Is that because I mean more to you than you wish to admit even to yourself? Me...a servant?"

The stark, bald truth of his words hit her hard. He *did* mean more to her than simply someone to keep her warm at night, yet it could not be so. *Should* not be so. Their passion would one day need to be set aside and Orlando would have to leave.

The light in his eyes suddenly went out. It was as if he'd just remembered something horrible, something he'd tried very hard to forget. "This is foolishness," he snarled and stalked off ahead of her. "I'm coming inside with you."

A groom appeared from around the side of the house. He ran to them, breathless. "Sorry, m'lady, I heard your arrival, but I was needed in the stables. I'll take Silver around for you?"

"Thank you, Warren. Oh, and one other thing." She glanced at Orlando's broad back. He was waiting for her on the bottom step but he had not turned around. "Is Mr. Monk in the house?"

"No, m'lady."

She told Bessie and Hendricks to take themselves off to the kitchen then went after Orlando.

"He's not here," she said, curt. "There'll probably be warm soup for you in the kitchen if you want some. I'll be perfectly safe with Jeffrey, alone, as I've always been."

She climbed the steps, passing him, and was met at the door by Jeffrey's house steward. He greeted her with a deep bow. When she turned around again, Orlando was gone. He had not made a sound.

he large study on the first floor of Sutton Hall hadn't changed much since Phillip's time. The wood paneling was not covered by tapestries or portraits to soften its masculinity and coffers of varying sizes squatted on the rushes near the wide desk. One of the coffers was triple padlocked as it had been when Phillip was alive. The only difference Susanna could see was the man behind the desk and the torn pieces of paper scattered across its surface and on the floor.

Jeffrey set his pen down in its stand and gathered up the pieces. "I don't have any more timber."

And good afternoon to you too, Cousin. "I don't want more timber. I simply wanted to thank you for what you've given me already. Your man, Monk, is a good worker."

"Is he?" he said absently.

"He's strong and efficient, much like Mr. Holt."

"Your thanks are welcome but unnecessary." He screwed up the bits of parchment into a wad and threw it onto the desk. It rolled off and fell to the rushes where it broke apart. "Is there something else?"

She sat down even though he hadn't asked her to sit. "Yes. I want to know more about your man, Monk. You tell me he's trustworthy—"

"Then what else do you need to know?" He rubbed his forehead and sighed heavily.

Infuriating man. "I need to know why he's been wandering into my outbuildings for no reason. I have not directed him to do so, yet he's been seen exiting the brewery and the bakehouse, and he spent longer than necessary in the stables too. Can you be sure he's not up to something?"

The look Jeffrey gave her was one of strained patience and exhaustion. She'd never seen him look so wretched. "Susanna, I understand that your feminine nerves make you worry excessively and that you cannot help that, but—"

"Oh good lord, Jeffrey, this is nothing to do with my femininity or my nerves. It is a simple question regarding a man in your employ. Anyone would be equally cautious under the same circumstances."

"Anyone would not be equally cautious. Any *man* would accept his help and let him roam where he wanted to. He and I are both doing you a favor, are we not? I can't see what harm there is in letting him take a look at your outbuildings. Perhaps he is observing their construction. Have you asked him?"

"No. Nor have I asked him why there is a letter in his pack from Lord Whipple."

His gaze flickered down to the scrunched up pieces of paper on the floor and back again. It was such a rapid move that if she hadn't been looking for any sign of recognition, she wouldn't have noticed it. "A letter?"

"Yes. A letter of introduction addressed to you, as it happens."

"Ah. Of course." He leaned back in the chair and stretched his legs under the desk. "Susanna, I'm appalled at your behavior. Why were you reading a private letter not meant for your eyes?" He shook his head. "You really have lost your way these past few months, haven't you?"

"Lost my way?" she spluttered. "Jeffrey, I have a right to know everything about the people I allow onto my estate."

"Your father's estate."

"While Father is unwell, I am both master and mistress of Stoneleigh, and as such, you should show me some respect."

"I am!"

"No, Jeffrey, you are not. Everything about this conversation is condescending." Walking out now would achieve nothing. Yet staying was proving just as futile and far more frustrating.

"You came to me," he petulantly pointed out.

"Yes. I did. Now, I will say this clearly since you seem to be having trouble understanding me. Lord Whipple addressed you in the letter, which means you must have an acquaintance with him."

"A passing acquaintance only." He leaned forward and slid a piece of parchment over the top of the letter he'd been writing. He rested his elbows on it and steepled his fingers. "He thought Mr. Monk may be of use to me, hence the introduction. Except it wasn't really an introduction. I knew Monk already. He used to live near me, although we didn't associate." This last he said with a wrinkle of his nose.

"And for what reason did Whipple recommend him to you?"

"That's private, Susanna."

Another block. Her only consolation was that Jeffrey seemed to be enjoying the interrogation as little as her. Despite the coolness of the room, sweat trickled from his temple, and he had not once maintained eye contact with her. A sure sign he was lying or, at the very least, holding back something important.

"Is there anything else?" he asked. "I'm very busy as you can see."

Busy being a toad. "Nothing else for now. Perhaps I'll get a better response from your man instead."

"Monk?" He shook his head. "I would advise you not to ask Mr. Monk too many questions about his past. I suspect he doesn't like talking about it."

"Who does? But if he wants to work at Stoneleigh then he must understand he cannot wander about until I am assured he is trustworthy. We may not have much worth stealing, but that is beside the point."

He heaved in another heavy sigh. "Susanna, you are a determined female. Were you this way with Phillip?"

"Only once." And he had made her pay for her determination in the most damning way.

She could see the thoughts ticking through Jeffrey's mind, wondering what she was talking about. She didn't care. He had his secrets, and she had hers.

Sometimes she wondered what would have happened if she had become more upset over Phillip's straying ways and his forbidding her friendships. Would he have hit her again? She doubted it. That incident seemed to shake him to the core. She probably could have asked him for anything after that and he would have given it to her out of guilt.

But she didn't have the heart to make him pay. She simply no longer cared for Phillip. It was like he'd stopped existing, except for the times he came to her bed to try and get her with child again. Even then she'd neither spoken to him nor looked at him. She'd simply spread her legs and closed her eyes until he was finished.

"Good day, Jeffrey. No, don't get up. I can see myself out." She glanced at the pieces of torn parchment still on the floor and left them behind with some regret. Jeffrey didn't want her to see them, and that meant the pieces could be important.

She made her way downstairs to the kitchen and gathered up her two servants. Orlando was in the stables where she found him helping out with the horses. He had his back to the entrance as he inspected a hoof, but he must have heard their approach on the gravel.

"If you're hoping Lord Lynden will pay you," she said, "then you're out of luck. He'll argue that he didn't formally employ you, and you're not entitled to anything."

"I don't expect pay," he said. "This poor animal was in pain, and the only man who seems to know what to do is out riding with the land steward."

Warren the stable lad nodded. "The head groom," he said for Susanna's benefit then, for some reason she couldn't fathom, he blushed to the roots of his hair.

Orlando lowered the hoof and rubbed the beast's back. "All better now, girl," he said softly. "Treat her with care, Warren, and make sure your master gets some of that paste I described. The wise woman in the village should be able to make it up for you."

"Aye, Mr. Holt." Warren led the horse away.

Orlando waited until she was back in her stall and then he strode right past Susanna. She followed him out of the stables to where Silver grazed on a feed bag and watched as he hitched her to the cart.

"Still in a bad temper I see," she murmured as he removed the bag and set it aside.

The look he gave her would have frozen hot water in an instant. "Find anything useful?"

"In a way." She didn't say any more because Hendricks had climbed up onto the cart and Orlando was helping Bessie to the seat. Susanna sat beside her.

It wasn't until they were back at Stoneleigh and alone in the stables that she finally spoke to him again. "Are you still angry with me?"

He lengthened his strokes as he brushed Silver's neck. "You need to be more careful."

"I *was* careful. I was also perfectly safe. And if you think Jeffrey would have allowed you to accompany me into his study, you don't know him. He would have turned you away without a second thought as to whether he'd hurt your feelings."

He stopped brushing. "You think that's what this is about? You think I care about getting my feelings hurt by your turd of a cousin-in-law?"

She gasped. He closed his mouth over hers, smothering her

protest. It was a hard kiss, urgent and hungry. His fingers curled into her cloak at her back, holding her in place against him.

But the hardness quickly melted away. His mouth turned soft, his kisses slow yet somehow still urgent, possessive. The change made her body tingle as if she'd been plunged from a hot pool to a cold one and back again.

He broke the kiss and gave his attention to Silver once more. His strokes increased their rhythm. "I'm sorry," he muttered.

"Don't be." She drew in a deep breath to steady her nerves. "You're angry, but I don't think it has anything to do with your position here at Stoneleigh or my safety."

He said nothing, just kept brushing Silver with long, regular strokes.

"Do you know," Susanna said quietly, "that I know as little about you as I do about Mr. Monk?"

He paused mid-stroke. "Sometimes you don't need to have background details to truly know a person. Sometimes being intimate is enough."

"I wish that were so, but I would be a fool to believe it." She had thought she'd understood both her husbands after making love to them the first time but discovered too late that she did not. "At least I've seen a letter of recommendation for Mr. Monk. I've not seen one for you." He didn't answer her and switched his attention to Silver's tangled mane. "I know nothing of your family, your childhood, or why you like to roam across the country in search of work."

"I told you all you need to make up your mind about me," he said, without turning around. "I've mentioned my sister to you and that my father was a gardener as well. I told you where I came from. As to why I like to roam...I simply don't like being in one place for long. I grow restless."

And yet that still told her nothing. Why did he become restless? Something must have led him to want to leave his family.

As to the rest, the more she thought about it, the less it made sense. He was an articulate, clever man who could read, and yet he wanted her to believe his father was a gardener? Orlando possessed no gardening gloves, little plant knowledge, and no letter of recommendation from his previous employer. That alone made her doubt him.

"If you don't want me here," he said, patting Silver's neck, "you can ask me to leave."

Not going to him and wrapping her arms around his waist was the hardest thing. Yet she refrained. She also managed to speak with a clear, strong voice. "I don't want you to leave."

His fingers flexed around the brush. He nodded once, curt, and started brushing again. "What did you learn from Lynden?"

The tension dispersed a little but didn't disappear entirely. "He's hiding something. There was a letter he'd torn to pieces that he didn't want me to see. He was also writing something that he hid from my gaze. I tried to think of a diversion to get him out of the study, but I doubt he would have fallen for anything. He seemed quite distressed, and a man in that state doesn't suddenly forget that he's protecting a letter from prying eyes and then leave it exposed."

"And did you mention Lord Whipple to him?"

She picked up the horse blanket from where it hung on a hook. "He said he's an acquaintance. I could get no more out of him on that front."

Orlando took the blanket and their fingers touched. A jolt of heat surged across her skin.

"Will you come to me tonight?" she asked, breathy.

He didn't answer immediately, but waited until after he'd arranged the blanket over Silver's back. "I—"

The sound of approaching footsteps stopped him. Hendricks appeared at the stable entrance. "Supper's ready, m'lady." His wrinkles formed a deep frown that he directed at Orlando. "S'pose you better come in and have some too."

"Go on," Orlando said. "I'll finish up here."

She followed Hendricks out without looking back.

SUSANNA FELL asleep despite her best efforts not to. She woke up some time later and crossed to the door leading to her parlor. To Orlando. "Are you still angry with me?" she asked as she opened the door.

It was dark in the parlor and no answer came from the direction of his bed. She padded across the rushes until her feet hit the mattress and dropped to her knees. She patted the blankets from foot to base then sat back on her haunches and stared into the blackness.

The mattress was empty. Orlando was gone.

* * *

IT WAS easy enough to get into Sutton Hall. Like many country homes, one of the service doors had been left unlatched. There was little need to secure a house when everyone knew everyone else. Besides, all the truly valuable items like the silver plate would be locked away. Orlando carried his boots past the larders, scullery, and kitchen, up an inner stairwell to where he guessed the master's apartments to be. Modern manors followed a similar layout with the best private rooms on the first floor overlooking the prettiest views. In Sutton Hall's case, the prettiest views were across the valley to the north, so it was that wing he investigated first.

There was enough moonlight coming through windows to make out furniture and doors as he carefully opened the first one off the landing. With any luck it would lead to Lynden's study. Beyond that would be his private chambers including his bedchamber and wardrobe.

But it was an empty room. He cursed his pride for not asking Susanna for directions. It was only now that he was faced with finding his way through a large house that he realized how foolish that pride was, particularly since he wasn't angry at her but at himself. *He* was the one who couldn't stop new and unwelcome thoughts from getting in the way of the task at hand.

She seemed to be having no such difficulty.

Bloody hell. Susanna's suggestion that she knew him as little as she knew Monk, and the implication that she didn't trust him, had sent him reeling. He may have lied to her, but she could trust him nevertheless. How could she not know that after what had passed between them during their lovemaking? Had she not felt what he'd felt?

Damnation. He wasn't supposed to *feel* anything.

Concentrate, Holt. If he didn't stop thinking about Susanna, he was going to find himself in the wrong room at the wrong end of a sword.

He tried the second door off the landing with more success. The moonlight streaming through the large window illuminated a desk, chairs, and coffers. The study at last. He went inside but left the door open a little. The desk was long and papers littered the surface. He read some, but they appeared to be estate accounts and letters to London tailors. No letter to or from Lord Whipple or anyone else Orlando recognized. He checked inside a casket on the far corner of the desk but it held only spare quills and ink. The only other casket on the desk was locked. The two large coffers on the floor were also locked. He tried the casket first.

The thin tools made of bone that Hughe had given each of the Guild members when they joined quickly opened the padlock. Orlando lifted the lid and angled the casket to the moonlight. Inside were dozens of pieces of crumpled and torn parchment.

He removed the small pack from his back and tipped the pieces inside. With the pack slung across his back and his boots once more in hand, he was out the door and down the stairs before the count of five.

"Halt! Who's there?" shouted out a voice. Monk.

Hell.

Orlando ran. Monk ran after him.

"Halt, fool, or I'll use my blade."

Try.

Orlando detoured into the kitchen and headed for the door leading outside, but someone had locked it. He pressed his back against the wood, assessed his options. It was dark and he could only just make out the shapes of the table, stools, pots, the fireplace. Monk.

"Do not move," Monk said. "I'm armed." Armed but foolish. He'd not raised a hue and cry to rouse the rest of the household. That was a mistake.

Orlando drew his knife out of the sheath strapped to his forearm and approached Monk carefully, slowly. Metal flashed in the other man's hand. He too held a knife. Another mistake. He should have brought his sword.

Why hadn't he? If Orlando had awoken to sounds of an intruder, the first thing he would have done was grab his sword, if he had one.

Perhaps Monk hadn't been asleep when he heard Orlando. Perhaps he'd been roaming around the house too with the less wieldy knife for protection. It explained why it seemed like he'd been waiting for Orlando in the service area when he ought to be sound asleep in a bedchamber upstairs.

Well, well, why was the mysterious Mr. Monk sneaking about his employer's house?

"Who are you?" Monk growled.

Orlando said nothing. Speaking would give his identity away. It was so dark in the windowless kitchen that even his blond hair would not be visible.

"I said—"

Orlando hunched over and charged. He hit Monk side-on, using his body to force the other man out of the way. Monk grunted and slammed against the wall near the door. Orlando ran out of the kitchen, past the larders and other service rooms toward the narrow passage leading to a different exit.

But he didn't see the object in his path. He tripped over it and skidded across the flagstone floor. Bloody hell! What fool had left a crate or whatever the hell it was in the way?

He got to his feet, keeping his pack close, but was shoved back down again by the full force of Monk's body. He managed to stand again only to receive a punch to the stomach.

Orlando couldn't breathe and pain rippled through his middle. The hit was a solid one. Monk knew what he was doing. Orlando swung back and his fist crunched against Monk's face. Monk grunted then lunged.

Orlando didn't see the knife until too late.

He leapt to the side but the blade sliced through his sleeves and slashed his arm. It stung like the devil, but he made no sound.

Enough. Time to end it.

Orlando ran off again, through another door, and found himself in a small room whose function he couldn't determine without light. Perfect.

Monk was right behind him. But instead of running, Orlando flattened himself against the wall near the door. Monk tripped over Orlando's boot. He went sprawling across the floor and crashed into what sounded like pails.

Before he could get up, Orlando stepped on his hand. Grunting in pain, Monk let go of the knife. Orlando snatched it up then hauled Monk to his feet, and hit him in the stomach. Hard. He didn't pull back.

Monk doubled over, gasping for air. He fell to his knees and that's when Orlando left. He didn't look back. Didn't need to. No footsteps followed, and he knew Monk wouldn't be able to breathe properly for some time.

Now all he had to do was sneak back into Stoneleigh without getting caught.

* * *

"You're awake," Orlando said, closing the parlor door behind him.

Susanna sat up on the mattress and gave him what she hoped was a withering glare, but was probably a complete failure. She was too relieved to see him to be angry. Yet her relief didn't disperse the doubts surrounding his disappearance.

"Where have you been?" she asked.

He dumped his pack on the floor and fell to his knees near her. "You waited up for me?"

He leaned in to kiss her. She swayed back and pressed a hand to his chest. His heart beat furiously beneath her palm and now that she looked closely, she could see beads of sweat across his temple. The blazing light from the candelabra on the parlor's mantelpiece also picked out a rent in his cloak sleeve.

"Where. Have. You. Been?"

God, she sounded like a shrew. He was not hers to command in this manner. He was a free man who could do what he wanted and go where he desired. He wasn't her husband or betrothed, and not really a servant. If he wanted to walk into the village in the middle of a freezing November night to have a tumble with one of the village women, then so be it. It wasn't her business and she had no right to be upset.

Yet she was. Upset and deeply, deeply wounded. She wanted to be the only one.

She drew her housecoat around her and stood. Orlando rose with her and clutched her arms. His gaze locked with hers and he frowned.

"I apologize," he said. "I was abrupt with you this afternoon and I shouldn't have been." He blew out a breath, shook his head. "I was worried about you and that produced in me..." More head shaking and he left the sentence unfinished.

He thought she was still upset about that? "Orlando." She wrapped her fingers around his upper arms but he jerked away. The hiss of air being sucked between his teeth sent a shiver through her. "You're hurt!" Now that she looked closely, the tear in his sleeve was edged with blood. "Take off your cloak and doublet."

He did, gingerly, to reveal a bloodied shirt beneath. "Looks like he did more damage than I thought."

"Who?" she asked, unlacing his shirt.

166

"Monk."

She paused. "Where did you come across him?"

"Sutton Hall." He shrugged. "Where did you think I went?"

She gave him a gentle shove in the chest. "I didn't think anything!" she lied. "All I knew was you weren't here." *Where you should be.* "And now you're wounded and there's blood everywhere! Foolish man. Why did you have to go up to the Hall anyway? What did you think you would achieve on your own in the dark? Foolish man!"

"You already said that." He kissed the top of her head then tilted her chin up so that she had to look at him. She tried not to cry. Tried very hard. But a tear and a sniff escaped before she could stop them. He swept the tear away with the pad of his thumb. "Ah, Susanna, it's all right. I know how to take care of myself."

She tugged on his torn sleeve. "I can see how good you are at taking care of yourself. Let me inspect the damage."

"As you command, fair lady."

"This is not a jest, Orlando. If Monk's aim had been better, this could have been much worse. Or what if he'd caught you? Jeffrey would see to it that you were arrested." A cold lump of dread filled her stomach. The punishment for theft was hanging. "Monk didn't see you, did he? Dear God, if he did...you have to go! Go now!"

He caught her hands as she frantically tried to push him away. His long, strong fingers held her fast. "Susanna, do not fret. He didn't see me. No one did."

She bit her wobbling lip. After a moment, when the tears no longer clogged her throat, she said, "Are you sure? Because you can leave tonight and be far away by dawn. I can give you food and money for a few days journey until you reach your sister in Salisbury."

He blinked rapidly. "You care for my safety that much?"

"Of course!" The vehemence of her response caught her by surprise. "I...that is, we are linked now, in a way. I do not take lovers lightly." Indeed, she'd never had a man outside the marriage bed. "There's a bond between us, Orlando, whether we like it or not. What it means...I cannot say."

He looked down, his eyelids lowered. He dropped his hands to his sides and scrunched them into fists.

She forged on. "All I do know is, seeing you hurt wounds me too. Knowing you're hurt because of me makes me feel ill."

His head jerked up. "Because of you? What do you mean?"

"You went to Sutton Hall to search Jeffrey's study for letters after I told you what I saw there this afternoon. It's no great leap to suggest you went to discover more."

"But that is not *your* fault, Susanna."

"Orlando, my problems are not yours. You seem to have appointed yourself my champion and although I'm flattered, I want you to stop. It's become too dangerous. You are a gardener."

"So you've reminded me. Often."

"Don't pout."

"I'm not pouting."

"And you *are* a gardener. If it bothers you to be called that, perhaps you chose the wrong profession."

"It seemed like the right choice at the time," he said through his clenched jaw.

She sighed. Men and their foolish pride. "Remove your shirt and let me tend your wound."

"Aren't you interested in what I discovered in Lynden's study?"

"I'm more interested in checking your injuries first."

He picked up his pack, opened it, and tipped the contents onto the mattress. Pieces of parchment fluttered down and settled among the three knives, a small club, flask, and sling that also fell out of the pack.

"Why do you need so many weapons?" she asked.

"Traveling alone can be dangerous." He sat down cross-legged on the mattress and gathered up the pieces of parchment. "Bring that clever mind here and help me puzzle this out."

"No. I'm going to tend to your wound. Remove your shirt." She stalked back into her bedchamber, picked up the ewer, basin, and a cloth and returned to the parlor. He'd removed his shirt and the sight of his broad, naked back halted her. His head was bent to his task and he didn't notice her staring at him. Oh my! She would never tire of his undulating muscles, the smooth skin, the strong curve of his spine. She could stare all day.

She set the basin down beside him and poured water from the ewer into it. She dipped a corner of the cloth in and set to work cleaning the blood away. He tensed at first but relaxed again when she wrapped her free arm around his chest and pressed her body into his back.

Both remained silent as they set to their tasks. Just as she tied a clean, dry cloth around his arm, he thumped his thigh. "Got it," he said, sliding the last few pieces into place.

"What does it say?"

"It's a letter from Whipple to Lynden." He read:

"Lynden,

Monk informs me there has been little progress, so I am informing you that time is running out. The next report I receive from him had better state his success, or we will all suffer for your cousin's ineptitude. I will not be able to save you. Fail and you lose it all.

It is up to you now.

Whipple."

"Fail," she echoed. "Fail at what?"

Orlando regarded her for a long time. "Susanna, I've heard of Lord Whipple before. I didn't tell you earlier because I didn't want to alarm you."

"Tell me what?"

"My father worked for his neighbor, and it was common gossip that Whipple is a Catholic."

A dangerous faith to follow in a Protestant country, although not illegal in England. Unless... "Do you think he's preparing to...do something terrible? Something treasonous?"

"I think it's likely given the secrecy surrounding these letters and Monk's presence here. Whipple may be involved in a plot to overthrow the queen and replace her with a Catholic monarch. I also think Lynden must be somehow embroiled in the scheme."

She felt sick. Surely not Jeffrey. "Impossible. He's not a devout man, and I don't think he cares much about any faith, let alone the Catholic one. And what do you think Whipple means by 'your *cousin's ineptitude*'? What does Phillip have to do with any of this?"

He drew her onto his lap and tucked her head under his chin. She rested her cheek against his chest and listened to his steady, rhythmic heartbeat. It calmed her and his warmth chased away the chill in her bones.

"I don't know. But we'll find out, Susanna. Together."

She closed her eyes and breathed in his scent. *Together.* Knowing he would be at her side kept the fear at bay, but not the newfound worry that she was the key to solving the riddle.

Finding out why might endanger both their lives.

CHAPTER 12

The rain cleared and the clouds parted just as Orlando finished breakfast. He helped Cook clean up then went out to the well to draw more water. He left her with a full pail and took another into the stables to add to Silver's trough. Susanna joined him there.

"Good morning," she said. Her movements were graceful yet languid and soft, like a contented cat. She must be as sated as he following their night of passionate lovemaking.

He smiled and caught her round her waist. "Good morning, my goddess."

"Orlando," she whispered, "someone might see."

"There's no one here." He stole a kiss before she gently pushed him away.

Together they took the tools out to the garden. Orlando set to work building a shelter following the plans from Susanna's French orange grower, while she tended to the trees themselves, checking their leaves, the soil at their base, and the trunks. He thought he even heard her speaking to them from time to time. Later, when Monk still hadn't appeared, she put her tools down.

"I'm going up to the Hall to find him," she said.

"I'll go. It's too dangerous and I was the one who—"

She put a finger to his lips. "Hush. Don't say it." She glanced at the arch. "Someone might be listening."

He kissed her finger, her wrist, her mouth. She didn't move away but sighed into him. He groaned against her mouth. "I want you," he murmured.

She reached up and dug her fingers through his hair, holding him against her. She moaned, low in her throat, and his groin pulsed in response.

At the edge of his awareness, something caught his attention. He broke the kiss, looked around.

"What is it?" she asked, sounding a little breathless.

"It felt like we were being watched." He strode to the arch and looked across the ruined formal garden at the front of the house, the gravel area leading to the outbuildings around the back, and the eastern wall of the house itself. He saw no one.

"Do you think someone was here?" she asked.

"I was probably mistaken," he lied. He didn't want to alarm her, but his instincts were never wrong. "Let's keep working. If Monk hasn't shown by dinner time, we'll both go to Sutton Hall." He didn't want to leave her at Stoneleigh where she was vulnerable without him, or let her go on her own. Not until Monk's, and Lynden's, intentions were clear.

His caution turned out to be unnecessary. Monk sauntered in soon after. "Where have you been?" Susanna asked, looking up from the plans for the orange tree shelter.

Orlando straightened. His grip tightened on the shovel. Monk came up to him, his shoulders square, his gray eyes dark with venom as they skimmed over Orlando's face to his right arm. Assessing if it suffered a cut? But Bessie had quickly mended the doublet that morning and it was thick enough to hide the bandage Susanna had wrapped around his wound.

"I was busy this morning," Monk said to Susanna. "My apologies for being late."

"Very well. You can start now."

He suddenly clapped Orlando on his injured arm, right over

the bandage, and pain burned up to his shoulder. *Hell.* The man had a grip on him like death.

Orlando gritted his back teeth and smiled.

Monk squeezed harder.

Orlando smiled more. His entire arm was on fire, but he would not show weakness to this man.

"Mr. Monk!" Susanna's shrill voice sliced through the crisp air. "Kindly cease your pathetic attempts to prove who is the stronger and pick up a mallet. According to these plans, we need to sink the supporting structure deeply into the ground first." She waved the diagram at him.

Monk let go and Orlando breathed out and in, conquering the pain.

"Plans?" Monk asked, crossing to where she stood near the pile of wood. "Did you draw them yourself?"

"No, they came from my French supplier." She handed the parchment to Monk and he inspected it closely, brushing his fingers across the drawing.

"Very good," he said. "I know a little about building, and these plans seem quite detailed."

"Then let's delay no further and get to work."

Monk smiled. "Yes, madam."

Orlando picked up a beam. He would keep as close to Monk as he could while the cur was in Susanna's presence. He doubted Monk would harm her in daylight in her own garden, but it was best to stay alert.

"Why were you late?" he asked.

"I told you," Monk said. "I had things to do. If you have a problem with my tardiness, I suggest you take it up with Lynden."

"How long were you standing at the arch there?"

"I wasn't standing anywhere. I came straight in."

The man was a very good liar. He looked directly at Orlando as he said it without even the faintest flicker of his eyelashes.

Or he was telling the truth.

They set to work. Orlando remained close to Monk and

Susanna kept her distance, thank God. Although she was always polite to Monk, Orlando could see her wariness around him, the watchfulness in her eyes, the tension across her shoulders. It must be distressing to think her cousin-in-law might have hired a man to kill her.

"M'lady!" Bessie called from the arch. Hendricks stood beside her, looking grave.

Susanna straightened and stretched her back. "Is it dinner time already?"

Bessie and Hendricks exchanged glances. "We need to have a word," the manservant intoned.

Susanna huddled with them. Orlando wished he were closer to hear but it was clear from the way the servants shot furtive glances at Monk that it was about him. Monk himself either didn't notice or pretended not to. He continued to dig.

Susanna dismissed her servants and trudged over to where Orlando stood leaning on his shovel. "Mr. Monk."

He turned at her sharp voice. "Yes?"

"My maid informed me that some of my papers have been disturbed."

Monk's grip shifted on the shovel handle. "You think I did it?"

"You were late this morning. Care to tell me what you were doing?"

Monk took a step toward them and Susanna sidled closer to Orlando. He wanted to put his arm around her shoulders and reassure her. Instead, he moved to stand between them.

"I was with Lord Lynden," Monk said, a hand up in surrender. "He'll confirm it if you ask him."

"What are you looking for?" Orlando growled. "What's in Susanna's papers that you need?"

"I told you—"

"Enough! We know you're lying. You've searched the outbuildings, you almost succeeded in climbing through Susanna's window, and now you've rifled through her papers." He squared up

174

to Monk, toe to toe. "Cease your lies, and give me an answer or I'll be forced to extract it from you."

Monk's nostrils flared and a muscle pulsed in his jaw. He kept his wintry gaze on Orlando, which in itself set him above most men. He would not be easily intimidated. This might get interesting.

"Call off your dog, Lady Lynden," Monk said idly. "His yapping annoys me."

"Not until you answer his questions," she said.

A strong breeze whipped through the garden, rustling the orange tree leaves and cooling Orlando's skin but not his temper. He was about to thump Monk to teach him a lesson when he spoke.

"Your arm is bandaged," he said. "I'd wager you were cut by a blade last night up at Sutton Hall. Correct?"

Very well, Orlando would play his game. "I was there to find out more about *you*. Why Lynden has employed you, where you hail from, and how you both know Lord Whipple."

Monk raised his eyebrows. "Lord Whipple?"

"Don't act the fool."

"Orlando," Susanna warned.

"It's all right. It's time to confront this eel." To Monk, he said, "I don't trust you. I never have. So I searched your pack and found a letter of introduction from Whipple."

Shadows passed over Monk's eyes. "You looked through my belongings?"

Orlando shrugged. "A necessary measure."

"I beg to differ."

"You'll be begging for your life soon enough if you don't tell me how you know Whipple."

"We had business dealings with each other. Complicated matters. You wouldn't understand, Mr. Holt, being a gardener."

"Even a gardener can understand murder, Mr. Monk."

Monk went very still. The throbbing vein in his throat was the only sign of movement. His gaze shifted past Orlando to Susanna then back again. "You think I'm here to kill her?" When Orlando didn't answer, Monk added, "It's quite a leap from rifling through her papers to murder."

Not when you know what I know.

"Yes, I suppose so," Susanna said. She came up alongside Orlando, her brow furrowed.

Hell. If she began to doubt that her life was in peril, she might lower her guard. And that could prove dangerous. Whoever had hired the Guild to kill her was going to be very angry when they discovered the deed not done. If Monk hadn't been hired as a back-up, then someone else surely would be.

"Perhaps you were wrong, Orlando, and no one is trying to...take my life," Susanna said quietly.

"We should remain vigilant, nevertheless. And there is still the fact this prick is sneaking around your house, looking through your papers."

"I didn't admit to that," Monk said, cheerfully. He leaned in to her with the sort of smile tweaking his lips that most men saved for wenches they wanted to bed. "Lady Lynden, are you sure your gardener is not suffering from madness? He seems to see wrong-doing where there is none, and murderers too."

White-hot light burst before Orlando's eyes and all he knew was that he had to wipe that cock-head's smile off or he *would* go mad.

The thud of fist on chin was the most satisfying sound. Monk reeled back, clutching his face in precisely the same spot Orlando had hit him the night before.

Susanna gasped. "Stop!"

He would have stopped too, but Monk recovered faster than he expected and ran at him, shoulder down. It caught Orlando in the chest and they went careening backward, locked in an embrace, and fell to the soft earth.

Rising above the thumps of fists and the grunts was Susanna's voice, ordering them to cease. Orlando managed to roll on top of Monk and went to grab the knife he kept up his sleeve, but Monk locked his legs around Orlando's hips and spun him over. The man was strong and fast, an unexpected combination. Orlando hadn't faced an opponent this good since Cole had suggested they challenge one another to keep their skills fresh.

Damned if he was going to let someone outside the Guild get the better of him. He saw an opening and dug his fingers into Monk's shirt. He dragged him closer and smashed his forehead against the bridge of Monk's nose. Monk let his guard down long enough for Orlando to shove him off.

He was about to get up when ice-cold water was dumped over his head and Monk's. He stood and shook his hair, sending droplets spraying across the onlookers—Susanna, Hendricks, Margaret Cowdrey, and her brother. Farmer Cowdrey held the empty pail, looking pleased with himself.

Susanna's eyes blazed like blue fire. "Have you two quite finished?" she asked, hands on hips.

"Madman," Monk muttered. Blood dripped from his nose and dark circles were already appearing beneath his eyes.

"What sort of animals have you employed, Susanna?" Farmer Cowdrey asked, still holding the pail.

Margaret said nothing, but looked Monk up and down then switched her searching gaze to Orlando. Her eyes narrowed. She bared her teeth. They were crooked and sharp.

"I'm beginning to wonder that myself." Susanna's sharply spoken words were aimed at Orlando. They felt like needles piercing his skin.

"Come inside, m'lady," Hendricks said. "You shouldn't be exposed to these scoundrels. Cook'll give you something nice and warm to calm your nerves."

"My nerves are calm, thank you. I am calm. It was a simple disagreement that went too far. Isn't that right, men?"

Monk nodded and dabbed at his nose with his sleeve. Orlando watched her closely. What was Susanna thinking? Did she believe Monk's suggestion that her life was not in danger? Had she begun to doubt Orlando?

Bloody hell. He needed to get her alone and talk to her, but with all her guard dogs surrounding her, it was unlikely to happen. It would have to wait until tonight. That's if she let him near her after this.

"You can't control them," Cowdrey said. "It's not your fault, no woman could." He set the pail down. "Susanna, this is why you need to marry again. It's a sign from God that a woman cannot and should not live alone."

She sighed heavily. "It's not a sign from God that I should wed, Walter, it's a sign that two men with inflated self-worth cannot get along."

"Susanna." Cowdrey went to take her hands, but she pulled away. Margaret stiffened and crossed her arms. Her glare was lost on her brother who only had eyes for Susanna. "You have unruly servants, your oranges require too much work, and you cannot sell enough marmalade to restore Stoneleigh *and* survive. Heed me on this. I have a head for business."

Margaret made a small sound in the back of her throat. Small white lines appeared around her mouth as she pursed it tight.

"My servants are not unruly," Susanna snapped. "And you are wrong on every score, Walter. One day I will prove to you that my head for business is as good as yours. I will send out more letters to more merchants. Better ones. Ones who supply the nobility or perhaps the queen's household itself!"

Walter frowned and seemed genuinely confused. "Wouldn't it be easier to let a husband take care of matters?" He looped his arm through hers, drawing her aside. "Susanna," he murmured but not low enough to stop Orlando from hearing, "my farm turns a good profit. I can buy you anything you need, your father too. We can employ your three servants and have all your orange trees transplanted to your own garden at Cowdrey Farm. I'll build you the best walled enclosure—"

"Stop, Walter. I cannot marry you."

"Susanna." His voice was firm, demanding. "You need a husband. You need me."

"You're a fool, Brother." Margaret's ice-cold voice ripped through the air like shards of broken glass. "She is a whore."

"What!" Orlando and Hendricks spluttered.

"Margaret!" Cowdrey snapped. "Hold your tongue, woman."

Only Susanna seemed unaffected by Margaret's accusation. She was like one of her orange trees, straight and proud, only the stray strands of her hair fluttering in the breeze.

"It's true. I saw her embracing her gardener earlier in a lewd manner."

Cowdrey made a choking sound and turned a bright shade of purple.

"Earlier?" Orlando said. "But you just arrived."

"No, I didn't," Margaret said. "I was in the village with my brother. He had business to conduct with a gentleman farmer from the next parish so I decided to take a walk as the conversation frustrated me." She gave Cowdrey a rather vicious glare. "We agreed to meet here." Her top lip curled and she looked at Susanna like she was something she'd scraped off her shoe. "It's time you stopped wasting your breath on *her*, Walter. I've let your infatuation go on long enough, but it needs to end. Perhaps now you can see why."

Another blast of white fire burst in front of Orlando's eyes, but he didn't move. Didn't breathe. Kept himself very still lest his anger consume him. If she were a man, however...

"You had better go," Susanna said to the Cowdreys. "We have nothing more to say to each other."

"Susanna?" Walter Cowdrey stared slack-jawed at her. "Is it true?"

Susanna said nothing.

"It *is* true," Margaret said. "I *knew* there was something about her. For years I suspected she was a witch the way she dazzled Phillip and then you. A witch and a whore. Now I have the proof. I saw them with my own eyes, Walter. It was disgusting, base." She spat onto the ground. "I warned you about her many times, and now you see I was right. Perhaps you'll put this pathetic infatuation behind you."

Susanna pressed her hand to her lips and her eyes filled with tears. Orlando moved to her, but Hendricks got there first. He touched her shoulder and that seemed to rally her. She tilted her chin at Margaret.

"I'm not sure what I've done to you to deserve such a lashing, but whatever it is, it has apparently upset you and for that, I'm truly sorry."

Margaret's eyes widened. Clearly it wasn't the response she'd expected. She spun on her heel, smacked her brother's arm, and stormed out of the garden. Cowdrey stood like a small, lost boy, looking down at his feet. After a moment, he rallied.

He removed his hat and scrunched it in his hands. "Susanna, I'm sorry for what Margaret said. I'll have words with her." He swallowed and his gaze shifted to the archway. Orlando suspected the last thing he wanted to do was speak to his tempestuous shrew of a sister. "She's got strange ideas in her head. She doesn't hate you. Not really."

"It's all right, Walter. You'd better go, or she'll come back and drag you out." She offered him a weak smile.

He bowed and left the garden.

"Well," Monk said. "That's one way to make everyone forget about our little stoush, Holt."

"Shut it," Orlando snarled without taking his gaze off Susanna.

"As you wish."

"Susanna—"

"*Lady Lynden,*" Hendricks cut in, "we should go inside for dinner. It might calm everyone's nerves." He glared at Orlando. "And give some of us time to think about the consequences of their actions."

Orlando *had* thought about those. Sometimes he thought about nothing else. Unfortunately, it didn't change anything. He continued to do the wrong thing. He simply couldn't help himself.

"Mr. Monk, will you dine with us in the kitchen?" she asked.

"Thank you," Monk said. "That's very kind and I accept."

"I'm not sure that's a good idea, Susa—m'lady," Orlando said.

"I agree with him for once," Hendricks said. "Having both of 'em in a closed space is asking for trouble."

"I promise to be on my best behavior," Monk said. "If Holt agrees to a truce then I think we can all consider ourselves safe for the time being." He raised both brows at Orlando.

"Clean yourself up first," Orlando said. "You're a mess."

"Aye," Hendricks said. "Cook's very particular about getting blood on the table."

Monk chuckled. He seemed to be enjoying himself, the cur. Susanna led them back to the house, her back stiff and her head high. Orlando followed, acutely aware that she'd neither looked at him nor addressed him since Margaret's outburst.

The worst of it was, he had no idea how to bring back the smile to her face.

* * *

SUSANNA WISHED everyone would stop their fussing. Between Cook plying her with warm broth, Bessie insisting she help to wash Susanna's hair, and Hendricks keeping a hawk-eyed watch over her, she was stretched tighter than a lute string. Only Orlando seemed to understand she wanted to be left alone. He'd spent the remainder of the day in the garden with Monk. He'd not spoken to her since midday's dinner, and they hadn't found themselves alone. What he thought about Margaret Cowdrey's accusation, she couldn't determine. Aside from his initial vehement defense, he'd remained quiet, thoughtful.

Susanna, on the other hand, felt numb to her core. Margaret Cowdrey had just called her a whore and a witch. She probably should be concerned that the entire village would know by the end of the week, but she wasn't. She felt nothing.

The knock on her bedchamber door stirred her. She rose and answered it. Orlando stood in his work clothes, his arms crossed, his stance formidable. But his eyes betrayed him. They were cloudy and troubled.

"Susanna." He reached for her.

Instinct took over and she stepped into his embrace. He was so solid, so real in a world where everything suddenly felt like an illusion, a conjurer's trick. Margaret's words, the uncertainty surrounding Monk, Walter's proposals...all melted away so that there was only this man and his strong heart pounding against her cheek.

They stayed like that for a long time. "I'm sorry," he said. His voice vibrated through her body, across her skin, and down to her toes.

She closed her eyes, drew in a deep breath then stepped away. "No. It's not your fault. None of this is."

"I should have kept away. I shouldn't have started this—"

"You didn't do it alone. *We* started it. Both of us." She wrapped her arms around herself, suddenly cold. He moved to her again but she stepped back, out of his reach. "No, Orlando. It has to stop." Her eyes prickled with tears but she willed them not to fall. "It was time we ended it anyway," she added, as much to convince herself as him.

He bowed his head and his hair fell forward, covering his eyes. "I know. I came to you tonight to tell you the same thing." He gave a short, humorless laugh and looked up, a ghostly smile on his lips. "It's harder than I thought it would be."

She kissed her fingertips and pressed them to his cheek. He caught her wrist and kissed her palm.

"It's for the best," he murmured. "Ending it now is for the best."

Was he trying to convince himself or her?

"Will you..." She cleared her throat. "Will you be leaving now?"

He suddenly looked up. "No! Not until we discover who the intruder is for certain, and what Monk and Lynden are up to. Susanna." He squeezed her hand. "I'm not leaving you alone while something is afoot. I will sleep outside your bedchamber until I know the danger is gone. In everything else, I am your servant to command, but not when it comes to your safety. In that, I'll make decisions I think will keep you safe whether you like them or not."

Her chest felt tight. Her heart hammered against her ribs, its beat echoing in her blood. She nodded and he gave her a small bow.

"Good night." He closed the door between them, shutting out the light from the candles blazing in the parlor.

The tears she thought conquered swelled and spilled, running unchecked down her cheeks. "Good night," she murmured.

Where earlier she'd felt numb, now she felt too much. And it was painful.

CHAPTER 13

*J*t was a cruel twist of fate that the next day was a Sunday. The entire village was at church of course, including Margaret and Walter, Jeffrey and Monk, and even the elegant, foppish stranger was back with his fat servant. Jeffrey spent much of the service admiring the gentleman's lushly embroidered silver and blue doublet. The gentleman didn't appear to notice, his gaze never wavering from the pulpit. Susanna's servants, including Orlando, sat at the back, and she felt exposed without them at her side. It didn't help that many of the parishioners watched her. Margaret, however, wasn't among them. She studiously kept her gaze forward, as did Walter.

Susanna made sure to be among the first to leave after the service. Unfortunately, she still had to wait to give her thanks to the curate. It was doubly unfortunate that waiting brought her near Margaret and her friends. Susanna didn't need to hear them to know they were discussing her—their pointed glares gave them away—but snatches of conversation reached her on the breeze.

"...ought to be married..."

"...shouldn't be allowed near our menfolk."

"...pretty face and wanton ways."

It only stopped when Walter pulled his sister aside.

Margaret's cronies were like her. They had been Susanna's companions when they were younger, but ever since she became of marriageable age, they'd ceased to pay calls and only kept up polite appearances around others. She knew they talked about her, but she could endure it because she had her true friends. Anne the chandler's wife, Joan, and Widow Dawson.

Susanna turned her back and tried to shut out their voices. She *would* endure this too. Their opinions didn't matter. They were just words. She *would* rise above them. What she'd shared with Orlando hadn't been dirty or shameful, but beautiful. It had filled her, blocked out past pains, and made her feel whole again. And cherished. Definitely that.

She looked around for him but couldn't see his striking blond head above the other parishioners.

"He left, m'lady," Bessie said without Susanna asking. "Said he would be back soon."

"Left? Where did he go?"

Bessie shrugged.

"He slipped away," Hendricks said, "right after the stranger and his servant disappeared behind those trees." He nodded at a stand of yew. "Holt walked off in the same direction."

Susanna frowned at the copse. He may have fulfilled her in bed and promised to protect her, but he was still a puzzle that needed solving. "Wait here for me." She strode off in the direction of the yew trees.

* * *

"WE ONLY HAVE A FEW MINUTES," Orlando said. "So talk."

"Is that how you get your women to open up?" Hughe asked. He wore a tall hat with more feathers on it than a bird and his doublet was embroidered with a silvery feather pattern. The outfit took ridiculous to a new level and Orlando would have teased him if they'd had more time.

"Shut it, Hughe," he warned.

"You're in a fine mood."

Orlando had to grudgingly admit, if only to himself, that he was. Seeing the bunch of marigolds on Phillip's grave had given him an unexpected gut-ache. Susanna rarely spoke about either of her husbands, but clearly she cared enough for her second one to tend his grave. Aside from the flowers, the marble headstone was clean, the weeds removed. It shouldn't bother him—the man had been her husband and was now very dead for God's sake. But it did.

"Someone will come soon," he said. "Believe me, my absence will be noticed today of all days."

"I heard the gossip. Bewitched, are you?"

Cole grunted from where he kept watch near a tree. "Makes a nice change."

"Just don't go leaving us like Rafe," Hughe said. "We can't cope with any more rejection, can we, Cole?"

"My heart's bleeding," Cole said blandly, without turning around.

"It's not a jest," Orlando snapped. "And I'm not leaving the Guild. Why in God's name would I want to do that?" He glanced past Cole toward the old stone church perched atop the rise. Parishioners milled about and he could just make out Susanna among them.

Was she enduring more of that malicious talk? Walter Cowdrey ought to have kept his sister home.

He ached to go to her and whisk her away but he needed to speak to Hughe and Cole. "Tell me what you found out about Susanna's first husband. How did he die?"

"Natural causes," Hughe said, suddenly serious and speaking quickly. "He ate too much, drank to excess, and suffered from melancholy after losing his fortune. Apparently he was also saddened that his beautiful wife didn't give him heirs."

"It wasn't her fault," Orlando growled. "Her second husband got a child upon her."

Hughe waved his hand. "So I think we can safely conclude Lady Lynden is innocent of murder."

Orlando blew out a breath. He already knew it, but hearing Hughe say it with such certainty meant that he would not try to eliminate her without Orlando's knowledge.

"So we're left with the question, who hired us to kill her and why?"

And would they hire someone else if the Guild refused?

"Monk," Orlando said. "The stranger up at Sutton Hall...he's definitely hiding something." He told them about the letter from Lord Whipple in Monk's pack and the one in Lynden's study, as well as Monk's wanderings around Stoneleigh.

"Whipple?" Hughe pursed his lips. "Interesting. You think this man Monk has been hired by Lynden to find something at Stoneleigh?"

"At Whipple's insistence, yes. It must be some incriminating papers, or why else would the earl be involved? The letter did say something about Lynden's cousin, Susanna's second husband."

Hughe began to pace, churning up the muddy earth and damp leaf matter with his blue velvet shoes. Not that Hughe would care. Later, back at the inn, he would make a show of caring and Cole would have to clean them. Picturing his big, serious friend stooping to cleaning another man's shoes would ordinarily make Orlando laugh, but not today.

"I don't think any of them are our client," Cole said. "The timing is wrong. Monk arrived here the same time you did, Orlando. If our client is watching, he would not have known that you wavered then. Perhaps now, however..."

"I agree," Orlando said. "Then why is he here? Is Susanna innocently involved in a Catholic plot?"

Hughe continued to pace. "She must be," he said. "Or her husband was. Monk's been looking through her papers, disturbing the letters that were sent to her from her grower on the Continent. Correct?"

"I believe so."

"Not love letters or other correspondence from Phillip?"

Orlando's gut knotted. "Not that I am aware."

"Letters from the Continent, a known Catholic sympathizer in Whipple... It must be the correspondence between them that Monk is trying to find, and most likely it's of a treasonous nature. But why involve Lynden? Was he Catholic?"

"Susanna didn't think so."

Hughe shook his head and resumed his pacing.

"Whatever the reason," Orlando said, "there is a letter incriminating Whipple or Lynden or both in Susanna's possession and that's why they desperately want it back."

"In which case, she must surely have read it by now and have grown suspicious."

"Not necessarily," Orlando said. "It could have been written in lemon juice."

"You say Monk has taken nothing from Susanna's belongings?" Hughe asked. "Not a single letter?"

"It appears they've just been trifled with but nothing was taken."

"I wonder why."

"Because what he wanted wasn't there." Oh. *Hell.* "The building plans."

"The what?"

"Plans for building a structure over her orange trees to protect them. Monk and I erected the foundations yesterday. He seemed interested in the plans, asking her who'd sent them, pouring over them more than necessary."

"As if he was attempting to read the invisible lemon juice writing." Hughe nodded. "So where are the plans now?"

"Susanna has them."

"Good. I think we should confront Monk."

"I'll do it after I escort Susanna back to Stoneleigh. I'm not leaving her alone and vulnerable, Hughe, no matter what."

"Agreed."

Cole glanced at them over his shoulder. "You need to protect orange trees? What's the point of growing them if they need protection? What's wrong with good English trees?"

"Shut it, Cole, and keep look-out," Orlando said. "Hughe, there's one other thing."

Cole looked back toward the church and swore. "Your lover is walking this way."

Orlando pulled Hughe further into the shadows. "Next time wear green and brown to blend in."

"Green and brown clash horribly," Hughe said, putting on his dandy's tone. "I wouldn't be caught dead wearing those colors together."

"Don't tempt me." He glanced back the way they'd come but he couldn't see Cole through the thick foliage. "I want to tell Susanna about my reason for being here."

"No."

"I won't mention the Guild or you."

"No!"

"Hughe." Orlando gripped his friend's arms. "I *need* to tell her. She's already suspicious about my presence. If she finds out more, if she discovers I'm lying..." He shook his head. How could he explain it when he wasn't even sure why he needed to break his vow of secrecy? He blew out a breath. A few more moments and she would be with them. There was no time to think anymore, he just had to say it uncensored. "I've already lost her as my lover. I don't want to lose her friendship too."

Orlando could feel Hughe tense. The cool, pale gaze sharpened. "Listen to me," Hughe said and Orlando had never heard such gloom in his friend's voice. "If you so much as hint to her about your work, you will have to leave the Guild. I can allow no compromises, no half-truths, nothing. The lives of all of us, your-self included, depends on our secrecy."

"She wouldn't tell a soul."

Hughe shook his head. "Do not make me remove you, Orlando. It really would break my heart."

Orlando didn't know whether he meant remove him from the

C.J. ARCHER

Guild or from the land of the living, nor did he want to find out. He had seen how ruthless Hughe could be and he didn't want to force his hand.

"I want your promise, Orlando."

When Orlando dropped his hands away and hesitated, Hughe grabbed him by the shoulders and shook him, hard. "Promise me," he ground out.

If Orlando disobeyed, there would be no more Guild for him. He would need to find work elsewhere, perhaps even return to London. No, he could never do that. Never face Thomas or his wife May again. Whatever he did, he was unlikely to find the sort of job that offered as much freedom as the Guild did.

"I promise," he finally said.

Hughe let go and wiped the back of his hand across his forehead. "No good can come of her knowing anyway."

"She comes," Cole whispered, slipping silently through the trees to join them.

Hughe and Cole disappeared deeper into the stand of trees. Orlando blew out a measured breath just as Susanna's soft footsteps thudded over the damp ground.

"Orlando? Are you there?"

"Here." He forced a smile when he saw her, but inside he felt so angry he wanted to hit something. Hughe's face came to mind. Those sharp cheekbones would make a satisfying crack under his fist.

"What are you doing here?" she asked, looking past him.

"Relieving myself."

She gasped. "In church grounds?"

"Is that against the law?"

She narrowed her eyes at him. They looked tired, with more small lines radiating from the corners than before. "It could be."

"I'm not sure these trees are even on church land. They're some distance away." He ducked under her hat and kissed her forehead because no one was looking and he just bloody well wanted to. Hughe might be able to control what Orlando could and couldn't say, but he was damned if he'd let anyone tell him to stop kissing her.

"Orlando," she warned. "Don't. What if someone saw?"

"There's no one here."

"What about those other men? The gentleman and his servant?"

"Were they relieving themselves too?"

She gave him a withering look. "Do not pretend you didn't see them. I know you met them in here. Why?"

"Susanna, don't fret. You've been through an ordeal and are hearing and seeing things that aren't there." He moved past her so he didn't have to see the skepticism in her eyes. "Let's go."

"No."

He doubled back. "Is everything all right?"

She nodded past him to the church. "I'll return the way I came, but you must go in the opposite direction. We cannot be seen together. If you walk through these trees, you'll come to the main road leading out of the village. We'll pick you up as we pass."

He nodded and touched her cheek. It was cold. "Are you all right?"

She blinked rapidly up at him but it didn't hide the sheen of tears. "I don't understand why...why they hate me so."

He folded her into his arms and held her against his chest. If she cried, she made no sound or movement. He couldn't even hear her breathing. After a moment she stepped away.

"I shouldn't have. I'm sorry."

"Susanna, if you need me, I'll not be far. Understand? Things may have changed between us, but you can trust me." *Except for when I must lie.*

"Thank you," she said, rather formally. She smoothed down her skirt, nodded once and walked back the way she'd come.

He watched her leave. Did she truly not know why Margaret Cowdrey wanted to make her as miserable as she was? Did Susanna not know how beautiful she was, and how jealous that could make other women?

It seemed so remarkable, yet he was beginning to think she didn't.

* * *

ORLANDO HAD LIED to her about meeting the two strangers among the trees. Susanna was certain of it. She wasn't sure how she knew since she had no proof, but she did.

What was he up to?

And did it bode ill for her or anyone she loved?

He'd told her she could trust him, yet that was probably a lie too. Since he'd lied about the strangers, and most likely about being a gardener, how could she trust anything he said?

"The service was nice today," Bessie said. She was squeezed between Susanna and Cook on the driver's seat, her good hat in her lap lest it blow off.

"It was too long," Cook said. "I've got to get back to my kitchen."

"The kitchen won't miss you for a while yet," Hendricks said from behind them where he sat with Orlando in the back of the cart. "Your soul comes first."

"My soul does all right, thank you, Mr. Hendricks. More than I can say for some others," Cook muttered.

"Eh? What's that about mothers?"

Bessie giggled and bumped Susanna, probably because Cook had jabbed her with her elbow.

Despite her anxiety, Susanna smiled. She appreciated their chatter. It took her mind off her other problems, although nothing could dampen her awareness of Orlando sitting behind her. Even after all his lies, his presence was still a comfort.

Which made her the biggest fool in England. First John, then Phillip, and now Orlando. It was time she learned from the lessons given her, beginning now. Today.

Suddenly Silver balked and veered sharply to the right. Something whizzed past Susanna's face, inches from her nose. A small blade.

Bessie and Cook screamed.

Orlando grabbed Susanna's shoulders. He was shouting.

Hendricks was shouting.

Out of the corner of her eye, shadows moved amid the trees, but she was too busy trying to control a terrified Silver to look closer.

"Get down!" Orlando ordered, taking the reins and pushing her forward onto the footboard at the same time.

Cook put her hands over her face. Bessie stopped screaming, but she clutched Cook, her eyes wide as Silver swerved to miss a tree. The cart, however, didn't. It bashed against the trunk, throwing everyone about and unnerving Silver more.

Orlando spoke soothing words over the din of the rattling wheels and his big, capable hands expertly persuaded the frightened horse to a slower, calmer pace. He handed the reins back to Susanna and leapt off while the cart still moved.

"Stay down!" He pulled a long knife from where it had been hidden under his sleeve then ran off into the trees. He returned a few moments later, his face stony. His gaze skimmed Susanna from head to toe as she sat on the seat once more.

"Are you...?"

She shook her head. "It missed."

Naked relief passed over his face before his eyes shuttered again.

"Wh...what happened?" Cook asked. She clutched onto Hendricks's hand so hard the poor man's fingers turned white.

"A knife," Susanna said. "It came from nowhere."

"It came from someone's hand," Hendricks growled. "A coward hiding in the trees."

Orlando ran back up the road and bent to inspect something near the bend. He returned carrying a small, thin blade. He was still holding his own knife, a rather lethal-looking weapon that he must have kept strapped to his forearm. Did he always carry it?

"Do you recognize it?" he asked her.

She shook her head. It was just a plain, simple knife that

anyone would carry. "Did you see anything in the woods?"

"A horse galloped off through the trees. The rider wore a long cloak with a hood, but that's all I could make out." He shook his head and stalked off. He paused a way up the road, swore vehemently then kicked up a clod of dirt with his boot.

"He and I are finally in agreement," Hendricks said heavily.

Cook looked at him and, as if she just realized she'd been holding onto Hendricks, snatched her hand out of his. "What an ordeal!"

Bessie wrapped her arm around Susanna's waist. "Are you sure you're all right, my dear?"

Susanna gave them all a reassuring smile. "Just a little shaken. Nothing that a warm cup of mulled wine won't cure." It would take much more than that to settle her nerves but it may help to settle theirs.

Orlando returned and placed his hand over Susanna's, still clutching the reins. It was only then that she realized she was shaking. "I'll drive," he said. His turbulent, unblinking gaze met hers and held it. The world seemed to close around them, shutting out the others and all ills so that there was only the two of them. Only this moment. Only the beating of their hearts, Orlando's strength, and the security of his presence.

"But...why?" Bessie's plaintive question jolted Susanna into focusing.

She climbed into the back of the cart with Hendricks's help. Orlando leapt up to the driver's seat and they set off at a fast clip.

No one answered Bessie. Susanna didn't have an answer anyway and she doubted Hendicks or Cook did either. Only Orlando might know why someone had attacked them, but Susanna wouldn't confront him in front of the others.

* * *

THEY ARRIVED BACK at Stoneleigh without any more incidents. The three servants went into the kitchen, but Susanna remained in the

194

stables with Orlando as he organized Silver's feed. She picked up a brush and set about soothing the last of the mare's nerves which seemed as jittery as her own. She watched Orlando from the corner of her eye and, despite the pounding of her heart, said what needed to be said.

"It's time you tell me what you're doing here at Stoneleigh."

He rubbed Silver's neck as the horse bent to the trough. "I was passing through and offering my services as a gardener—"

"Enough, Orlando." Her voice was low, level, and yet it held all the fury and anguish boiling inside her. She regarded him, Silver between them, but he was not looking at her. "I'm tired of your lies. You are not a gardener. You were not simply passing through. You have a reason for coming here and I want to know what it is."

His hand stilled on Silver's neck. The pulse in his throat throbbed. "Susanna. Please. Don't ask me."

The raw plea in his voice cooled her anger, but she forced herself to remember his deceit. He was a charmer, used to lying and getting his way by saying the right things in a way he knew would work on her. She would not allow them to affect her anymore.

"Tell me," she said.

He walked around Silver and grasped her shoulders. She shook him off and his hands fell limply to his sides. "Susanna, I can't tell you. I want to, but I've been forbidden."

"By that man? The gentleman? Who is he?"

His only answer was a slow shake of his head as he lowered it.

"I want you to leave."

His head snapped up. "No. It's too dangerous for you on your own."

"You may be the reason I am in danger."

"Is that what you think? That I am the one trying to harm you? I was in the cart with you when the blade was thrown."

"I don't know what to think. But the trouble began when you arrived, and I don't believe in coincidences."

"Nor do I. Usually. But...I am not trying to hurt you, Susanna.

You know that. Your heart is telling you the truth." He placed his hand beneath her left breast and her traitorous heartbeat quickened in response. "Listen to it. What does it say?"

She stepped back, out of his reach. *Be firm. Be strong. Do not fall for his words.* "I have followed my heart so many times and it has always led me astray. Always." Her voice cracked. She cleared her throat and forged on. "It's time I stopped listening and began thinking."

He reached for her but quickly dropped his hand back to his side again. "Susanna, I am not like your husbands. I am not..." He trailed off, looked away.

"Not what? Not lying to me? Not fickle in your affections? Or not going to change so that the man I...cared about becomes unrecognizable?" A kind of madness gripped her and wouldn't let go. The words shot from her mouth, intending to wound. If they did, he gave no sign of it. He stood very still, his eyelids half-closed like shields, his mouth set firm. "Which lie would you like to tell me now, Orlando?"

He took a long time to answer. "I want to tell you why I'm here," he eventually said. "But I can't. You're right and I am not passing through, nor am I a gardener. But I am on your side. Throw me off your land if you wish, but I *will* find a way to watch out for you until the danger has passed. I will protect you for as long as necessary, whether you like it or not. Whatever my previous reason for being here, guarding you is now my new mission. And that, Susanna, is no lie. Someone tried to kill you today and—"

"Your foppish friend?"

"Not him."

She believed him. Or perhaps she *wanted* so much to believe him that his tone rang true.

Fie! She couldn't even trust her own instincts anymore. "Then who? Monk?" She scoffed. "If he wanted to kill me, he would have done so already. He's had opportunities."

She'd expected him to argue the point, but he only nodded.

"If it is not Monk and not your friend..." She swallowed, but the lump in her throat remained. "Then it must be you."

It was as if he expected it and had braced himself for it. There was no change in his stance, his face. "And haven't *I* had many opportunities too? In your bed, for example. Or here, right now."

His words were like body blows and she took a step back. Breathed.

Then suddenly it all clicked into place. "You have been hired by someone, you and your friends—Monk, the gentleman stranger, and his servant. Not to kill me, but to frighten me. Hired by Walter Cowdrey perhaps." She nodded quickly. Oh yes, it made a lot of sense. "He thinks that if I am scared enough, I will agree to marry him." She snorted. "He doesn't know me at all if he thinks fear will induce me to wed."

The muscles high up in Orlando's cheeks worked. He stared at her, anger and concern gone, replaced by thoughtfulness. She crossed her arms and stared back.

"Will you do me one thing?" he asked. "One last thing before I leave Stoneleigh."

"What?"

"I need the names of the London shopkeepers you sent your letters to."

It wasn't at all what she'd expected him to say. "Why?"

"Because..." Without seeming to move, he was suddenly a little closer. "Because I know some London merchants and many high-end shopkeepers. I want to see if they are among the ones you've already contacted." He fidgeted with Silver's mane. "There's no point writing another letter to them if they've already received one."

He was going to help her? After what had been said? She couldn't quite believe it.

Or was it just another ruse? Just another lie to get her to trust him?

"How do you know them?"

"I can't tell you."

She turned and walked off. He caught up to her and jerked her around to face him, pulling her against him. His breath came in jagged bursts as if he'd been running. Her blood rushed through her body, pounded between her ears.

"Susanna, I have lied. I admit it. And I know you don't believe me when I say I don't want to hurt you."

"Yet you have," she whispered. "Just as you hurt me now."

His fingers sprang apart, letting her go. She didn't tell him she hadn't meant physical pain. "I am going to make it up to you. I'll find you a shopkeeper to take your marmalades and succades. I promise you."

She really should have left him then, walked away. But her heart was cracking and her legs wouldn't work. And God help her, she believed him. She believed him.

He cupped her cheek and bent his head. He hesitated, giving her a moment to escape if she wanted to.

She didn't want to. It was just a kiss. One last kiss for her to remember him by.

His lips were impossibly soft, yet the kiss held more power than any other. An ache wrapped around her insides and settled like a shroud over her heart. God it hurt.

When he pulled away, it hurt more.

"I'll get the names of the merchants for you," she mumbled.

"I'll return for them later. There's something else I need to do first. Stay in the house while I'm gone. Don't let anyone in, including people you know."

They parted outside the stables, his warning ringing in her ears. She watched him walk off down the drive to the main road, and let out a long, shuddering breath once he was out of sight. She trudged back to the house where Bessie waited for her at the front door, a sealed letter in her hand.

"We found this slipped under the kitchen door when we arrived home," she said.

Susanna opened it with trembling fingers, her mind not on the task. But it soon was.

Holt is an assassin. I hired him to kill you.

CHAPTER 14

Orlando beckoned Warren the stable lad with a crook of his finger. The boy came running to where Orlando was half-hidden by the shadows near the stable wall.

"Mr. Monk's inside the big house," Warren said, jerking his head at the Hall.

"Thank you," Orlando said. "But I wanted to ask you something first."

"Me?" The lad squared his shoulders and cleared his throat. "Ask away, Mr. Holt."

"You worked here when the previous Lord Lynden was alive, didn't you?"

"Aye. Been 'ere two years now."

"How was he as a master?"

"As fair as any other. I didn't 'ave much to do with 'im. Mostly 'e didn't see me and 'e never spoke to me direct. Only time I was in 'is presence was at Christmastide when we all dined together. I think 'e never liked it, but it was custom and the mistress prob'ly insisted."

"Was he a devout man?"

He shrugged. "Went to church on Sundays, just like the rest of us."

"What about the current master?"

"Same thing. Goes to church on Sundays."

"And Lady Lynden...did she...was she a good mistress?"

The lad blushed. "Aye. The best. She always had a kind word. Always said good mornin' to us, no matter how beneath 'er we was. When me Ma was sick, she gave me the day off and sent me 'ome with a basket. Sent the wise woman round too, she did, and paid 'er."

"Did her husband know?"

"Aye. Well, not at first." He pulled a face. "Later 'e found out and 'e railed at her. One of the maids said he shouted and said terrible things to 'er. Told 'er not to see none of 'er village friends no more. Said she was above that."

Bloody hell. "What did she say?"

"She said she would keep 'er own friends. After that..." Warren shook his head and huffed.

"Did he..." God, it hurt just to think it let alone say it. "Did he hit her?"

"Aye. The maids said he did. Terrible thing, it was. None of us could believe it. She never 'urt no one. And, well, we didn't know it until later, but she was with child. She lost it."

Orlando knew about the lost baby and the damaged womb from Widow Dawson, but this...the reason for the loss was new to him. He felt sick to the core and so very, very angry. An anger that could never be vanquished because the perpetrator of Susanna's heartache was already dead, and not by Orlando's hand.

If he did not need to speak to Monk, he would have gone back to Stoneleigh and taken her into his arms. The need to hold her, cherish her, and to take away her pain, was unbearable.

Yet he knew she would not let him near. She no longer trusted him, and considering what he'd hidden from her, she had every right. He had lied to her, bedded her, and engaged her affections for his own amusement and purpose. Why in God's name *would* she trust him?

Perhaps she was right and parting was the only option left to them now. It would certainly dampen the raw emotions he felt when he was near her, and dampen them he must. Distance and time, that's what he needed. It never failed to cure bruises of the body, so why not of the heart too. His conscience may take longer to forget the ills he'd bestowed, but he was growing used to carrying guilt of one kind or another. It was an old companion.

Walking away from her would be difficult, but not as difficult as staying. Staying would do neither of them any good. Susanna needed to make her own way in the world as the heiress of Stoneleigh and he needed to see new places, meet new people, have adventures with his brothers-in-arms. Stay active and free from boredom and trouble it caused.

The one good thing he could still do for her was seek out a London shopkeeper to sell her wares to noble customers. But first he needed to see the list Cowdrey had given her. If, as Orlando suspected, the names were false, then Cowdrey would feel the sharp end of Orlando's wrath.

His mind was awhirl as he waited for Monk to leave the house. He helped Warren and the other lads in the stables, remaining near the entrance to see who came and left. Every thought he had returned to Susanna and the look on her face as she'd accused him of lying. The churning in his gut grew worse. If he could take every lie back, he would.

But wishing was futile. Things wouldn't have been any different to what they were now except perhaps it was easier for her to banish him, easier for her to shrug off any feelings she may have harbored for him. He could live with her hatred. Absolutely. It was much, much better to bear her hatred than her love.

Love. Hell. Now he was beginning to sound like Rafe Fletcher. Love might suit his good friend, a man who was ready to settle into an unvarying life, but it would not sit well on Orlando's shoulders. He wasn't ready. He never would be.

"What are you doing here?" asked Monk, standing in the open doorway, blocking out the gloomy light.

Orlando leaned on his broom. "You weren't at church this morning."

"Report me to the parish then."

"Not worried about your soul?"

"My soul went to Hell years ago."

Another one. He and Cole should become acquainted. What a fun evening around the fire that would be. "I'm not here to save your soul or muck out the stables." Orlando returned the broom to the corner. "Come with me."

He strode past Monk, out the door and away from the house. Monk followed, his steps light on the gravel. It seemed he was a man used to sneaking about.

"If you're taking me somewhere to kill me, get it over with," Monk said. "I'm a busy man."

Orlando stopped when they were far enough from everyone and there was nothing but open spaces around them. They could not be overheard. "I'm not going to kill you after the grooms saw us leave together. How big a fool do you think me?"

"Are you sure you want me to answer that?"

Despite everything, Orlando laughed. "You sound like a friend of mine."

"Get on with it, Holt, I'm busy." They stood a little apart, just out of each other's reach. Monk crossed his arms and glared at Orlando from beneath his hat.

"Busy trying to steal the plans from Susanna Lynden?"

The brief flare in Monk's eyes told Orlando he had the man's attention. It was a small sign and most would have missed it, but he was trained to look for such things. Monk was good at hiding his emotions, but not that good. "What plans?"

"Don't play the fool with me. You're not."

"Ah, flattery. I hear you're famous for it."

Orlando's fingers twitched with the need to run him through with his blade. "Shut your mouth, or I'll shut it for you."

"How can I answer you with my mouth shut? You cannot have it both ways."

"You showed great interest in the plans to build the structure over Susanna's orange trees. Why? What's written on them?"

"Written on them? You saw for yourself—"

Orlando's fist slammed into Monk's jaw, but he eased back at the last. The blow didn't knock Monk down, but it would leave a nice bruise. "Answer the bloody question."

Monk gave a harsh laugh. He didn't touch his jaw. "You have a good fist, and you're fast. For a gardener."

"How did Lord Lynden become involved with Whipple?"

Monk's humorless smile disappeared. "I don't know what you're talking about." He turned to go.

"Yes, you do. And I'm going to help you get the secret letter."

Monk paused, turned. "I can get it myself."

If he could, he would have kept walking.

"I'll get it for you," Orlando said, "but first you have to answer one question and make a vow."

Monk's brows shot up. "No request for money? For payment of some kind?"

"Money holds no interest for me."

"Then *you* are the fool," Monk snarled, bitterness screwing up his mouth. "Money is everything in this world. Everything."

Orlando shrugged. "If you say so. But I'm not concerned with payment. All I want from you in return for the plans is the answer to one question: have you been hired to kill Susanna?"

He frowned. "No."

"You answered very quickly."

"That's because I didn't have to think about it. I'm telling the truth."

"Promise me you'll not harm her."

"I have no reason to harm her. If she gives me the plans."

"You'll get the plans. You can give them to Lynden or Whipple, or whoever is afraid of their treason being discovered. I don't care about that. I only care that Susanna is not your target."

Monk folded his arms again. "I have no target. My orders do not stretch to killing anyone, Lady Lynden included.

Although I've come close to wanting to slit your throat on occasion."

"The feeling's mutual." Despite his words, Orlando was beginning to like the man. "Who do you work with?"

"No one."

"Ever killed anyone?"

"That would be against the law, Holt."

Orlando tipped his hat. "You're right. Good day, Mr. Monk. If I catch you breaking your promise, I'll kill you. Understand? I'll deliver your letter to you when I have it." He walked off, not toward the main road but across the fields in the direction of Stoneleigh.

"Make it soon," Monk said to Orlando's back. "Whipple's patience is thin and his nerves are weak."

"He shouldn't have committed treason then, should he?"

Crossing the fields was faster than taking the main road, although muddier. It began to rain hard. Drips fell from the brim of Orlando's hat, down his neck, and soon he was wet through. The proud, grand structure of Stoneleigh was a welcome sight. The stone walls themselves looked welcoming, the wings stretching like arms to embrace him. He could almost smell Cook's broth and feel it warming his insides. Susanna would be there too. Perhaps she would not walk away when she saw him. Perhaps she'd forgiven him and come to realize he spoke the truth when he said he wouldn't harm her. Perhaps she would not make him leave tomorrow.

Despite his earlier conviction that leaving was the best thing for them both, the thought had him walking faster. Then running. He ran across the last field, jumped the fence, and didn't care when he landed in a puddle. Susanna would forgive him. He had the rest of the day and all night to convince her.

He wiped the soles of his boots on the steps leading up to the kitchen door and went to open it. Locked.

"Cook! Cook, open up, it's me, Holt. My stomach's growling for a bowl of your broth."

No answer. He knocked.

"Go away!" It was Hendricks's voice, but it took Orlando a moment to realize where it was coming from. "Your things are in the stables."

Orlando stepped back from the small porch and looked up. Rain splashed in his eyes, but he could just make out the open casement window and Hendricks looking down at him.

"My things?" Orlando called back. "What do you mean?"

"I mean, you are to leave Stoneleigh. This instant."

A dreadful foreboding pressed down on Orlando's shoulders. He felt heavy, as if he were drowning in a flood and couldn't swim up to the surface. "Where's your mistress? Where's Susanna? What's she got to say about this?"

"The doors have been locked by her orders. Leave now, Mr. Holt. And do not come back." The window slammed shut.

Orlando stood in the kitchen garden for some time. He didn't know how long. Minutes, perhaps, or hours. The rain stopped at some point but he was dimly aware that it made no difference. He was wet to the bone and so cold he'd gone numb. He stared up at the window then at the door, willing them to open, for Susanna to appear.

She did not.

Did she truly expect him to leave? Now? When danger was so close?

Did she not understand that he *couldn't* leave?

He sat on the ground near the thyme and stretched out his legs. Some time later, as dusk threw itself over the day, the coldness finally got to him. He shivered. The cut Monk had inflicted on his arm ached like the devil. He drew up his knees and tried to make himself as small as possible when it began to rain again.

But he would not move. Not even to get his pack. It was better off in the stables staying dry anyway.

He rested his chin on his knees and calculated how long it would be before the cold became unbearable. He could watch the

C.J. ARCHER

eastern side of the house from the stables, but it would be easier to hear an intruder if he was inside Stoneleigh.

He rubbed his hands up and down his arms but it failed to warm them. At least he was thinking again, and that was a good thing. Except for when he thought about Susanna and why she'd suddenly locked him out. He had no answers to that. He only hoped she'd armed herself. He could not watch the whole house from the outside all of the time. But he could patrol it.

* * *

"WHY IS HE STILL HERE?" Susanna paced the length of the great hall where Bessie and Hendricks had joined her. Cook remained in the kitchen, preparing supper. Her two servants had pleaded with her to stop pacing, to find something to do to take her mind off Orlando, but she could not. "What's he doing now? Has he moved yet?"

"Not yet, mistress," Hendricks said.

Orlando's reaction to being locked out of Stoneleigh was not the one she'd expected. Her initial fear that he would be furious had quickly vanished, along with her worry for her household's safety. He was capable of breaking her door down if he wanted to get in and harm her, yet he did not.

Holt is an assassin. I hired him to kill you.

She knew it was the truth. It made sense. His lies, the hidden knife, the fighting skills he'd displayed against Monk. And then there were the attempts on her life—the blade thrown from the trees as they drove home from church, and the intruder several nights ago. If the note spoke the truth, and she knew in her gut that it did, Orlando must have orchestrated those events which meant he was working with someone. But who?

And why?

All these things crowded her mind, yet she also knew that he could have killed her many times over. They'd been alone together often and he'd not so much as laid a finger on her except in passionate embrace.

Her stomach rolled. She wanted to be sick. She didn't know what to believe any more.

"M'lady?" Hendricks steadied her with a hand to her elbow. "Sit. You'll do yourself no good worrying about him. He's not worth it."

He was right. So why did shutting Orlando out in the freezing cold feel so wrong? Why was her heart tearing in two?

"I'll build up the fire," Hendricks said.

"No." Susanna continued her pacing. "Leave it. And no candles." It had grown dark and was raining again. Rain splashed against the windows and tracked down the glass in rivulets. She folded her arms around her body, but it didn't stop another shiver. She was cold, but Orlando must be colder.

Hell. She'd not covered the orange trees for the night. With all the events of the day, she'd forgotten them. Hell and damn.

Cook waddled in, wringing her hands in her apron. "Supper's ready. Shall I bring it in here?"

"Go into the kitchen," Susanna told them gently. "All of you. It's warmer there."

"You come too, my dear girl," Bessie said, putting an arm around Susanna's shoulders. "Come now, you need to eat and get warm."

She shook her head. "I'll stay here." Where it was cold, but dry at least.

There was a thin silence while the servants all exchanged glances in the semi-darkness.

"What about him?" Cook asked quietly.

"What *about* him?" Hendricks snapped.

"Shall I give him some broth?"

"He doesn't deserve your pity. He's no better than a rat and that's how he should be treated."

"Stop it," Susanna said, weary. "Give him some broth, Cook. If he's still there." Perhaps he'd gone into the stables, or finally left altogether.

"He's still there," Cook said gravely. "Poked my head out a window before to see. He's just sitting and watching the house."

"He'll catch his death in this weather," Bessie said.

Oh God. Susanna put her face in her hands and tried to shut out the image of him lying cold and dead on her doorstep in the morning. "Give him a blanket too."

"M'lady," Hendricks said, "is that wise? Once you feed a stray dog and offer it comfort, it never leaves."

"He is not a dog, Mr. Hendricks, or a rat. Get him a blanket."

"Perhaps I should speak to the master."

"No! Leave Father in peace."

He blanched. She'd never spoken to him with such harshness, and the poor man looked completely taken aback.

So be it. She would not have Orlando becoming ill because of her. Besides, the longer he remained out there, the more she suspected it was too late for Hendricks's warning anyway. Orlando had received too much comfort from Stoneleigh already. He was no longer a stray.

The three servants reluctantly left and Susanna was relieved to be alone again with her bleak thoughts. Instead of trying to chase them away, she embraced them. In a strange way, they were a solace.

THE KITCHEN DOOR opened and Cook appeared, holding a bowl. Steam spiraled off it in a seductive dance. Orlando's stomach growled.

"This is for you." She thrust the bowl out further. "Hendricks is fetching a blanket."

"Thank you." Orlando's bones groaned in protest as he stood. He angled his hat over his eyes but it did little to keep out the sleety needles of rain slicing his already frozen skin. The wind had picked up as darkness fell and the cold he'd felt before was nothing to what he felt now. His jaw ached with the effort to stop his teeth chattering, and his body hurt all over. He was certain he would shatter into thousands of pieces if he were struck.

Soon he wouldn't be able to feel his toes or fingers. He needed the broth then he had to move if he was to survive the night.

Cook gasped when he drew nearer under the small porch. "Look at you!" Deep lines scored her thick brow and if he didn't know better, he would have thought she was in pain too. "Get this into you." She shoved the broth at him. The wooden bowl was hot in his hands and he almost spilled it.

He set it down near his feet. "I'll let it cool a little first. Thank you, Cook."

"If she could see you now, she'd not let you suffer like this." Tears filled her eyes and she sniffed. "Poor thing." She took his hand in between her big ones and rubbed hard. It helped and he smiled his thanks.

"Why did she lock me out?" he asked.

She switched hands. "There was a note telling us...well, saying what you were. An assassin."

"A note? From whom?"

She shrugged. "It didn't say. There now...better?"

"Yes. This note...did she recognize the hand?"

"No, but it was a childish scrawl, so the writer could've been trying to hide themselves."

"And Susanna believed it?"

Another shrug. "Why wouldn't she? You *are* an assassin, aren't you?" Her gaze held no sympathy anymore. It was direct and accusing. "And someone *did* hire you to kill her, didn't they?"

He didn't answer and Cook grunted and dropped his hand.

"Go now. Leave Stoneleigh tonight. Your presence upsets her, and you're not doing yourself any good turning into an icicle out here."

Hendricks's long face appeared over Cook's round one. He tossed a blanket at Orlando. "Cook's right. You must leave."

The door widened and Bessie appeared. She cringed as she

took in his appearance. "Oh dear lord, this isn't right. Look at him! He's wet through. He'll catch his death."

"Good riddance," Hendricks muttered.

"Mr. Hendricks, where's your Christian charity?"

"Where's *his*? And don't either of you tell me he deserves my sympathy. He doesn't. He's a killer. Get out, Mr. Holt, and don't come back."

Orlando bent and picked up the bowl. It was a little cooler, but its warmth still burned his frozen fingers. He relished the pain almost as much as he'd welcomed the coldness.

"No. I can't. She's in danger." His gaze locked with Hendricks's and the servant shut his mouth. "Not from me, from the person who wants her dead. I can protect her better inside the house, but if that's not possible, I must remain outside."

"Oh, Mr. Holt." Bessie wiped away a tear. "Please find somewhere dry to go. I can't bear to think of you out here. Nor can she."

"Hush," Hendricks hissed.

But Orlando's heart kicked inside his chest and began beating with a strong, steady rhythm. Perhaps, despite everything, she did care.

But it was almost too much for his weary soul to hope for.

ORLANDO STOOD on a path in the center of Stoneleigh's neglected formal garden and didn't move. From her bedchamber window, Susanna could just make out his blond head in the pathetic moonlight. He must have removed his hat, or perhaps it had fallen off when he last circled the house. He'd been around dozens of times since she'd retreated to her room, each time his pace slowing, his shoulders hunching further. He must be extremely cold, yet he didn't use the blanket she'd ordered Hendricks to give him.

Fool. Madman. Utter, utter, stupid bloody *fool*!

She pulled the edges of her housecoat tighter at her throat. With no fire burning in the hearth, the chamber was freezing.

What must it be like out there in wet clothes, driving rain, and a wintry wind?

He was quite still except for the ends of his damp hair fluttering in the wind. The collapsed borders and overgrown hedges of the once beautiful formal garden surrounded him. She couldn't see them but she knew the weeds outnumbered the decorative plants. It was difficult to tell if he was looking up at her window, but even if he was, he couldn't possibly see her, half-hidden in the dark as she was.

He suddenly set off again and she counted to one hundred and seven slowly, the time it had taken him to circuit Stoneleigh last time. One hundred and seven passed. One hundred and ten, one hundred and fifty. Two hundred.

Where was he?

She peered out her window, but there was no sign of him. She went out to her parlor and looked through the windows there, then the other windows on the first floor all around the house. The only ones she left alone were in her father's rooms. He was blessedly unaware of the drama that had unfolded at Stoneleigh and that was exactly how she wanted it.

With her heart in her throat, she returned to her bedchamber. Another check out the window proved he had not returned. Perhaps he had finally gone into the stables and found some dry straw. Or perhaps he had succumbed to the cold.

Oh God, oh God.

She could no longer bear it. She threw off her housecoat and quickly dressed in her gardening men's clothes and her warmest cloak. She ran down the stairs to the empty kitchen. Cook and the others had long ago gone to bed. Susanna would not wake them. It was her choice to lock Orlando out, just as it was her choice to let him back in.

If this a trick to get her outside where she would be vulnerable, then so be it. It was a risk she was willing to take because if he was telling the truth and he didn't intend to harm her, the thought of him freezing to death was too horrible to think about.

She threw open the door. Wind and rain lashed her face like sharp talons and the cold stung her eyes. Oh lord, he was out there somewhere in this?

"Orlando?" she called. "Orlando, where are you?"

No answer. The blanket Hendricks had given him lay in a wet crumpled heap on the porch. She flipped up her hood to cover her head then ventured out through the kitchen garden.

She checked the outbuildings first, but there was no sign of him. She circled the house but couldn't find him. At least he wasn't lying in any obvious places in a frozen heap. She called him, but the wind stripped his name from her mouth before it was barely out and carried it away. After her second circuit round the house, it was hard to distinguish the tears on her cheeks from the rain.

She was about to go around again when a movement in the walled garden caught her eye. She ran to the arched entrance. He was there, tying the corner of one of the canvases to the newly built frame.

"Orlando," she choked out.

"Susanna!" A gust of wind dragged the untied edge of the canvas out of his hands.

"Leave it," she said as he caught it. "Come inside."

He shook his head. "There's no point now. I'm already wet."

"Orlando, please."

"Nearly finished." But he fumbled with the twine and she realized his fingers must be terribly numb.

She took the canvas from him. It was the last corner to be secured. He'd covered all the trees, somehow managing the canvases on his own despite the wind and his wretchedness.

"Come inside," she shouted into the gale. But when she reached the arch and looked back, he hadn't moved. He stared at her.

"Orlando, come on! You need to get warm and dry."

"Are you sure?"

She nodded and if he noticed her hesitation, he didn't show it.

He followed her. She bent her head against the rain but he didn't bother.

They crept back into the house and up the stairs, leaving puddles behind on every step. Worry dogged her as she watched his painfully slow pace, but not doubt. In her heart, she knew she was doing the right thing.

She only wished her head agreed with her.

CHAPTER 15

*S*usanna opened the door to her bedchamber and was surprised to find a fire crackling in the hearth. Bessie knelt and applied another log.

"Thank you," Susanna said. "Did I wake you?"

"I was already awake and heard you go out. Thought I'd better get this ready for when you both came back."

Both? She'd known Susanna would bring Orlando back to her room? Susanna wanted to hug her.

"Thank you," she said again. "You may go."

Bessie hesitated. "Are you sure?"

Orlando laughed softly. "Bessie, I'm so cold. I'm not capable of doing anything to Lady Lynden tonight unless it's to fall asleep on her."

"It will be all right," Susanna said gently.

"If you need anything, I'll be in the guest chamber nearby," Bessie said. "Just for tonight." She bid them good night.

Susanna shut the door. The fire's warmth embraced her, made her fingers and nose tingle. Bessie had left a jug and cups on a table and blankets piled on the rushes near the fire. Her mother's fur-lined coat was laid across the foot of the bed.

Orlando still stood by the door, as if he was unsure where to go or what to do. It was the first good look she'd got of him since seeing him in the walled garden. His hair hung damp and limp around his face, his eyelashes were clumped together and his lips had gone blue.

"You're getting the rushes wet," she said. "Come by the fire and take off your clothes."

He began to remove his cloak, but his movements were stiff and awkward and his fingers shook. "I can't."

She helped him out of his cloak, jerkin and doublet, then peeled off boots, netherstocks, and hose and finally his shirt until he was gloriously naked. And shivering violently.

"Oh Orlando," she whispered. "Look at you, you big fool."

He managed a one-shoulder shrug. "I'm not the one who locked the doors."

"But you were the one who refused to seek shelter in the outbuildings." She wrapped a blanket around him and directed him to sit on another she set out in front of the fire. "You would have been perfectly warm snuggling up to Silver."

"She smells of horse." He sat and drew up his knees beneath the blanket. Susanna placed two more blankets around his shoulders but he caught her hand. "Forget about me, you need to get out of your clothes too."

"I will, but you're still cold."

"I'll warm up faster when I see you naked."

"That won't stop you catching your death."

"No, but it will make death so much sweeter."

She turned her back and removed her clothes then wrapped the fur coat around her shoulders. She breathed in the scent of the lavender that Bessie had stored with it to keep the moths away. The fur was so warm, so blessedly warm.

"Come here," Orlando murmured.

She knelt beside him and touched his cheek. Another shiver wracked him. "You're still frozen," she said.

"I can think of a way to warm up."

"So can I. I'll get another blanket."

He caught her arm. "Lie with me, Susanna." His voice was full of the heat his body lacked. "It's the best way to warm up and you know it."

"It may also be the most foolish way."

He tucked a damp lock of her hair behind her ear. "Then call me a fool." He shucked the blankets off then helped her out of the coat. He laid it over the blanket covering the rushes and indicated she should lie down. She stretched out on the coat, the soft fur caressing her skin, sliding between her fingers and toes. He lay beside her and arranged the blankets over them both.

He groaned when their bodies touched. "Better," he murmured. "Much, much better."

His body rippled with another shiver and she wrapped her arms around him, held him close. He nuzzled into her throat and soon his skin felt warm against hers. His soft breathing became deep and rhythmic as he fell into slumber. She closed her eyes but did not sleep. It wasn't because she feared him. She did not. Not anymore. But an overwhelming sadness consumed her. Orlando Holt had lied to her from the very beginning and he'd done it so convincingly.

How could she believe anything he said ever again?

Some time later, as the sun cracked through the clouds, he woke up. He looked at her from beneath heavy lids. "You saved me," he murmured.

She withdrew her arms and shifted a little away. He didn't try to close the gap but the sleepiness vanished. "If you'd gone to the village or to the stables, I wouldn't have needed to."

It was a long time before he spoke again. "Susanna...why didn't you tell me about the message? Why didn't you give me a chance to explain?"

"Explain? Ha!" She sat up and dragged one of the blankets with her but the edge was stuck under his hip. "How can I believe your explanations, Orlando? You have lied to me at every turn. I cannot trust a single thing you say anymore."

He propped himself up on his elbow and frowned at her. "Is that what you think?"

"You would have come up with an explanation that sounded perfectly reasonable. That's how you do it, isn't it? Tell me something I either want to believe, or something that is close enough to the truth that it's plausible." She wrenched the blanket out from under him and flung it around herself as she got up. "I will not be treated like a fool."

"I don't think you're a fool, Susanna. I never have."

She stoked the glowing coals in the fireplace and laid kindling over the top. He came up behind her and kissed her throat.

She pushed him away. "Stop it. I don't want you touching me." Touching led to making love and that led to her believing she could trust him. She would not make that mistake again.

He sat back down on the fur cloak. She knew because she could feel the loss of him and hear the rustle of blankets and his small sigh. She stayed near the fire to warm up and banish the cold that had seeped into her again.

"I have a brother," he said. "He lives in London. I don't have a sister in Salisbury. I don't have a sister at all."

"Is this supposed to make me believe you now? You think telling me about your family will cancel out the lies?"

"No. I know I've lost your trust and I know I'll have to work very hard to win it back."

She swung round. "It is *not* a prize to be won nor is it something you can retrieve like a lost buckle at the bottom of a pond."

He swallowed hard and nodded once. "My brother's name is Thomas. We don't get along anymore. My mother died five years ago, my father a year before her. He was a merchant who imported goods from the Continent and the Orient. My brother took over the business when he died."

"I don't need to hear this." But a part of her *wanted* to hear it. A very large part. She turned her back on him and pulled the edges of the blanket closer at her chest even though the fire blazed.

"My father was an ambitious man. He prized money and position above everything. Our house was—is—large. We employed many staff. My brother and I had London's finest academic tutors, as well as fencing and archery masters, our own horses... Whatever a boy could want. We were indulged, and I'm not too proud to tell you that indulgence almost ruined me. In a way, Thomas was fortunate. Inheriting the business and the responsibilities of our family and his new wife gave him purpose. He didn't follow the same path as me."

"What path was that?"

"The one that led to me almost throwing my life away. Thomas set me to work in the warehouse. I counted goods until my eyes felt like they'd fall out. I talked to merchants who were just like my father—greedy and self-important. I despised it. Day in, day out, I worked in that windowless warehouse and at night I sat through endless dinners so my brother could rise through the Guild's ranks as Father had done. I don't blame Thomas for wanting to become Master of the Guild. It was bred into him as eldest son that he would one day achieve it. I don't blame him at all for putting me in a place that drove me mad."

"You went mad?"

"In a manner. I could feel myself leeching away, all my drive and desires just fading. I felt like I was suffocating, like the walls were closing in around me. If that's not madness, then I don't know what is."

"What changed? How did you get away?"

"My frustration led me to the alehouses, and that led me to fights and women. A lot of both, I'm sorry to say. I spent time at the Marshalsea Prison for affray."

Susanna gasped, but covered her mouth when he winced at her shock. "Is that why you left? To escape your reputation?"

"Not quite. I came out of prison and continued my life as it was before. Nothing had changed. Until one night I ended up in the bed of a woman who'd led me to believe she was a widow."

"She wasn't?"

"Her husband was very much alive. As was his brother. They

learned my name, but instead of setting upon me, they went to my house. I wasn't home, but my family was. They beat Thomas and terrified his wife May and the maids until thankfully, some of the male servants overpowered them. When I found out what happened, I hunted them down."

"And?"

"And I did what I felt was necessary to keep my family safe. Then I left London immediately. I knew my brother would survive by then, but I couldn't face him or May. I'd become the sort of man I despised and I needed to leave that behind. Start afresh."

He spoke with detachment, like a narrator but one who lacks passion for the story. Was it his way of protecting himself from the memories and the loss of his family?

"Is that when you became...an assassin?"

Orlando held his breath. It was the question he'd been dreading. Her reaction, he dreaded even more. "I'm not supposed to tell you that."

She blinked at him with those big, beautiful eyes that were usually so vibrant but were now cloudy. Despite everything he knew about her, her life, and the hardships she'd endured, there was innocence in them. She was no fool, but she was too trusting. It was one of the things he adored about her.

"Then don't," she said, turning away.

"I'm not supposed to, but I will." Hughe be damned. If he found out and wanted Orlando to leave the Guild, then so be it. Orlando could always work alone, or perhaps band together with Monk. He simply could not have Susanna distrusting him anymore, and the only way to gain her trust was to tell the truth in everything.

She rested her chin on her drawn up knees, the blanket still around her. The room was much warmer now and he dropped his blankets to his waist. The flare of desire in her gaze burned brightly, albeit briefly, before she had it under control.

"Hughe saw me kill the brothers."

"Hughe?"

"The gentleman you saw in Sutton Grange and then at church. His name is Hughe St. Alban, the earl of Oxley."

"You call this Lord Oxley by his first name?"

He shrugged. "He doesn't stand on ceremony with the members of the Guild."

"The Guild?"

"The Guild of Assassins."

Her face paled. "Oh. Yes. Of course." Her fingers curled tighter into the woolen blanket.

"I was Hughe's first member, Rafe was his second, and Cole the third to join. Rafe has moved on, but Cole and I remain. You don't need to fear them, Susanna. Or me. We don't kill indiscriminately. Every one of our targets is deserving and thoroughly investigated first. We don't eliminate anyone unless we are absolutely certain of their guilt. No exceptions or mistakes. That's why you are still here today. I didn't believe you killed your husbands and there was no proof."

"What!" She sat up straight and the blanket slipped off her shoulders, exposing the swell of her breasts. Would she let him kiss her there? "What do you mean?"

"An anonymous person commissioned us to kill you. They claimed you murdered both of your husbands, but your crimes were overlooked because of your position within the community. Our client said you were a danger to other men, and especially your next husband. He paid us well, with the promise of more to come."

"This client..." she whispered. "He did not make himself known to you?"

"No. The way our network is set up, it's possible for people to employ us without ever giving away their identity. It's how we like it. Without that anonymity, most would not seek us out. This is not the first time we've had a false claim, but it is the first time we've feared for our target's safety."

She lifted the blanket again and pressed the edge to her lips. "Why? Why would someone want me...?" Tears sprang to her eyes, and he desperately wanted to move closer but didn't think he would be welcomed.

"I don't know, but I feel like I'm closer to finding out," he said. "Do you understand now why I couldn't leave last night? A locked house would hold no difficulty for someone intent on doing you harm. The only reason I didn't force my way inside was because I didn't want to scare you any more. You were terrified of me by then and going against your wishes would have worsened your fear."

She closed her eyes and rested her forehead on her knees.

"Susanna..." But there was nothing more to say. Except... "Despise me if you will. I deserve it. But please, do not fear me."

She lifted her head and wiped her damp cheeks with the blanket. He shifted closer but she shook her head. "I don't fear you, Orlando. I did, briefly, but not now. I fear...my reaction to you."

"What do you mean?"

The sad, faraway look in her eyes boded ill. Very, very ill. "I think you already know I did not enjoy happy marriages. I have the misfortune of attracting men who like me for reasons other than my character. My husbands wooed me, charmed me into marriage, and used a different but no less potent charm on my father so that he agreed to the unions. It was only after the weddings that I learned the true nature of both my husbands. They wanted a pretty wife; they did not want *me*. They thought I would be biddable once I was wed, and eager to please them and help further their interests. But I didn't like their politicking and being pretty wasn't enough in the end. John blamed me for not charming his influential friends, and Phillip blamed me for the same as well as for my low connections in the village. My friends. He..."

She swiped at the tears falling freely down her cheeks. Orlando sat beside her but did not touch her. She wouldn't want that.

"One day he was so angry because I defied him to visit my friend Joan. He pushed me and I fell."

"I know. And I know you lost the baby because of it."

She blinked at him. Her damp lashes clumped together above

her ocean-blue eyes. "It was the second I'd lost and it...ruined my womb."

"Susanna, I'm sorry. I'm so sorry."

"I hated Phillip after that. I hated him so much. He was not the man I married. He'd become a monster. They both did. Why, Orlando? Why does marriage change men?"

"I don't know."

"Was it me?" she whispered. "Was it my fault?"

"No, Susanna. Don't think that."

"John once said he spent his fortune so he could buy me things. Phillip also. A woman like me should have jewels and beautiful gowns, he said."

"Then they were fools. They didn't know you well enough to know what you wanted was to be loved and cherished beyond money or property or things. I pity them. They threw away the perfect woman, all because they did not understand her."

She stared at him, her wide, damp eyes filled with an intensity and wonder that clawed at his insides.

And scared him.

He let her go. "It's just a theory," he said. "Pay me no mind when I'm in this melancholic mood." Susanna had a way of casting a spell over him, making him forget what was important, what he'd worked so long to achieve, ever since leaving London and his family behind—freedom of mind and body.

"I'm going to leave Stoneleigh as soon as the danger to you is passed," he said as much to himself as to her.

She said nothing, but he felt her watching him as he inspected his damp clothes. It was agony not to turn around.

"It's for the best," she said, her voice sounding small and distant. "For both of us."

"Yes. It is." He breathed deeply. The damp-wool smell of his cloak filled his nostrils. He probably should do something with it —spread it out in front of the fire or hang it up—but for some reason he couldn't stop staring at it. Damned rain. He shivered, but he wasn't cold anymore. Not like he'd been last night, wet to his skin and frozen to the bone. If Susanna hadn't relented, if he'd stayed all night out there...

But she had and that was worth something. Wasn't it?

She gently plucked the cloak from his hands. He didn't know she'd come up beside him. "Most of your clothes are still wet. You'll have to remain inside until they're dry." She laid the cloak on the rushes while he retrieved two chairs from the parlor and set them near the fire.

"That'll give you time to do something for me," he said, arranging his jerkin over the back of one of the chairs. "Two things, actually."

"Oh? Does this have something to do with the list of London merchants? I still don't see what relevance it has to who threw the knife at me yesterday."

"It may have no relevance." Or it may have a lot.

"The names are in the casket on my writing desk," she said. "I'll get them for you. What was the second thing?"

"I need to see the plan for the orange tree house."

She wrinkled her adorable little nose. "Why?"

"Because I confronted Monk yesterday and finally got some answers."

"You didn't hurt him, did you?"

"Not much."

She gave him a crooked smile. "Tell me what Monk said."

He did. He told her about the connection between Whipple, Monk, and Jeffrey which led to her late husband's involvement. It was easy to see the moment she realized the implications of it all. Her face drained of color.

"Phillip? A traitor? I...I don't believe it." She sat on the chair and shook her head over and over. "He never displayed any tendency to treason. He wasn't even Catholic! Are you sure he was involved?"

"Lord Whipple is sure and the message written in lemon juice on the plans will probably prove it. That's why Whipple wants it back, and why Jeffrey has agreed to give Whipple's man Monk all the help he can."

She frowned. "Why does Jeffrey want to help Whipple? If he's caught, it'll only throw suspicion on himself when he wasn't part of the original plot."

"Because he'll lose Sutton Hall if that letter falls into the hands of the authorities. Traitors have their lands and property stripped from them. It can be done posthumously."

"Losing Sutton Hall would devastate Jeffrey, as it would have devastated Phillip. So why did he become involved with Lord Whipple at all? It doesn't make sense."

"Phillip was an ambitious man by all account. If he thought Whipple had a good chance of succeeding with his plot then anyone who helped him would receive considerable advancement under a new monarch. It was quite a gamble, but he must have thought it one worth taking."

"A pox on him! On all men." Her glare was pointed. "You too."

"Me? Why?"

"Because you're just like the rest of them. You've charmed me, bedded me, and lied to me. It is more or less the same."

She might as well have run him through with a rapier, the stabbing in his chest hurt so much. She was right. He wasn't so different.

"You need to cover yourself," she muttered. "It's...distracting."

It took a moment for his mind to grip onto the new topic. "I'm not the only naked person in this room and you're not the only one who's distracted."

"I'm covered with a blanket at least."

"I think you can see how much that doesn't matter."

Her gaze shifted to his groin and a light blush infused her cheeks. "Hmmmm." She rose. "I'll fetch the plans then tell Bessie we need your pack from the stables for your dry clothes."

She bid him to leave her so she could dress and he wrapped a blanket around his waist and waited in the parlor until she joined him. A little while later, she did, wearing women's clothing again and he had to admit he preferred the sight of her in men's trousers than the voluminous skirt.

"Here," she said, handing him the plans. "See what you can make of it."

She left to speak to Bessie and he set the plans on the desk while he lit a taper. Carefully waving the taper beneath the paper, he watched as the lemon juice turned brown and revealed the writing.

"What have you discovered?" she asked upon returning. The sweet, heady scent she added to her bathing water enveloped him, and it took a moment before he could focus again.

"It's as Monk said. It's a correspondence from an Englishman now living in France and addressed to Lord Whipple. It includes some words of a treasonous nature, but no actual details of a plot as such. It would be enough to put Whipple in danger if it was discovered, and anyone else associated with the correspondence."

"Phillip."

Orlando nodded. "I suspect your orange grower, like you, was unaware his letters were being used in such a way."

"Claims of innocence wouldn't have been enough to exonerate us in the eyes of the authorities."

"Perhaps not."

She sank heavily to the floor and put her head in her hands. He crouched beside her but dared only touch her elbow. "How could Phillip do such a thing?" she whispered. "How could he endanger me so, and himself, for the promise of advancement?"

Orlando didn't have an answer for that. He'd never understood the need of some men to further themselves, or become richer. How could those things fulfill a man? They were just an extra noose.

"He was a fool, your husband." Orlando had no desire to throw away a perfectly good life in the hope of improving it. Not at the expense of the people he loved.

Love. Bloody hell.

"So you don't think Monk was the one trying to kill me?" she asked.

He helped her to her feet. "No. Jeffrey had no reason to want you dead."

"I don't know why he didn't just ask me to look at the letters. If he'd explained the situation, I would have given him free access to all my correspondence."

Orlando watched her as she opened one of the caskets on the writing desk and sifted through some papers. There was much to admire, and not just in her form. She had quickly rallied herself after her disappointments. She was not one to dwell on matters, or feel regret and hatred for the wrongs done to her. She appeared determined, however, not to make the same mistakes. He couldn't blame her for that.

Yet it didn't stop him from wanting to hold her, kiss her.

"Here it is," she said, handing him a list of names. "Those are the merchants I wrote to in London."

He scanned the names. He didn't recognize a single one. "These are not London merchants," he said, giving the list back to her.

"But Walter Cowdrey gave me those. He's had dealings with them in the past."

"Then Walter Cowdrey has lied to you. And I'm going to find out why."

CHAPTER 16

*S*usanna couldn't believe it. Walter had lied to her. Another one.

John, Phillip, Orlando, and now Walter. Was there any man she could truly trust?

"Why?" she whispered. "Why would he do it?"

Orlando pressed a hand to her back and directed her to sit in the chair at her writing desk. "I don't know," he hedged, "but I think it was to keep you poor."

"W-what? Why would he do that?"

"To force you into marriage."

"Force me?" No, Walter was much too sweet, too good. He had never done anything wrong or cruel in his life. He was reliable, his reputation beyond reproach.

To think he was no better than the others...

Orlando's hands wrung hers, his fingers kneading the knuckles. "Susanna, think about it a moment. You are on the brink of ruin here at Stoneleigh. Any poorer and your situation would be desperate. As it is, you have hope while you still have your marmalades and succades to sell. Destroy that hope and you're left with nothing. He wants you to turn to him in your need, and wed him."

"But even if I didn't find any buyers for my orange stuffs, I wouldn't marry him. I don't care enough for him and I've never married for money. Not once. Poor foolish Walter," she muttered.

"You feel sympathy for him?"

"A little. I certainly can't hate him."

He dropped her hands. "No?" he rasped. "After he deceived you in such a way?"

"*You* deceived me. And I don't hate you."

He folded his arms over his broad chest, still so wonderfully naked. "It was not done willingly, I assure you."

"Unless your life was in danger for revealing your secret, you were willing."

He barked a laugh and turned away. Her heart plunged to her toes as a sinister thought embedded itself in her mind. "It's not, is it?"

"Hughe is my friend," he said without facing her. "Don't worry about me."

It wasn't an answer.

"When your clothes are dry, we'll confront Walter together," she said.

He spun round. "*I* will confront him. It's too dangerous for you to leave the house. You must keep all the doors and windows locked in my absence."

"I should be the one to speak to him, Orlando. Your methods might be a little...strong for the likes of Walter. He's a gentle man."

"Is he?"

"What do you mean?"

He rested his hands on his hips and looked to the ceiling. "Susanna, you need to prepare yourself for the fact that Walter is the one who hired the Guild."

"No. No!" It wasn't possible. Not dull-witted, safe, reliable Walter Cowdrey. "He claims to love me, why would he want to kill me?"

"It's possible he commissioned us in order to intervene and

look like he'd saved you. What woman can resist a hero?" he said, wryly.

"You think *he* threw the knife at me just to make me think I'm still in danger?"

"Perhaps," he said, carefully.

"But it could have struck me."

He said nothing. Nor did he keep eye contact. The churning in her stomach became a painful twist. "Orlando, what is it? What are you thinking?"

"You won't want to hear it."

"Tell me anyway. I *need* to know."

He conceded with a brief nod. "I think that it's possible he truly wanted to go through with the act. So no one else could have you," he added quietly.

"No one else...?" Oh God. Oh God, not Walter. "But...but he has always been so good to me. So helpful." She buried her face in her hands, but she did not shed a tear. She couldn't believe Walter would want her dead, yet he had tried to ruin her chance of financial freedom. That alone was deceitful. He deserved no tears.

"Whether or not it was Cowdrey, I do think the person who employed the Guild to assassinate you threw the knife," Orlando said. "He grew frustrated with our lack of action and took the task into his own hands. Walter Cowdrey appears to have a motive, of sorts. I'm sorry, Susanna. I know you consider him a friend."

There was a knock on the door and Orlando answered it. Bessie gasped and covered her eyes. "Mr. Holt! Put on some clothes." She held out his pack.

"Thank you," he said, taking it.

Bessie peeked through the gap between her fingers. "I'll fetch your breakfast."

She shuffled off and Orlando shut the door. "Susanna, I'm sorry your faith in Walter has been destroyed, but I can't pretend that I care. He may or may not have tried to kill you, but he *has* steered you in the wrong direction regarding those merchants."

"Just as you have steered me wrong?" But that wasn't fair and she knew it. Orlando had not tried to block her in order to keep her tied to him. "I'm sorry," she muttered. "I'm...overwrought."

He stepped toward her but stopped and crossed his arms, his hands high up under his armpits. "I'm going to make it better for you," he said. "I promise."

She nodded. "Just don't kill anyone."

"I'll try not to."

* * *

IT'S ALWAYS the quiet ones who prove the most dangerous. So Orlando often found. The flamboyant and loud may boast of their deeds, but they rarely turned out to be as terrible as they claimed. The average and unassuming were different. They didn't boast and they appeared pleasant enough on the outside, helpful even, yet they could do the cruelest things. Walter Cowdrey was one of those types. He was a good man, so Susanna had said. But Orlando disagreed. Cowdrey was definitely a liar, and perhaps a killer. It was time to find out for sure.

He rode Silver to Cowdrey Farm. His dry clothes didn't stay dry for long thanks to the light sprinkling of rain. He'd suffered no ill effects from the previous night's banishment, not even a sneeze, although the nagging doubt that Susanna may not let him back in upon his return remained with him the entire journey.

Cowdrey Farm was a sturdy rectangular stone house with little in the way of garden out the front. There was no lawn, border hedges, or raised beds. Indeed, the only plants were a few clumps of hawthorn that held no pattern whatsoever and a scraggly patch of flowers under one of the ground floor windows. The house itself appeared to be surrounded by more mud than gravel and Orlando's boots were thick with it by the time he walked around to the stables.

He handed Silver's reins to a groom and asked after the master. The lad directed him to the milk house past the barn in the nearby field. Orlando thanked him and glanced up at the main house.

Margaret Cowdrey's stern face peered down at him from a first floor window. He tipped his hat, but she gave no response in return.

It was some distance to the milk house and took him several minutes of clomping through mud to reach it. Inside, he spotted Cowdrey standing over one of the milkmaids, giving her instruction. She looked to be no more than thirteen and uncertain of her task.

He scowled when he saw Orlando. "What do you want?"

"I want to talk to you about the list of London merchants you gave Susanna. Among other things."

Cowdrey flinched. For a moment Orlando thought he'd have to say his piece in front of the milkmaids, but then Cowdrey led him outside. It had stopped raining, but the gray clouds hung low and expectant. He wanted to get home to Stoneleigh before they dropped their load.

"Speak," Cowdrey said.

"I've lived in London almost my entire life," Orlando said. "I worked for my brother, a merchant who imports goods from the Continent and other foreign parts."

"So?"

"Most of the things my brother imports are spices and food-stuffs that aren't available here in England, and most of his customers are grocers in London. I don't recognize a single shop-keeper on the list you gave Susanna."

Cowdrey removed his hat and wiped his forehead with the back of his hand. "There must be a lot of merchants in London. You cannot know them all."

"Actually, my brother's business interests are extensive. When I worked for him, I talked to almost every London merchant at one point or other, and those I didn't speak to, I knew by name."

Another flinch from Cowdrey. The man grew twitchy. "So you're not a gardener. I'm sure Susanna would like to know."

"She already does."

"She ought to throw you out."

"She did."

Cowdrey pressed his lips together. "Then you are wasting my time." He began to walk off but Orlando grabbed his arm, spun him around. "Release me, Holt. You're a liar and a cur. If Susanna wants nothing to do with you then neither do I."

"You didn't let me finish. Susanna threw me out, but then she allowed me back into the house. That's when she showed me the list of names you gave her and I told her they're false. She knows you're lying, Cowdrey. She also knows why."

Cowdrey jerked his arm out of Orlando's grip. If the man ran, so be it. Orlando would simply have to chase him. The exercise might warm him up.

"What lies have you been telling her?" Cowdrey snapped.

"I haven't lied. Not about this."

"Ha! You admit you are a liar, and yet she believes you now?" He poked Orlando in the shoulder. It was annoying. "What would she say if she knew you," *poke*, "were the one who lied about the shop-keepers?" *Poke.*

Orlando grabbed the finger. Twisted. Cowdrey winced but didn't cry out despite the pain he must be feeling. Orlando let go. "Keep your fingers to yourself unless you want them snapped off. I promised Susanna I wouldn't kill you. I don't like breaking promises, but I could make an exception in your case."

Sweat dampened Cowdrey's brow. He shook out his hand then put it behind his back. "What do you want?"

"Two things. First, I want you to stop pestering Susanna with offers of marriage."

"Bah! Be gone! Get off my land. You cannot come here and order me about. You're an arse. Susanna has been fooled by your manner and your pretty looks—"

"Leave my looks out of this. I'm rather sensitive about them, if you must know."

"I'll set her straight. She'll listen to me because I've known her all her life and she knows I wish her no harm."

"No harm? You deceived her in order to ruin her."

"I gave her those false names out of kindness."

"Kindness? You think it kind to force her into poverty?"

"You think it kind to let her believe she can fix Stoneleigh on her own? The task is enormous even for someone who knows what they're doing. She has no money, no skill at building, no one to do the labor."

"Hence the need to sell the products made from her orange trees so she can employ someone."

"You think that will bring in enough?" He snorted. "And you call yourself a merchant."

"My brother is the merchant, not me. I care little for money."

"Then you are as foolish as Susanna. Selling her marmalades and other orange stuffs will get her a few pounds, no more. Stoneleigh will fall into ruin soon, and she will starve if she continues with her stubborn refusal to remarry. I am her savior. *Me*." Spittle bubbled at the corners of his mouth. He spoke fast, his words falling over each other in his haste. "There is no one richer in this parish. None among her acquaintance have more land than me. None. Letting her think she can live off the meager income from a few jars of marmalade is worse than the small lie I told because it gives her false hope."

"It is still hope. And I said I care little for money, not that I don't know the value of it. The sale of this crop will help her buy more trees and protect the ones she has."

"She will be happier if she forgets it all. Happier with *me*. She won't need to work herself to the bone or worry about money. I'll take care of her. The sooner she comes to realize her plan is hopeless, the better off she will be." Cowdrey's chest rose and fell with his labored breathing. He'd shown more passion, more character in his speech than he'd shown in every conversation Orlando had witnessed. Yet the man was still a prick.

Orlando's heart raced, his anger welled inside him until he couldn't contain it any longer. "I don't know if she can do it on her own," he said, "but God's blood I want her to succeed, now more than ever. And if you loved her as you claim, you'd want her to succeed too. With you or without."

Love. Bloody hell, not again.

Orlando pressed his thumb and forefinger into his eyes. He was tired and there were too many thoughts racing through his head. It was impossible to make sense of them all.

"I am merely protecting her," Cowdrey said.

Orlando stared at him. The man honestly believed what he was saying. "Then where were you when someone tried to kill her?"

Cowdrey's head jerked up as if Orlando had hit him. "What do you mean?"

"There have been incidents. The latest one occurred yesterday on the drive home from church. Someone threw a knife at her." It was one thing to break his vow and tell Susanna about his work for Hughe, it was entirely another to tell this man. If Cowdrey was innocent, he didn't need to know, and if he was guilty, he'd probably already guessed that Orlando was the assassin he'd hired.

"A knife?" Cowdrey's face turned white. He staggered backward. If it was an act, it was a good one. "Who...?" He stared slack-jawed at Orlando. "Who would do such a thing to her? She's never hurt anyone."

Orlando crossed his arms. Waited.

Cowdrey's eyes widened. "You think I did it? You filthy swine! Is that what you told her?" He clasped Orlando's cloak and tried to drag him closer. He was strong, but not strong enough. "Now she thinks it's me! I wouldn't harm a hair on her head. Susanna is a...a thing to treasure. Like a...a precious jewel. A pearl!" His fingers twisted in Orlando's cloak and he shook him. "I would not harm her. I only ever wanted to protect her from the world's ills, as any gentleman would after setting eyes upon her. A woman as beautiful as Susanna is rare and..."

"Precious? A pearl?"

Cowdrey punched Orlando in the shoulder but did not let go of his cloak. "Do not mock me."

"Are you finished?" Orlando asked, curling his fists at his sides.

"Go back to Stoneleigh and tell her it's not me." Cowdrey's eyes had a wildness in them and his voice rose to a high pitch. "Understand? Make sure she knows I am not the one trying to harm her."

"There now, that's the problem I have with you. Or one of them."

"What?"

"If you loved her, your first thought shouldn't be to make your innocence known to her, it should be to find out who is trying to kill her before he does it again."

Cowdrey's face screwed up, distorting his features. "What do you know of love? You're no better than a vagabond."

"Vagabonds can have feelings too."

"You dare to jest at a time like this." Cowdrey snarled and shoved at Orlando's chest.

Orlando stepped one foot back for balance. "Unhand me."

Another shove, but Orlando was braced for it and didn't move. Cowdrey bared his crooked teeth. Orlando sighed. He was going to have to remove him the hard way. Since Cowdrey was too close to get a punch in, Orlando slammed the hardest part of his forehead down on the bridge of the other man's nose.

Cowdrey let go with a squeal of pain and covered his smashed face. Blood dripped through his fingers.

"You're fortunate," Orlando said.

Cowdrey merely glared at him.

"You're fortunate because I don't think you're the one trying to kill Susanna. If I did, you'd be bleeding from more places than your nose."

"You're a madman!" Cowdrey shouted. "I know you want her for yourself, but you can't have her. She's mine!" He lunged but Orlando stepped aside and Cowdrey stumbled forward, almost falling into the mud.

"She's no one's," Orlando said. "The sooner you realize that, the happier you'll be."

"Get out! Get off my land, you pizzle!"

The milkmaids had come to the door of the milk house, their

aprons pressed to their mouths, their eyes wide with horror. None came to Cowdrey's aid. Orlando tipped his hat at them then turned and walked away across the field back to the house. He listened for footsteps approaching but none came. Cowdrey remained behind.

He collected Silver from the groom who was none the wiser to his master's agony and looked up at the window where he'd seen Margaret earlier. She was gone. He walked Silver a little way then mounted and glanced back at the house once more. Cowdrey Farm was a bleak place. Susanna would hate living in the austere, blocky house with no garden to speak of except for the bedraggled little patch of marigolds.

Marigolds. The same flowers that were on Phillip's grave.

Bloody hell! Susanna hadn't put them there, it was Margaret. Had she been in love with Phillip? Is that why she hated Susanna so much? Surely not enough to kill her almost a year after his death.

Orlando steered Silver back to the stables. "Tell me," he said to the groom, "did your master and mistress ride to church yesterday or drive?"

The boy shrugged. "She drove the cart, 'e rode."

Damn. Orlando had seen someone leave the woods on a horse after the attack, not a cart.

"She rode 'ome," the lad added.

Orlando's heart stopped. "On her own?"

"Aye. The master come 'ome in the cart and she rode Gilly. She's a good 'orsewoman. Rode out just now on Gilly, in fact."

"Which way did she go?"

"To the village."

Stoneleigh was on the way to Sutton Grange. Orlando spurred Silver on, but the mare was old and slow and Margaret Cowdrey had a good lead. He hoped to God Susanna didn't let her in the house.

CHAPTER 17

Susanna saw Margaret arrive from her father's bedchamber window. She rode with purpose, bent low over the horse's neck, her skirts rippling around her legs. Susanna didn't rise to greet her, nor did she tell her father they had a visitor. Orlando had instructed her not to let anyone in the house while he was absent and had given the same instructions to the servants. Margaret would leave when no one answered.

A few minutes later, Bessie peeked around the door. "Mistress Cowdrey's here to see you."

"How pleasant," her father said from his bed where he was propped against pillows. Susanna had thought he was asleep.

She gave him a smile then picked up her embroidery basket and followed Bessie out to the landing. "Mr. Holt said no visitors. Not until he returns."

"Aye, but it's Mistress Cowdrey. Surely he meant only men."

A shiver chilled Susanna's spine. She put her basket down but picked up the small knife she used for snipping threads. She tucked it up her sleeve. "Just in case," she said to a wide-eyed Bessie.

"Oh, m'lady, you don't think..." Bessie gave a small yelp then covered her mouth with her hand. "I'll tell her to go."

"No, it's all right. I'll talk to her." If she was the one trying to kill Susanna, then asking her to leave might only serve to enrage her and put the servants at risk.

She reached the bottom of the stairs and entered the great hall just as Margaret emerged from the parlor adjoining it. She had her arms folded and her cloak draped over them, hiding her hands. Susanna kept her distance. Bessie remained at her back. "You may go," Susanna said to her maid.

Bessie didn't move.

"Margaret," Susanna said, smoothly. "This is a surprise. What brings you to Stoneleigh?"

Margaret's eyes were unblinking, yellow-green orbs. "My brother."

"Is everything all right? He's not unwell, is he?"

"Don't play the simpleton with me," she hissed.

The hairs on the back of Susanna's neck rose. Behind her, Bessie drew in a sharp breath. "Bessie, go." To Margaret, she said, "State your business then leave."

Margaret's upper lip lifted in a sneer. "It feels good, doesn't it?"

"What does?"

"Being mistress in your own house. You're even luckier than most. You are both master *and* mistress here at Stoneleigh." Her mouth flattened, her eyes sharpened as her gaze bored into Susanna. "Yet you want to take over Cowdrey Farm too."

"Uh, no. I don't. I'm not going to marry your brother, if that's your fear. I don't love him."

"Love? Ha! Did you love Phillip? Or your first husband?"

"I was...drawn to them. Foolishly, as it turned out. They were not the best of husbands."

Margaret spluttered out a laugh but it was harsh and cruel. "Perhaps if you'd been a better wife he would have treated you with more kindness. Phillip was a true gentleman." Her nostrils flared and the sheen of unshed tears covered her eyes. "He was a good man and you ruined him with your willfulness and your disregard for *his* needs. I told him so. I warned him he was making a mistake choosing you over me."

Good lord! No wonder Margaret was so bitter. She had been in love with Phillip, but he had rejected her. "You think you would have been a better wife to him? You are less biddable than me, Margaret. Do not pretend otherwise."

"I would have changed for Phillip's sake. I would have done whatever he needed of me. I would have been the best wife to him. He still chose you."

"That is hardly my fault. Many, many times I've wished he hadn't."

Margaret took a step forward. Her eyes were slits from which she watched Susanna the way a feral cat watches a mouse. "You lying *witch*. You set out to seduce him and you got what you wanted."

"I did not—"

"I've *seen* you, Susanna. The way you look at men with lustfulness, tempting them with your pretty face and the sway of your hips. You lure them as a siren lures her victims with her voice."

"Nonsense."

"You wanted to tie them to you so you could take over their estates. That's why you killed them, isn't it?"

Susanna was prepared for the accusation, but it still came as a shock. It took her a moment to gather her wits.

"She never did such a thing!" Bessie cried.

"Hush, it's all right," Susanna murmured.

"You tried to bend them to your will," Margaret went on, "but they would not bend so you ended their lives to earn your widow's portion."

Good lord! Did she truly believe such madness? "If that were the case, I would have already accepted your brother's offer of marriage. He is the most docile of them all and Cowdrey Farm extensive. If I wanted a husband I could manipulate, I would choose Walter. But I have not."

Susanna didn't see the hand coming until too late. The slap

stung and sent her stumbling into the wall. Bessie steadied her and angled herself between Susanna and Margaret, but Susanna set her aside with a gentle nudge. Margaret's direct gaze looked straight past the maid as if she wasn't there.

"Fetch Hendricks and Cook," Susanna said quietly to the maid.

"I'm not leaving you with her."

"You have to. Go. Now."

Bessie rushed off, glancing over her shoulder until she reached the end of the hall and had to turn the corner. Susanna let the handle of her knife drop down into her palm.

"My brother would be perfect for your needs," Margaret said, her words twisted with bitterness, "except for one thing. He has me." She tapped her chest. "*I* would not let you get the better of him. *I* would not let you overrun Cowdrey Farm with your ridiculous orange trees and your wanton ways. It's *my* place as much as his and you know that. You *know* you can't control Walter while I'm there, that's why you've rejected him thus far. But I know your kind. You bewitch men to the point where they're soon begging and will do anything to have you. Walter is on the verge of marrying me off because of you. Me! His beloved sister, the mistress of Cowdrey Farm. The one who spent years experimenting with new techniques, planting different crops, striking deals with merchants as far as London. I am the reason for Cowdrey Farm's success, not him, and you will not take it away from me with your simpering prettiness and whoring. I'm not going to marry. I am not leaving. Ever."

Susanna let the insults roll off her. Margaret had bottled up her anger for so long, she needed to let it escape. Perhaps this outpouring would help her. Perhaps she would not try to kill Susanna after all.

"The farmer Walter has been meeting with in the village...is that who he wants you to wed?"

"His lands are half the size of Cowdrey. I'll not accept him, and you will not force Walter on the matter."

"I've rejected Walter time and again," Susanna said. She had to keep using logic, keep Margaret thinking and not acting on violent impulse. "Why would I change my mind now?"

"He's not a complete fool, my brother. He's been slowly thwarting your plans for financial freedom to make you need him more. I admire him for his fortitude and cleverness, if not his tastes in women."

"You mean by tricking me into thinking I'd written to London shopkeepers when I hadn't?"

"That is the final touch, and a deft one, but there were others. Withholding his men so that you couldn't make repairs on Stoneleigh, not giving you the tools necessary for such tasks or giving you faulty ones. He made sure you suffered setback after setback and that they were costly ones."

It was a relief to hear the admission, just as much as it had been when Orlando told her about the merchants. Susanna had always thought the delayed repairs on Stoneleigh were in some way her fault, but now she knew they were not and it lightened her heart.

"I can assure you," she said, "that you have just made marrying Walter even less appealing. I certainly won't wed him now."

Margaret stepped closer to Susanna, backing her into the wall. "Yet he will persist and persist and persist because that's the sort of fool he is."

"Then confront *him*, not me."

"Oh I will. But first, I have something to take care of. Something I've wanted to do in a very long time." Before the last words were out of her mouth, she lunged. The cloak fell away and the blade Susanna suspected she'd hidden all along thrust up.

Susanna darted aside, lost her balance and fell. The knife struck the wood paneling behind her. She called out to alert her staff. Footsteps came running. Her name was shouted from somewhere deeper in the house. Margaret heard them too. She pulled the knife out of the wall and struck before Susanna could regain her balance.

The blade sliced through the forearm Susanna put up to shield herself. She screamed. White hot pain tore up her arm. She scuttled across the wooden floor on her rear, kicking at Margaret's feet and feeling for the handle of her own knife.

Her back smacked against another wall. Trapped.

Margaret stood over her, knife raised, cold fury glinting in her eyes.

"Susanna!" Orlando. The desperate cry ripped from his throat as he took in the scene. But he was at the other end of the large room. Too far.

He ran, blade in hand, fierce determination etched into every line on his face.

But he would not reach them in time.

With a shrill cry, Margaret plunged. Susanna struck upward with her own knife at the same time. It caught Margaret in the chest just below her shoulder, not close enough or deep enough to strike her heart.

Yet Margaret's eyes widened in shock. Her grip loosened on her blade's handle, dropping it. She fell forward as her hands scrabbled at her back. Orlando was there now and he caught her before she could fall on Susanna. He lowered Margaret to the ground. A knife protruded from her back. Blood oozed from the wound.

"Susanna!" Orlando picked her up and drew her to his chest. It pounded furiously, matching the beat of her own. "Susanna." He held her against him as he inspected her injured arm. It hurt like the devil but the cut wasn't deep and had already stopped bleeding. "I couldn't get to you," he muttered into her hair. "I'm sorry, sweetheart. I'm sorry. I shouldn't have left you. I shouldn't have—" A shudder cut him short and he never finished the sentence.

"I'm all right, Orlando. Is she...?"

"Yes."

Susanna closed her eyes and wept into his chest. He settled on the floor and cradled her in his lap. She was vaguely aware of others surrounding them, covering Margaret's body, wrapping something around Susanna's injured arm, but she lost track of time and place. It became just her and Orlando, his hands lightly skimming her, checking for other injuries, his lips pressed to her forehead and the pulse of life throbbing in her veins.

She didn't want the moment to end.

"What in God's name happened here?" The voice belonged to Jeffrey, and it shattered Susanna's cocoon. She extricated herself from Orlando although he kept hold of her hand as they both rose.

Jeffrey and Monk stood at the far end of the great hall. Cook, Bessie and Hendricks hovered nearby, looking uncertain and anxious.

"Who's under there?" Monk asked, nodding at the blanket.

"Margaret Cowdrey," Orlando said.

Monk merely nodded while Jeffrey went white. "Margaret? What happened to her?"

"I killed her," Orlando said.

Jeffrey took a small step back and hid partially behind Monk.

"She was going to kill me," Susanna said, showing him her injured arm. It had stopped bleeding, but it still hurt. Some of Widow Dawson's salve should soothe it.

"Aye," Hendricks said. "Mr. Holt saved her." He gave Orlando a firm nod.

"Dear God," Jeffrey muttered. He must have realized he was in no danger because he crossed the length of the hall and lifted the edge of the blanket. He pressed the back of his wrist to his mouth and nose. "Where's Farley? I need to speak to your father, Susanna, and find out what really happened."

"Father wasn't here. He's asleep and knows nothing of this. We'll tell you what happened." She did, leaving nothing out.

"Can anyone confirm your story?" Jeffrey asked.

Susanna stretched out her arms, indicating Orlando, her staff. "All of them can. You doubt me, Jeffrey?"

"No, no," he said quickly. "But as justice of the peace, it's my duty to gather all the facts, and not from Mr. Holt himself but an independent witness."

"We can vouch for what occurred here," Cook said. "Saw it with our own eyes, we did. All of us."

Jeffrey turned his back on her. "Anyone of *standing*, Susanna? Or is it just yourself? Because I'm not sure your account is all that independent since you clearly...like the killer."

"Jeffrey, you are being ridiculous. Margaret Cowdrey came at me with that knife there." She pointed to Margaret's weapon.

Monk came up behind Jeffrey, fists at his sides, his level gaze on Orlando. Orlando appeared still, calm, but she could feel the ripple of pent-up emotion in their linked hands. He let go and dread filled her.

"Susanna," Jeffrey said on a huff, oblivious to Orlando's dangerous mood, "I have to do this properly. The witness account of mere servants is not as weighty as—"

Orlando's hand whipped out and he grasped Jeffrey's jaw. Jeffrey yelped and struggled to get away but failed. "Hear this. I killed Margaret Cowdrey because she was going to kill Susanna. That is how you'll record it. Only after that will we release the plans for the orange tree shelter to you. Do you understand me, Lord Lynden?"

"Plans for the orange tree shelter?" Cook echoed.

"Hush," Hendricks said. "He knows what he's doing."

"I'd agree if I were you," Monk said to Jeffrey, rubbing the shadowy bruise on the left side of his jaw. "Mr. Holt is not someone you'd like as your enemy."

"Yeth, yeth!" Jeffrey said through lips squashed together by Orlando's grip. "I agwee."

Orlando let him go. "There is no need to investigate this further, no matter what Mr. Cowdrey says when he finds out."

Jeffrey shifted his jaw from side to side, checking if it still worked. "Agreed. As long as you give me the plans."

"I'll ride out to see Walter," Susanna said quietly.

"But your arm, m'lady," Bessie said.

"It's all right. It's not too deep."

"I'll go with you," Orlando said.

"And I," Monk said.

"We don't need you." Orlando took Susanna's hand. It was big and solid and she gratefully closed her fingers around his.

"Nevertheless, two thugs are better than one."

"I'm capable of taking care of myself and Susanna against Cowdrey."

"Madmen can be stronger than they appear," Monk said with a shrug. "And I suspect he'll be very mad."

"Then we'll all go," Susanna said before Orlando could argue. She led them both out the front door while the others remained behind, but stopped on the front porch. A chopping sound came from the east. "Do you hear that?"

Orlando let go of her hand and ran in the direction of the sound. Monk was on his heels and Susanna followed. As soon as she rounded the house, she realized it came from the walled garden. Her heart plunged into her stomach.

Her trees!

"No! *No!*"

She ran, but Orlando and Monk reached the archway first. What she saw cut her deeper than any blade could. Walter Cowdrey swung an axe at the trunk of one of her oldest, strongest orange trees. Wood cracked and groaned. The tree toppled, scattering unripe oranges and leaves onto the ground as it hit. Nine other trees lay beside it. Only two remained standing.

Susanna's knees buckled. She fell to the ground. "*No!*"

Orlando tackled Walter before he swung the axe at the next trunk. Walter grunted as his face slammed into the dirt and Orlando forced his arms behind his back. The axe lay out of reach. Monk must have taken over after that because Orlando was at Susanna's side in a heartbeat, holding her.

A terrible shrill cry spewed from the depths of her. "My trees!" All Mama's years of hard work, gone in moments. The planting, pruning, fertilizing, harvesting, loving, and the nights spent covering them, worrying if they'd made it through the frost. All gone. "Mama."

She shut her eyes, bent over and sobbed into the earth. It felt like her heart had been ripped out of her chest and smashed by Walter's axe. The pain was so immense it pushed her down and finally buried her altogether. Not even Orlando's arms holding her made a difference.

Her beautiful trees were dead.

Eventually, when there were no more tears inside her, she looked up and fixed a glare on Walter. He stood beside Monk. Dried blood smeared his nose and mouth and fresh blood dripped from a graze above his eye. His gaze focused entirely on Orlando and he snarled like a wild dog. He looked like a man who didn't yet know he'd lost.

"You filthy, heartless wretch," she said, swiping at her wet cheeks. "How could you do this to me?"

Slowly he turned to her. There was very little of the Walter Cowdrey she knew in his eyes and a lot of Margaret. "How could *I* do this to *you*? What about what you have done to me? I have loved you forever, Susanna. I have waited and waited. I have given you every kindness, offered you a comfortable life at Cowdrey Farm, and you have repaid me by humiliating me and whoring yourself with...*him*."

Susanna's limbs weighed her down but she hauled herself to her feet with Orlando's help. There would be no reasoning with Walter in his current state. She turned to leave, Orlando supporting her.

"Come back here!" Walter shouted. "I haven't finished! Do not walk away from me, woman."

She didn't have the heart to argue with him. She just left. At the archway, her three trusted servants waited silently, their weary brows furrowed in concern. Orlando passed her into Bessie's arms, and the three servants steered her away from the walled garden. She didn't realize Orlando hadn't followed until she heard Walter shout.

"She's mine!" It was followed by a blood-curdling scream like an ancient tribal battle cry.

Then nothing.

"Orlando?" she called.

No answer.

She pulled free of Bessie and ran back to the garden. "Orlando!"

He caught her beneath the arch, lifting her off the ground, and she buried her face in his neck. Her body shook uncontrollably. She couldn't stop crying. "I thought he hurt you," she said, clutching at his jerkin.

"No." His voice sounded thick and unnatural, not at all like his usual deep, self-assured one. "He's gone, Susanna."

She peered past him. Walter lay on the ground beside the last tree he'd felled. Monk stood beside him, a blood-soaked knife in his hand. He looked up, and she was surprised to see so many naked emotions in his eyes, from shock and horror to disgust. He swallowed hard, blinked, and they were gone. His gray eyes were clear once more.

Orlando lowered her to the ground and clasped her face in his hands. He gently kissed her. It was excruciating in its sweetness because it wasn't enough. Not nearly enough. She craved him and the comfort only he could offer.

"You need to go inside and warm up," he said. "Cook, some broth for everyone if you can. Bessie, see to Susanna's needs. Hendricks...take the ladies inside while I help Monk here."

Susanna wiped her cheeks. She was still crying. She couldn't seem to stop. Where before her heart felt like it had been ripped out, now it was a pulpy mess. Her trees were gone. Margaret and Walter were dead after trying to do her harm. And above it all was the knowledge that it was time for Orlando to leave.

* * *

ORLANDO WATCHED the little party until they were inside the house. They passed Lynden on the way. He'd remained inside with Margaret's body, but now he approached the walled garden with a frown.

"Why is Susanna crying?" Lynden asked as he approached.

"Take a look in there," Orlando said without removing his eyes from the door through which Susanna and her servants had disappeared. He'd seen unhappiness in others before, but never had it echoed within him as it had done watching Susanna grieve for her trees. His very bones ached with it and his heart couldn't bear any more of her tears. If he could banish her sorrow, he would do it in an instant.

"Not another one," said Lynden, from inside the garden. "What happened this time?"

Orlando passed under the arch and his gaze connected with Monk. The man had turned out to be a swift, capable killer. When Walter had grabbed the axe and made to throw it at Orlando and Susanna, Monk had slit his throat cleanly. If Orlando didn't already know it was Monk's first kill, he would have discovered it from his reaction afterward. He'd looked ill.

Orlando could sympathize. It may have been some years since his first kill, but he remembered it vividly. And if he hadn't, killing his first woman today would have been enough of a reminder. He still couldn't unknot his tangled feelings on the matter of Margaret's death, and he doubted he ever would.

"It doesn't get easier," Orlando told him, "but you will grow used to how it feels and find a way to justify it to yourself." He clapped Monk on the shoulder.

Monk looked down at Cowdrey's body. "He tried to kill Lady Lynden," he said. It wasn't quite true—it had been impossible to know if it was Susanna or Orlando he wanted to hit—but Monk was right to tell Lynden that she was the target. His sympathy probably wouldn't stretch to an attempt on Orlando's life.

"That's the problem with beauty," Lynden said on a sigh, turning away and wrinkling his nose. "It breeds jealousy. She needs to be married. It'll make everyone's life easier, including her own. Her father will be able to die in peace knowing a husband is taking care of her again."

"I'm not sure she'd agree with you," Orlando said. He wasn't sure he agreed with him either, but there was a logic in his words that couldn't be denied. He wished it wasn't so.

"I suppose it'll be up to me to find her another husband," Lynden said. "With Walter gone, she'll need to look out of the parish to find an eligible man. I know a knighted gentleman who may soon be in need of a new wife. His current one is on her deathbed. He already has children too. Susanna might like that." He nodded, pleased with himself.

"She doesn't want to marry anyone," Orlando said, dully. "Nor does she have to."

Lynden snorted. "Don't be ridiculous. She does have to. Look what happens when a woman like her doesn't have a husband." He waved at Cowdrey's body without looking at it. "Utter chaos."

Orlando's fists closed at his sides. He needed to work off some excess tension and thumping Lynden would make him feel better. He stepped toward him, but Monk caught his arm.

"Not now," Monk said quietly. He nodded at the arched entrance. "We have company."

Hughe and Cole stood just inside the walled garden, taking in the scene. Cole appeared unaffected by the sight of the body, but Hughe gasped and pressed his long fingers to his mouth. He wrinkled his nose and turned away. It was almost the identical way that Lynden had reacted and Orlando would have laughed if he was in a better mood.

"Good day," Lynden said, bowing. "Lord Oxley isn't it?"

Hughe nodded and flapped a hand at the body. "Is that...blood?"

"I'm afraid so," Lynden said. "There's been an unfortunate accident. Or two."

Hughe made a gagging sound in his throat. "Perhaps I'll return at a better time. Come, Cole."

"Wait!" Lynden trotted over to him and bowed again. "Come inside for refreshments. Stoneleigh's parlor is warm and contains no dead bodies."

"You might want to avoid the hall, however," Orlando said.

Cole, still dressed in the disguise of fat servant, raised an eyebrow at him.

"Ugh," Hughe said. "Perhaps I'll remain out here in the fresh air."

"The lady of the house, my cousin by marriage, would be very pleased to have you call upon her. I think if you meet her you'll want to stay a while longer, my lord Oxley. She's quite...charming."

Orlando could hit him before anyone could stop him. It would be done in the blink of an eye.

"Ah, yes, The Beauty," Hughe said. "I've heard of her. Perhaps you could bring her out here to me. I'd like to inspect her."

Lynden bowed elaborately and backed out through the arch. "I'll fetch her now, my lord."

Once he was out of earshot, Orlando turned Hughe around to face him. "Inspect her? She's not a horse."

Hughe cleared his throat and raised both brows at Monk.

"Don't mind me," Monk said. "I'm practically one of the family."

Orlando introduced them. "I think he could replace Rafe well enough," he said about Monk.

"No one could replace Rafe," Cole said. Of all of them, he seemed to feel the loss of their friend the most, which took Orlando by surprise. Cole was the loner of the band. He never discussed his past, never let his feelings show. When it came to killing, he did it without emotion or regret. In their quiet moments, they shared their hopes for the future, but not Cole. Perhaps he didn't have any.

"That's glowing praise coming from Orlando," Hughe said to Monk. "I'm staying at The Plough until tomorrow. Come and see me if you're up for adventure."

"And a little bit of killing," Cole added. "It's not easy. The training alone is rigorous and Hughe is a cruel task-master when he wants to be."

Monk laughed. "Him?"

"Don't let the lace and feathers fool you," Orlando said. "He may look like a dandy, but his heart is made of impenetrable rock."

"And I have the strength to match," Hughe said lightly.

"Do you think you have the stomach for it?" Cole asked.

"That depends," Monk said.

"On what?"

"How much is the pay?"

"Probably more than you've ever seen in your lifetime," Hughe said.

"Then I'll take it."

"You think money will buy you respectability?" Cole asked darkly. "Trust me, it does not."

"That's what everyone who *has* money says," Monk said, equally dark.

And with that simple observation, Monk had quite possibly struck a trait of Cole's that Orlando had never seen. He would have a lot of money saved from his work with the Guild, but hardly enough to be considered wealthy, not like Hughe. Yet he gave money away at every village, or sometimes he simply gambled it and once, left some behind. Money never concerned him. Did he have more than he was willing to admit to?

While Monk and Cole glared at each other, Orlando confronted Hughe. "Now that you have another member," he said, "I don't feel so bad to be leaving."

"What?" Hughe blurted out.

Cole swore. "Not you too."

"I broke the pact. I had to tell Susanna."

Cole sighed. Hughe dropped his head, so that Orlando couldn't read his face.

"I don't understand," Hughe said, finally looking up. He looked drawn, exhausted. "Why?"

Orlando shrugged. How could he explain the need to tell Susanna everything? It had been a compulsion, and in the end, there had been no choice. If he hadn't told her about himself, he might have ended up as mad as Cowdrey. "Because she deserved the truth from me, and I simply couldn't lie to her anymore."

Hughe closed his eyes and drew in a deep breath. He opened them again and Orlando was a little saddened to see the bleakness in their depths. "Very well. But you can't stay with us. Your identity has been compromised."

"I know." Orlando clasped the arm Hughe offered.

Cole shook his head and stalked off, but he got no further than the arch and returned. He clapped Orlando on the shoulder then quickly embraced him. "I always knew you were a bloody fool."

"Goodbye, Brother," Orlando said. "Stay out of trouble."

"Unlikely." Hughe also gave Orlando a parting embrace then they both left.

Lynden rushed across the gravel toward them, waving his hands. "Stop! My lord, where are you going? You haven't met Susanna yet!"

"Another time," Hughe called out then spurred his horse onward.

Lynden puffed heavily as he watched them go. "She would have been ready in a few minutes. If only he'd waited."

"She wanted to come out and meet him?" Orlando asked, more disturbed by the thought than he should be.

"No. But I could have coerced her."

Monk gripped Orlando's shoulder, hard. "Help me get the bodies onto the cart. I'll drive them back to Cowdrey Farm."

"I wonder who inherits," Lynden said. "Wonder if he'll want to sell."

"Are you in a position to buy?" Orlando asked.

"I might be, but not all of it."

"Leave the land that abuts Stoneleigh to Susanna."

"She cannot afford it."

"Not yet."

Monk gazed at the felled orange trees. "Not for quite some time. Even if you do sell the products in her stables, the remaining trees won't produce enough of a harvest to live off let alone make a profit."

"Don't worry about that," Orlando said. "Just promise me now, Lynden, before a witness, that you'll leave some of the Cowdrey land for Susanna if it's offered for sale. If you don't, I'll have to keep that letter."

"Er, uh, right. Very well. Agreed. God's blood, I never knew how much of a fool my cousin was until I spoke to Whipple and learned of his treachery."

"You don't plan on continuing the communication?"

"No! Good grief, I want to rise but not that way. I quite like my head on top of my shoulders, thank you. It sets my ruff off nicely. I also like my estate. Sutton Hall was never meant to be mine, but now that I have it, I want to keep it. Whipple told me it would have been confiscated if Phillip's treason were discovered." He made an O with his mouth and blew out a slow breath. "It has been interesting having you here, Mr. Holt, but I can't pretend I'll be sorry to see you leave. The sooner you're gone, the sooner life can return to normal again."

"Normal," Orlando echoed. "I have no idea what you could possibly mean."

CHAPTER 18

*H*ow was Susanna going to tell her father? It was heartbreaking enough seeing those beautiful trees lying on the ground, but it would be nothing compared to his reaction. He'd loved his wife and after her death, he'd cared for the trees while Susanna lived elsewhere. They were a living reminder of her mother's nurturing soul.

Gone.

Susanna wondered if she would ever stop crying, and if she did, would the ache in her heart end too? She doubted it.

"Here, m'lady, take this," said Bessie, passing a cup to Susanna.

Susanna took it between both hands. The warmth thawed her numb fingers and the strong spicy aroma cleared her head a little. She sipped and the mulled wine burned as it went down. Cook had made it stronger than usual and it banished her tears but not the sorrow.

"Thank you," she said to the three anxious faces. "I'll be all right. Don't worry about me."

"But we do worry," Bessie said, sitting beside her.

"Them poor lovely trees," Cook said on a sigh.

"We've still got two," Hendricks said, falsely cheerful.

"Aye, there'll be enough oranges on two trees to fill up some of the marmalade jars."

Some but not many. Susanna gave them a weak smile. "Thank you. All of you."

She listened as the servants prepared dinner and chattered about plans for the garden. She appreciated their attempts to lift her spirits, but it was only when Orlando entered the kitchen that she realized she hadn't been paying attention and had no idea how much time had passed.

"Monk is taking the bodies to Cowdrey Farm," he said from the doorway. "And Lynden returned to the Hall."

"Thank you."

"The rushes in your great hall will need changing."

"We'll do it," Bessie said quickly. When neither of the other servants moved, she grabbed the hand of each and dragged them out.

"Me too?" Cook asked, brandishing her wooden spoon.

"Aye, you too."

Orlando slid onto the bench seat beside Susanna and took the cup from her. He set it down on the table then grasped both her hands in his. "Are you all right?"

She nodded. "A little shaken. Thank you, Orlando. You saved my life. Margaret would have..." She bit her wobbly lip. There would be no more tears. Not over Margaret or Walter.

He squeezed her hands and kissed the knuckles. His eyelids fluttered closed and he breathed deeply. "Thank God you're all right," he murmured. "I couldn't bear it—"

"Don't." She withdrew her hands. Listening to his words would undo her again, and she had to stay strong for what came next. "When are you leaving?"

The question seemed to startle him. He blinked rapidly. "Soon. But I will return."

"Why?"

"Because I'm going to help you plant new trees." He looked at her as if she'd lost her mind. "First things first. I'm going to

London, and I'm taking all of your marmalades and succades with me. I'm sure Lynden can lend me a cart for the journey."

Now she really was dazed. "I don't understand."

"I'm going to find shopkeepers to stock them. Not just this batch, but any future harvests too. Correspondence will take too long. It'll be easier to visit them in person. Indeed, I have one fellow in mind. His customers include maids from Whitehall Palace. Succades and marmalades made from exotic fruits are precisely what the queen and her ladies demand. All of the nobility will be serving your produce to their guests soon enough."

"You know a great deal about London ladies."

"I've studied their buying habits long enough." He smiled and her heart cracked. He was so handsome. So kind.

And such a good liar.

What if he took her products and never returned? What if he sold them and didn't bring back her money? It felt traitorous to think such a thing, yet she couldn't help it. The man had proved himself worthy when it came to saving her life, but as to trusting him...no.

"I can't let you do it, Orlando."

"Why not?"

"I...I just can't."

He shook his head, dismissing her. "Listen. I know you want to do everything on your own, but sometimes you have to let others help."

"I cannot accept any more help from you."

He stared at her for a long time then finally looked down at the bench between them. He blew out a breath, then another. "Give me a sample then. A few jars of each. I promise you I'll find someone to stock the rest. Until we sell all of it, you can live off my money. Hughe paid well, and I've had nothing to spend it on all these years. I sent it to my brother with instruction for him to use it as he saw fit. There may be some left, or there may not be." He shrugged as if it didn't matter.

"You're offering it to me? Good lord, no! I don't want it. You may need it if Hughe throws you out of the Guild."

"He already has."

"Then I certainly cannot accept your money now."

"You can and you will. Susanna, you need it to rebuild this place. The money from the oranges will not be enough, especially as next year's productivity will be down severely with the loss of the trees. It'll be hardly enough for you to live off, let alone fix what needs fixing."

"Orlando, stop it! Stop this at once." She rose and paced the kitchen. "I cannot accept your money, or your help. I am not your responsibility, nor is Stoneleigh." She put up her hands when he began to speak. "I'm very sorry you're not working for Hughe anymore, but you must find work elsewhere. Not here. I can't pay you and I don't think your presence is...in either of our best interests. Not anymore." There. She'd said it. It was a weight off her mind.

So why did she feel like her heart had been gouged out, leaving behind a hollow cavity?

Tears stung her eyes again and she turned to go. Orlando caught her and swung her around. The blue of his eyes flashed bright and fierce with an intensity she'd never seen before. "Would it make any difference if we were married?"

Everything went still. The blood froze in her veins and her heart ceased to tick. "Is that a proposal?" she whispered.

His smile was lopsided and devilish. "Yes."

"But..." She shook her head, tried to clear it. "Are you sure?"

"I'm sure. I want to stay here, with you. I've had enough of killing. Stoneleigh has felt more like a home in this last week than anywhere. Because you're here, Susanna, and I want to be with you." He cupped her face and she almost wept again.

"Orlando..." She fought the tears but one escaped. He wiped it away with his thumb. "Orlando, I can't have children."

"I know. And I don't care."

"You say that now..." She shook her head and moved out of his reach. It wasn't about the children, not really.

"Why not let me decide that for myself?" There was no smile in his voice but she didn't look up. She couldn't face him.

"Please," she whispered, turning away. She didn't want him to see her tears. There was only so much of his kindness she could take and remain strong. "We are not getting married, Orlando. Not now and not when you return."

"Susanna?" His low, rumbling voice came from close behind her. He said nothing else but she could hear his hard breathing, feel him tense as he waited.

"I have made terrible mistakes in the past," she said, squeezing everything within her to hold in the tears and keep herself from shattering. "All of them were because I listened to my heart and not my head. I ignored the warning signs and ignored common sense. I won't make that mistake again. Not with a man who is a liar."

He didn't answer for a long time and she almost turned around, even though she knew he was still there. She could feel his presence as powerfully as if he were in her arms.

"I am not like them," he finally said. "I've lied to you, yes, but never with the intent of hurting you. Not after I...got to know you."

She turned around because what she had to say must be said to his face, not with her back turned like a coward. "How can I be sure, Orlando? How do I know you're not lying now and will run off with my orange products but not return with the money? How do I know you do not want Stoneleigh for yourself, or you simply want to possess me like John and Phillip did? How do I know you wouldn't change after we wed, and become a different man, the man you've buried underneath all that charm? How can I convince my head as well as my heart?" She was rambling but didn't care. The words spewed out of her and she couldn't have stopped them even if she'd wanted to.

"You have to trust me."

"Why should I when you've given me no cause?"

"I have, Susanna. I have."

She braced herself against the tide of emotion welling inside her like a flooded river. "No, Orlando, I can't trust you because you're lying again. You don't want to wed me."

"I do!"

She shook her head. "I think your offer was made as an afterthought, when I said I cannot accept your money or your help."

He said nothing, and it wasn't until that moment that she knew for certain she was right. He didn't want to marry her, he merely felt obligated. "I'm going to help you rebuild, Susanna. I *will* return in the spring. I promise you that. I care for you deeply. I won't turn my back on you now."

She drew in a shuddering breath. Dared herself to believe. She *wanted* to believe him. He'd done so much for her already. His help in the garden had been invaluable and his dealings with Jeffrey, Walter and Monk had always been done with her best interests at heart. Why would he do all that only to steal from her now? Why would he make promises he didn't plan on keeping?

"Very well," she said. "You may take all of my marmalades and succades with you."

He let out a breath. "You won't regret it, Susanna." He clasped her shoulders, the gentle pressure reassuring, easing some of the tension within her. "And I will return in the spring with your money. That is my promise to you." He let go of her and walked out of the kitchen.

She sat back down on the bench seat, buried her face in her hands and tried not to hope too hard. The money would be a welcome relief, but not as much as Orlando's return. She didn't think she could bear not being with him again.

* * *

1 Month Later

"THANK YOU. I APPRECIATE YOUR HELP," Orlando said to his brother sitting across from him at the dining table. It was decorated with laurel and ivy leaves for Christmas and a large fire warmed the room. The children had already run off to play with their gifts, but May, Thomas, and Orlando remained seated, picking at their feast.

Thomas saluted Orlando with his wine glass. "Pleased I could do something since it seemed so important to you." The grocer Orlando had in mind to stock Susanna's orange stuffs had died last year, so Thomas had found another, one who agreed to give free samples to the palace maids. Before long, the court ladies demanded the exotic delights and orders flooded in. All of Susanna's marmalades and succades had been sold.

Orlando hadn't been sure what to expect from Thomas after all this time. Resentment? Anger? He'd displayed all those emotions back then, but now, he just seemed happy to have Orlando back.

But it was difficult to tell for sure. The wound that had left a deep, ragged scar running from the corner of his eye down to his mouth had rendered the right side of his face immobile. He'd got the scar in the attack.

The attack that had been Orlando's fault.

"If there's something I can do for you in return, please name it," Orlando said.

"There is actually." Thomas licked his thumb and pointed a quail bone at Orlando. "You can come back to work for me. I'm in need of a good man. Someone I can trust."

Trust again, rearing its head. Strange how his brother trusted him too much after he'd caused him so much trouble, yet Susanna didn't trust him enough when he'd saved her life.

Ah, Susanna. God he missed her. It had been weeks since he'd left Stoneleigh. The roads had been poor and it had taken him longer than expected to arrive home.

Home. No, not that. Not now. The house had May's stamp all over it, and his brother was clearly the master. There was no place for Orlando there.

"I can't," he said. "I'll be leaving in the spring."

"You can choose what you want to do this time," Thomas went on. The left side of his mouth, the good side, lifted in a smile. It was the first Thomas had given Orlando since his return and it was a relief to see it. "Perhaps work with the customers. You had them eating out of your hand as I recall, back before..." He set the quail bone down and picked up a cloth to wipe his hands.

"Before you left," May finished for him. She clasped the pearl and agate pendant hanging from a gold chain around her neck. "We really would like you to return to work in the family business, Orlando. Thomas...needs your help."

"Oh?" Orlando looked from one to the other but neither met his gaze.

"Times have been difficult of late," Thomas said. "Having you work beside me again would be invaluable."

"I can't," Orlando said.

"Because of what happened? Orlando, I don't blame you for this." He tapped the scar with his finger.

"You used to."

"We don't anymore," May said. "It wasn't your fault. And you shouldn't blame yourself either. Orlando, we need you now. You were so good with the customers, so natural. It was never the same after you left, we never had quite as many orders."

"I'm not really sure how you did it." Thomas shook his head. "But there's no denying the figures."

"I hated it," Orlando said. "Hated every moment of the work." How could he make them understand? "All I wanted to do was get away, anywhere. I needed to *do* something."

"You can have more responsibility this time and more to do," Thomas said. "Indeed, I'll let you do what you want, work when you want. Just...come back."

Orlando drained his glass, closing his eyes as he did so. Hell. Of all the ill-timing. "I've promised Susanna I'd return in the spring. I can only help you until then."

"Is she the orange grower in Hampshire?"

Orlando nodded.

"Are you going to marry her?" May asked.

Orlando studied his trencher and Susanna's words echoed through him: *We are not getting married, Orlando. Not now and not when you return.*

"No," he said. "I'm not going to marry her."

"If you're not going to wed her, you should forget about her." May touched the pendant nestled against her bodice. "Please, Orlando, stay."

"Don't beg, May. He's made his decision." Thomas rose and left without a farewell.

May watched him go and sighed. "Thomas hasn't been the same since that day. He worries more. He doesn't trust his workers like he used to, doesn't trust anyone. The business is suffering because he's trying to do everything, and he works harder than ever." She closed her hand around the pendant and leaned forward. "You owe us, Orlando. For what you brought down on this house, on Thomas. Your loyalty should lie here, with your family, and not with a woman you're not going to wed."

She too left and Orlando sat alone in his brother's dining room while his brother's servants cleared the dishes away. His heart felt leaden, his head woolly. He finally had a chance to atone for what he'd done to Thomas and May, what he'd caused to be done to them. And Susanna had refused his offer of marriage. May was right. Orlando's responsibilities lay with his family, and he only had one of those.

Ah, Susanna, forgive me.

He would send her the money owing her and a message that he would come when he was able, perhaps in the summer.

But summers were a busy time with cargo-laden ships coming and going, and autumn would be little better. Indeed, most of the year would be busy, and Orlando planned on being as involved as possible. There would be no growing bored this time, no retreating to alehouses and wenches for amusement. He would do his utmost to help his brother. It was the least he could do.

He thought about what Susanna would say and how she

would look when she read his letter. A shudder wracked him and he scrubbed his hands down his face. His whole body groaned with an ache so deep it hurt worse than any wound he'd ever received.

Why did doing the right thing feel so utterly and miserably wrong?

* * *

Four Months Later

"You're a difficult man to catch," Rafe Fletcher said, snatching the paperwork out of Orlando's hand. He seemed to have appeared out of nowhere in the warehouse. Or perhaps not nowhere. Orlando had been too intent on checking his customer's order to notice him.

"What brings you here on this freezing afternoon?" Orlando asked, taking the papers back.

"You promised me we'd go for a drink."

"I haven't forgotten." He waved in two dock workers carrying a crate between them and indicated they should deposit it with the others stacked against the far wall. He dipped the pen into the inkwell on his small desk and marked the crate off his list. "I've been busy, Rafe, but I promise I'll join you soon. Perhaps on Saturday."

Rafe removed the papers once more. "We're going now." He beckoned Orlando's assistant over and handed him the papers.

The assistant looked to Orlando. Orlando sighed. "I'll be back later." He walked out of the warehouse with Rafe, past the cranes and sailors and the dock workers rolling barrels and lifting crates. It already grew dark and they would be making their way home soon, probably while Orlando headed back to the warehouse in search of something more to do. "One drink only," he said. "I'm very busy."

"Too busy to have more than one drink with an old friend? Or are your worried that going to taverns might lead you back to your old ways?"

Orlando glanced at him sideways. "No. I know I won't start a fight by bedding the wrong sort of woman. I have no desire to bed any sort of woman." Except Susanna.

Hell. He hadn't thought about her in a long time. A few minutes at least.

"Sounds like you're in dire need of a drink after all," Rafe said.

In the Golden Mermaid's taproom they ordered ales and sat in the corner. Most of the drinkers sang along with a lute being played badly by a toothless old sea dog in the corner, and other men planted kisses on wenches attempting to entice them to an upstairs room for a shilling. Orlando shut them out, but that only led to him thinking about Susanna and what she'd be doing. Preparing her garden for spring, no doubt. Hopefully she'd used some of the money he'd sent her to buy more orange trees from her supplier.

Did she think of him? Did she stay awake at night regretting her decision not to marry him as much as he regretted not fulfilling his promise to return?

Breaking that promise clawed at him every day.

Yet Thomas wanted him. Susanna did not.

"So who is she?" Rafe asked.

"What?" Orlando frowned at his friend sitting on the stool across from him.

Rafe chuckled and shook his head. "Who's the woman who's got you pining like a dog locked out of the house?"

"Susanna." Orlando groaned. "And don't talk about being locked out of houses. It brings back bad memories."

"Susanna, eh? Tell me about her."

"There's nothing to tell."

"You never were a good liar, Orlando."

"That's not what I've been told."

Rafe folded his arms and regarded him. "You're my friend,

Orlando, and I don't like seeing you like this. That's why I'm going to give you some advice."

"I don't want your advice nor do I need it."

"Go back to your Susanna."

"I am. I promised her I would, so I am." God's truth, he would do what he could to fulfill his promise. He had to.

"When?"

Orlando stared into his cup. "As soon as Thomas can spare me."

"And what will you do when you get there?"

"Help her repair her house, her garden." He shrugged. "Whatever is needed."

"But not marry her," Rafe said.

"She doesn't want me."

"Doesn't she? Or does she just want to know that you're committed to *her* and not the house? Or that you won't turn around and blame her for trapping you into a life you may one day find dull?"

"Know everything about women now do you?"

"More than you, my friend." Rafe laughed. "Never thought that'd happen, eh? You're supposed to be the expert."

"Shut it."

"Take my advice or leave it, I don't care. I'm just trying to help you because I don't like seeing you a blathering mess."

Orlando straightened. "I'm not a mess."

Rafe snorted and lifted the cup to his lips and drank. "Thanks for the company, as miserable as it was," he said, thumping the empty cup down on the table. "I have to go. Write to us and we'll come visit you in the country. Lizzy would love Hampshire. The baby too when it's born."

"Can't stay away from her for long, can you?"

"No, nor do I want to. That's the thing about being in love, Orlando, you don't want to stay away. Ever. You want to be with her all the time. Every moment of every day. If you're not holding her in your arms, you're thinking about holding her. That's what love is. It's bloody inconvenient but there's nothing much you can do about it, except tell her and hold her whenever you have the chance. Just *be* with her, wed or not."

Orlando closed his eyes but it felt like the floor was shifting beneath him so he opened them again. He felt drunk but he'd not even finished one drink. "Bloody hell."

"What?"

Orlando met his friend's steady gaze. "You've just described how I feel." He wanted Susanna. He wanted to live with her, be with her, love her. He couldn't imagine a life without her. There was no point in chasing freedom when everything he wanted was at Stoneleigh. Being without Susanna was no kind of freedom at all. It would be a miserable hell.

Rafe slapped him on the back. "So you're in love. I suggest you go to Susanna and tell her. If she doesn't agree to marry you, make another arrangement that suits you both. You're a difficult man to remove and she'll probably give in eventually." He laughed.

"You're all kindness."

Rafe hauled him to his feet and clasped Orlando's shoulders. "Goodbye, my friend, and don't worry. Being in love isn't the end of the world." The hard planes of his face softened. "Indeed, I am having the best adventure of all."

Orlando sank down onto the stool again. "I can't leave. Thomas needs me here. I owe him."

"What happened back then was not your fault." Rafe's voice was unusually soft but still compelling. "Believe me, you cannot change what happened, but you should not pay for it for the rest of your life. Your brother is a man with his own family and he must take care of them on his own. Susanna is your family now, in all but name. I can see it in your eyes. You hate not being with her. If I were you, I'd do whatever it took to get her back, even if that meant letting my brother down."

"Thank you." Orlando stood and embraced him. "Give my love to your Lizzy."

Rafe drew him away. "He's not your responsibility any more,

Orlando. Understand?" He clasped Orlando's arm in farewell then strode off through the boisterous crowd.

Orlando followed him out some time later with two certainties: One, he'd drunk too much, and two, Susanna was worth any sacrifice.

* * *

THE SAPLINGS HAD TRAVELED WELL. Sir Francis Carew had kindly sent three of his young orange trees when Susanna had written of the disaster that had befallen Stoneleigh. As a favor to her late mother, he didn't ask for anything in return. The money Orlando had sent had bought three more from France, but they hadn't arrived yet. There'd been enough to hire a reed-thin lad to help too.

"Ahhh," said her father from his chair by the orange trees. "Can you smell that, my dear?"

She breathed deeply, her face turned to the bold afternoon sun. "Spring. My favorite time of year."

"Mine too. The scent of blossoms and new growth never fails to make me feel young again. It reminds me of your mother," he added wistfully. "Come here, my dear, and hold your old father's hand."

She did and followed his gaze to the lad digging in the garden bed. He grunted a lot and sweat poured from his brow but he kept at the task without complaint.

"He's a good worker," her father said.

"Yes."

"But not as good as Holt."

"No."

Farley squinted up at her. "You miss him."

She smiled and patted his hand. The skin stretched across the back felt as dry and thin as an autumn leaf. "He was a good worker, like you said."

"He was more than that to you. Don't deny it, Susanna. I might be old, but I still have eyes and ears. You think you hide things from me but you can't." His eyes did indeed seem clear and clever today, as if he'd seen into her heart and knew all her secrets. Perhaps he did.

"I don't know what you mean." She withdrew her hand and ignored the lump lodged in her chest. It was always there, ever since Orlando left, but it was only during the moments when she thought about him that sadness threatened to overwhelm her.

He had promised to return, yet spring was well under way and he had not come back. He'd sent the money and a letter to explain the situation he'd discovered upon his return to London. She understood. Of course she did. He had a duty to his brother and none to her. She'd refused his offer of marriage after all. It was her own fault.

Yet she had never stopped waiting and watching. Never stopped hoping.

The niggling thought that she'd been right to refuse him lingered. He'd spent long enough at Stoneleigh, long enough to need to travel again. In time, she suspected he would leave London too, but she doubted he would return to her. He was the sort who needed to move ever forward, never back.

It was best to stay active and not let herself think beyond the day's tasks otherwise melancholy would set in. If she thought about the future she was likely to burst into tears and she'd shed enough over the last five months to drown in.

"A little deeper," she said, kneeling on the ground near where the lad dug. It was the next best thing to digging the hole herself. "Before we put the sapling in—" She stopped. Someone was whistling outside the wall. Her heart ground to a halt then restarted with a vengeance.

He came back.

"Who's that whistling out of tune?" her father asked, turning in his chair. The blanket slipped off his lap as he half-rose.

"Out of tune? Mr. Farley, you wound me. I rather thought I was a good whistler." Orlando stood beneath the ivy-covered arch, smiling. Susanna couldn't tear her gaze away. He was beautiful with his merry eyes and maddening dimples. The sight of him made her want to alternately weep and laugh and swoon, all at once.

"Holt!" her father said. "Susanna, it's Mr. Holt. I told you he'd return."

"Good afternoon, Susanna," Orlando said, his smile drifting a little.

"Good afternoon," she said.

"Have you been well? Did your arm heal?"

"Quite well and yes it did. And you?"

He simply shrugged. "I see you've found yourself some help in my absence. I'm glad."

The lad gulped audibly. He'd stopped digging, and she indicated he should keep going.

"He's been a Godsend," she said.

"Then you should keep him on."

It was like walking through a briar patch without boots and trying to avoid the thorns. If Orlando wanted her to keep the lad, that meant he wasn't staying to help. She wouldn't be sad. She'd known all along that he'd just pass through, if that. But she still wanted to cry. Perhaps she would let the tears flow tonight when she allowed herself a few minutes to think and remember and dream. Still, it was best if she didn't speak, just until she knew her voice wouldn't break.

Her father slapped the arms of his chair and pushed himself up. Orlando went to aid him, but Farley waved him away. "You two have things to discuss." He gave Susanna a sharp glare.

"Do you need help getting to the house, sir?" Orlando asked.

"No, I can walk now that it's spring. I always feel better in the spring. It's the best time of year. New life and all that." He patted Orlando's arm and beckoned to the lad. "Take the chair inside."

Young and old left the walled garden and Susanna was alone with Orlando. She didn't know how to begin so she said the first thing that came into her head.

"You came back."

"I said I would." He cocked his head to the side. "You doubted me?"

She lifted one shoulder. "I...didn't think one thing or the other."

The smile he gave her was a typical Orlando Holt smile—an intriguing mix of imp and rogue. When she'd first met him, it had irritated her. Now she wanted to kiss it.

"Did you receive the money I sent?" he asked.

"Yes, and thank you for introducing me to your customer. He has already written and asked for whatever crop we can produce this year. I mean it, Orlando, thank you. I'm sorry I doubted you."

He pulled her to him, slamming her against his body. "I'll accept a kiss as an apology."

She made a small sound of protest. "Not so hard."

He stepped away and held her at arm's length. "Did I hurt you?"

She shook her head.

He frowned. His gaze moved lower, to her stomach. "Susanna..." Lately she'd returned to wearing women's clothes and he touched her bodice at her waist. His jaw went slack. "Susanna..." he whispered, wonder in his voice. He flattened his palm against her belly. "You're...with child."

She bit the inside of her lip but it wobbled, darn it. "Yes. I'm going to have your baby in about four months."

"But...you can't."

She lifted one shoulder. "It seems I can after all. I was going to write to you in London." When she found the right words.

"Your father...he knows?"

"I haven't told him, but I suspect he's guessed. I was going to tell him once my clothes no longer hid the bump. Bessie, Cook, and Hendricks guessed long ago."

"Hiding something like this from them would have been impossible." He laughed and threw his arms around her. It felt delicious and warm to be wrapped up in him again, and a riot of sensations swamped her, chief among them relief and sadness in equal measure.

He removed her hat and buried his face in her hair. "Ah, my sweetheart, I've missed you so much." He kissed her forehead and stroked his thumbs across her cheeks. "We'll marry as soon as the bans are read."

"Orlando," she said, gently extricating herself. If she didn't say it now, she may never say it, and it had to be said. "Orlando, I cannot marry you."

His smiled faded and a crease formed above the bridge of his nose. "Why not?"

"Because nothing has changed."

"Nonsense. Everything has changed! We're going to have a baby." The frown deepened. "Susanna...don't. Don't push me away. Not now. Surely the baby changes how you feel."

She turned away and lowered her head. Despite her resolve, her tears slipped down her cheeks unchecked. She felt him come up behind her but he didn't touch her.

"Is it because I broke my promise and didn't return immediately? I'm sorry for that. Thomas needed me and I...I thought I could atone for what happened years ago. But I can't. What's done is done. Thomas needs to be strong now. I did give him a lot of the money I saved. Hopefully he can hire some good workers to help him. I'm not going back, Susanna. I'm staying here, with you."

"It doesn't change how I feel," she said.

"I don't understand."

"You felt obligated before you left, just as you felt obligated to help your brother." She swung round and was struck by the misery etched into every line of his face. She forged on. "You think promising to take care of me, as if I'm some kind of responsibility, is what I want?"

"You *are* my responsibility, Susanna, whether you like it or not. You and our baby."

"I don't want to be your *duty*, Orlando!"

"Let me finish. You are my responsibility because I love you."

Her breathing sounded loud in the silence, echoing between her ears. "Love?" she murmured.

"Yes," he said, a tentative half-smile curving his lips.

"No."

His smiled slipped off. "What?"

She folded her arms across the swell of her belly. "Love is not for the likes of you, Orlando."

He stepped toward her but she held her hands up, blocking him.

"Whether you are or aren't, we cannot marry. Not because of the baby, not because you want to help me, and not because you wish to protect me. My reasons for denying you haven't changed. I will not tie you to me, or to our child. Marriage would be a slow death for a man like you. An honorable, good man who would fulfill his obligations when all he really wanted was to be free." She swallowed hard. "And I couldn't bear to see you turn into the sort of man I despise because of me."

"Susanna, stop it. You know nothing of what I want, or what I need."

"You said so yourself. You need your freedom lest you grow bored and cause trouble as you did for your brother years ago."

"Susanna, listen to me." He gripped her arms and lowered his head so that his intense gaze was level with hers. It held her rooted to the spot. "*You* are my freedom," he said. "Not the Guild, not wandering the world and not this baby. It's you."

A great shudder wracked her. "Me?"

He nodded. "I made up my mind before leaving London that I would return here and do my utmost to make you my wife. If you refuse me, I'm staying anyway."

"You...you will? Even if we don't wed? Even if I don't want you as my lover?"

"Not being intimate with you would kill me, but I defy you to resist my charms for long." He gave her his infamous lop-sided smile. "My charms are extensive, I'll have you know."

She gave a half-sob, half-laugh. "I know."

"I don't want to go anywhere else, Susanna." He was suddenly serious again. "Why would I, when you're here? Wherever you are is where I want to be, even if that's the same place for the rest of our lives. I could never grow bored with you." He pecked the end of her nose. "You're such a complicated creature it would take me a lifetime to discover all your secrets. What greater adventure is there?"

She blinked up at him for a long time, trying to determine if he told her the truth. He was such a good liar. So very, very good.

"You don't trust me," he said heavily.

"I do." It was the truth. She did trust him, with all her heart. He'd come back as promised—there was no greater evidence that he spoke the truth. "But why the change? Five months ago you were afraid of becoming a wastrel and bringing ill tidings to your family's door. Are you no longer afraid of that?"

"I'm not. I spent a lot of time with Thomas while in London. He forgave me for what happened that awful night. May did too. He said he'd come to understand me a little better over the years, and understood my need to be active. That's why when he asked me to stay this time, he offered me the freedom to do as I pleased, to work where I wanted to work, and have more responsibility. So I did. I learned every aspect of the business and I realized that I could do it and not grow bored. I could stay there for as long as I wanted and there'd always be something different to do, if I chose to do it. The thing is, I chose not to. I chose you. I *want* you."

"Oh," she whispered. Her throat was too tight to say any more.

He'd chosen her.

"When I left, Thomas gave me his blessing. He also gave me some advice. He told me to keep active and engage in something I enjoy to stay out of trouble." He leaned in and kissed her lightly on the lips. It triggered an ache, low in her belly.

"And what do you enjoy?"

She felt him smile. It was pure wickedness.

"Ah, well then." She stretched her arms around him and he responded by holding her gently. "It's fortunate that you and I have the same interests."

He kissed her. Thoroughly. It took her breath away and made her want to lie with him, right there on the earth.

"Come," he said, taking her hand. "I want to ask your father for your hand before you change your mind. Then I'd better ask Hendricks."

"Very wise. But I'm not going to change my mind."

"Oh?"

"Why would I when your..." She dropped her gaze to his groin. "...charm is so appealing."

He looped his arm around her waist and hugged her to his side. "Just as long as you never grow bored of my charm."

"Don't worry. There's no chance I'll grow tired of *your* charm. It is rather extensive, so I've been told."

He tipped his head back and laughed.

LOOK OUT FOR

The Rebel
The second ASSASSINS GUILD novel.

THE REBEL sees Assassins Guild member Cole lose his memory and forget the terrible events of his past, only to fall in love and remember everything at the worst possible moment.

To be notified when C.J. has a new release, sign up to her newsletter. Send an email to cjarcher.writes@gmail.com

A MESSAGE FROM THE AUTHOR

I hope you enjoyed reading this book as much as I enjoyed writing it. As an independent author, getting the word out about my book is vital to its success, so if you liked this book please consider telling your friends and writing a review at the store where you purchased it. If you would like to be contacted when I release a new book, subscribe to my newsletter at http://cjarcher.com/contact-cj/newsletter/. You will only be contacted when I have a new book out.

ALSO BY C.J. ARCHER

SERIES WITH 2 OR MORE BOOKS

After The Rift

Glass and Steele

The Ministry of Curiosities Series

The Emily Chambers Spirit Medium Trilogy

The 1st Freak House Trilogy

The 2nd Freak House Trilogy

The 3rd Freak House Trilogy

The Assassins Guild Series

Lord Hawkesbury's Players Series

The Witchblade Chronicles

SINGLE TITLES NOT IN A SERIES

Courting His Countess

Surrender

Redemption

The Mercenary's Price

ABOUT THE AUTHOR

C.J. Archer has loved history and books for as long as she can remember and feels fortunate that she found a way to combine the two. She spent her early childhood in the dramatic beauty of outback Queensland, Australia, but now lives in suburban Melbourne with her husband, two children and a mischievous black & white cat named Coco.

Subscribe to C.J.'s newsletter through her website to be notified when she releases a new book, as well as get access to exclusive content and subscriber-only giveaways. Her website also contains up to date details on all her books: http://cjarcher.com She loves to hear from readers. You can contact her through email cj@cjarcher.com or follow her on social media to get the latest updates on her books.

Printed in Great Britain
by Amazon